CW01151610

THE FACE IN THE GRAVE

R. Kenward Jones

Also by R. Kenward Jones

The Face in the Grave
Buried at Sea
Tabitha *(forthcoming)*

THE FACE IN THE GRAVE

R. Kenward Jones

Published by Watertower Hill Publishing, LLC
www.watertowerhill.com

Copyright © 2024 by R. Kenward Jones. All rights reserved.

Cover and internal artwork by Susan Roddey
at The Snark Shop by Pheonix and Fae Creations.
Copyright © 2024 JLFoxBooks, LLC. All rights reserved.

No part of this book may be reproduced in any form without prior written permission of the author and publisher—other than for "fair use" as brief quotations embodied in articles and reviews.

Author's Note
All character and names in this book are fictional and are not designed, patterned after, nor descriptive of any person, living or deceased.
Any similarities to people, living or deceased is purely by coincidence. Author and Publisher are not liable for any likeness described herein.

Library of Congress Control Number: 2024061824

Hardback ISBN: 979-8-9902033-4-1
Paperback ISBN: 979-8-9902-33-5-8
eBook ASIN: B0D3ITPRXF

Printed in the United States of America
10 9 8 7 6 5 4 3 2 1

This book is dedicated to the Spirit who spoke to my spirit in my darkest moment and called me back into life and light out of darkness and hopelessness.
He is the voice of creativity and creation and without Him I would not be able to breathe, or write, or live.
My hope is found in nothing less...

Table of Contents

Foreword i
Chapter 1 - Tony and Syd 1
Chapter 2 - Welcome to the Family 7
Chapter 3 - Frights and First Wives 13
Chapter 4 - Shirley's Words.. 19
Chapter 5 - Making an Unmade Man....................................... 23
Chapter 6 - Touching Off a War.. 27
Chapter 7 - Daddy Issues and DNA 33
Chapter 8 - Shirley Checks Out.. 37
Chapter 9 - Precautions.. 41
Chapter 10 - Parable for a Mobster 47
Chapter 11 - No Reason... 51
Chapter 12 - Tony's Funeral 53
Chapter 13 - Dynomark 57
Chapter 14 - The Bubble of Normal Breaking 67
Chapter 15 - The Book 71
Chapter 16 - Shirley Comes Home 77
Chapter 17 - Surfing Safari... 81
Chapter 18 - The Tunnel in the Sky 89
Chapter 19 - Coffee and Tsunamis... 95
Chapter 20 - Meet the Parent 101
Chapter 21 - The Phone 109
Chapter 22 - Tony's Place 115
Chapter 23 - Shots Fired 121
Chapter 24 - Gordon's Revenge... 129
Chapter 25 - Striking Resemblance 133
Chapter 26 - Pastor Jack.. 141
Chapter 27 - Surveillance and Surprises 145
Chapter 28 - An Outrageous Plan 149

Chapter 29 - The Groundskeeper's Sleep 153

Chapter 30 - Entering and Breaking 157

Chapter 31 - Graverobbers Interrupted 161

Chapter 32 - The Face in the Grave 167

Chapter 33 - Closed Coffin 175

Chapter 34 – Getaway 181

Chapter 35 - Pursuer 185

Chapter 36 - DNA of Connection 189

Chapter 37 - Depth in the Dark 193

Chapter 38 - Rat Trap 201

Chapter 39 - Unlucky 207

Chapter 40 - Lion's Den 213

Chapter 41 - The Right Bait 217

Chapter 42 - Antarctic Survival 221

Chapter 43 - Jumping Without a Chute 227

Chapter 44 - Parting of Ways and Means 231

Chapter 45 - Flight 239

Chapter 46 - The Money Talks 243

Chapter 47 - Money Keeps Talking 247

Chapter 48 - Above the Clouds 249

Chapter 49 - Opening King Tony's Tomb 251

Chapter 50 - Seed Phrase 255

Chapter 51 - Unhappy Endings 261

Chapter 52 - A Strange Family Reunion 267

Chapter 53 - Off the Mountaintop 271

Chapter 54 - A Final Accounting 277

Foreword

Sandy

There was this story about a woman. I can't remember her name, but her face could launch a thousand ships.

She was beautiful. Must have been some face. That kind of face would be worth a lot of money, wouldn't it?

But my old man? He was no beauty. Not heinous or anything, but not a handsome man.

Mainly it was the nose that took a left turn off a stop sign post when he was kid and never went back right. But he had nice tan-brown eyes that were deep-set and friendly.

Girls followed those eyes like grains of iron follow a magnet; they got him dates with the girls who got past the broken nose. Bedroom eyes. That's what my mom said about Dad.

She fell into those eyes and dragged me in with her. I guess that's not quite true since I didn't exist at the time, but it's close enough for a starting place in this story.

Yes, my father's eyes got him in trouble, and the rest of us with him. The magnetism worked so well he ended up with two different wives in two different bedrooms in two different cities, and eventually two houses with two families.

Two complete sets. Two complete lives.

Well, I guess that's not true either. He had another life that neither wife or family knew about.

Turns out I didn't know the half of my father's life; where he really spent his weeks, sometimes months, away on business, who he was with, or in the end even what business he was in.

My father's life was like one of those Hollywood sound stages. When you opened the wrong door you found out it was all plywood and black cables.

Sometimes a man's death is a door that opens backstage. It shows what was real and what wasn't.

At least my old man's death was like that. It's taken a lot out of me, sorting through his soundstage life. I'm going to write this down and hopefully get some of the anger out. And the confusion. And the hurt.

But back to the face thing.

My dad's face was no beautiful thing—nothing like that woman and her ships—but turns out that face was worth somewhere north of 750 million dollars.

Carla

My dad dropped dead without a word. He dropped dead without a sound. If there's a wall between this life and the next he didn't hit it, he just came to a gap in it and fell through.

One minute he was here, the next he was not. Funny enough, he was sitting up, eyes open, the three of us eating dinner, hands on either side of his plate.

He just… stopped. Stopped being with us. Stopped being.

I was used to my dad not being with us. He spent lots of time being other places—as it turns out, even being a different person.

I don't want to sound like I'm complaining too much. When he was with us, he was with us. He was a good dad. That's going to be hard to show when I tell you the whole thing, but I want to say it here before I tell too much.

And I want to say it now—get that part straight in my heart and my mind because he wasn't a good man, and I don't want to forget the good part.

Lord knows I'm going to live with the bad for the rest of my life.

So, no matter what else, I want to say he was my dad when he was my dad and it was real to me.

Doesn't every child grow up to find out their parents were at least two things: a black and white coloring book outline we colored in, and a human with flesh and blood and a past, and closets full of stuff maybe they don't even know about themselves?

The flesh and blood that was my dad came to us when I was three. I'd be lying if I said I remember this, but I'm sure I don't remember any other man so he's my dad like any other girl's dad.

Unless you want to start claiming you knew your dad when you were three.

We lived in a small town in the Shenandoah Valley at the foot of the Blue Ridge Mountains. When I say small you may not appreciate how small I'm talking about.

It's called Brand's Flat. There's no marker or sign or zip code to identify it. It's more of a suggestion than a place.

The people who live there have the rare ability to know all about each other and mind their own business; an ideal place to be known just enough and not too much, to have all the help you need but only when you ask for it.

Between Jericho Road on one border and Desper Hollow Road on the other, split by the narrow run of Christian's Creek, about one hundred and fifty people lived.

Most worked in the factories in the county—Little Debbie and McKie, and before it shut down, DuPont. Businesses sorted it out a long time ago: bring your factories to a place with settled folks who have a work ethic, the kind who are suspicious of unions, and you can write your own ticket.

Pay a little over minimum wage and you have a happy worker.

That all changed when the first union came to the county. It was the same year my mom, Rita Henry, met the man who became my dad.

She got a flat coming home from McKie. It was out on 64 and raining. He stopped and helped. That was it. Not romantic, just practical. He was just at the right place at the right time.

That flat tire was a metaphor for her life, our life, right then. No spare. No way to move from that dangerous, uncomfortable place. No idea how to change anything. Then there he was.

When I asked her years later to tell me the story—it was when she was chewing me out for accepting a ride home from high school with a boy she didn't know—I asked her why she got into a car with a complete stranger. She said it was his eyes.

There was kindness there mixed with not a little magnetism.

I knew some boys who had one or the other. One might make you get in a car with them, the other might make you get into bed with them. I guess my dad had enough of both.

She got home that day, I got a dad, we got the nicest house in Brand's Flat, and we got a new name: Dyson.

Chapter 1 - Tony and Syd

Tony Diderrick was a busy man. He told you he was busy without using words. He looked busy. He was motion. He was a human blur.

When he was a freshman in high school he worked two jobs. When he was a freshman in college he worked three jobs and managed a little side hustle for a guy named Syd DeVito, a Jersey kid who came south to take care of a family business, the kind of business that is strictly family and strictly out of sight.

Tony was good with numbers, industrious, and insanely, possibly maniacally, taciturn. For the people he worked with, loquaciousness was the original sin, the sin for which there was no forgiveness in this life or the next. Tony was no sinner.

The way he got hooked up with DeVito was this: the two were taking accounting in their second year at Old Dominion University when Syd began organizing a student government campaign for a guy you've heard of—Daniel Treeright—yeah, that's the man, one and the same.

The Face in the Grave

Syd started collecting money here and there to pay for some "things"—Syd's definition of things was as wide as the ocean.

He wanted to keep these contributions on the down low, but accounting and numbers were not his strong point as evidenced by his failing grade in accounting coming up on midterms.

Never one to let a little thing like integrity get in the way of progress, Syd took steps to ensure he would not only pass the big exam, but pass it with a high enough mark to save him from repeating the course.

Accordingly, he recruited the person in class who had the most on the ball to create a bulletproof crib sheet for which he paid one hundred dollars up front. Tony, to whom accounting came like breathing, gladly produced the sheet and pocketed the money, no questions asked.

On the day of the exam, which was held in the small auditorium in Constant Hall, Tony agreed to deliver the goods prior to start time. He was a punctual man. Precise. He had to be in order to juggle all of his spinning plates. Syd was not.

Fifteen minutes after the rest of the class began sweating out the test, he walked in and looked for a seat. Arriving late, on an exam day, he drew everyone's attention. He retrieved his copy of the test papers, scanned the room for Tony, and found him sitting near the back.

Here's where the trouble began. Tony arrived early, chose a seat close to where he'd seen Syd sit previously, and settled into his own last-minute preps for taking the exam. He paid no attention as the class filled up and the seats around him filled in.

By the time Syd DeVito arrived, there were no spots close enough for Tony to make passing off the crib sheet easy. Compounding this, DeVito eschewed many rows of obviously open seats as he made his way to where Tony sat.

He finally settled into a seat one row back and two spots over from him. It took another five minutes for the class to settle back down, like a flock of birds that had been disturbed finally finding a place to light.

The prof of Accounting 201 that semester was a stout blonde woman named Shmidt who had a hairdo matching both her name and her build. She was an accounting zealot who insisted everything in her world add up to the penny.

Her mental columns were as straight and clear as the figures in her grade book, and she did not like Syd DeVito. He annoyed her with his brash manner, loud voice, and swaggering walk.

Syd DeVito was a hanging decimal point, a number out of place in her otherwise neat columns. She would happily flunk him given half a chance, and his performance thus far had given her more than that. Syd's late entrance and meandering search for a seat caught Professor Shmidt's attention.

As far as she was concerned, he may as well have been walking up the stairs to the Accounting 201 gallows. When he turned in another of his sloppy exams, she'd throw the lever and the trap door would swing open below him.

Tony was as unaware of the prof and Syd as he was of the ticking of the clock or the whirring of the air handler. He had the ability to bring all focus onto one thing at a time to the exclusion of everything else, and numbers were the easiest thing upon which to focus. Syd's attempts to get Tony's attention with restrained throat clearings and coughs may as well have been directed at a deaf man.

It was a full twenty minutes before he emerged from his test-dream state and glanced around. He saw Syd, staring at him, perturbed, waiting on the agreed-upon crib sheet so he could begin taking the exam.

Rising with a vague idea of delivering the sheet to DeVito after he turned in his own exam, he unbuttoned his breast pocket and pulled it out far enough to assure himself it was indeed there.

Yes.

He slipped along the aisle, nodding at DeVito, hoping to communicate for him to sit tight, he'd be right back, but Syd, growing more anxious by the minute at the prospect of running out of time, got up and followed Tony to the front, assuming they'd make the exchange outside the auditorium.

Professor Shmidt, who had been watching the two and picking up the cues teachers have sniffed out from time immemorial, followed the two with her eyes as they approached.

"Done already?" she asked Tony.

"Yes," Tony said.

"How about showing me what's in your pocket?" Shmidt said.

The Face in the Grave

Syd, who had been trying to time his exit with a nod and a "I'm just stepping out to go to the bathroom" to coincide with Tony dropping off his exam booklet, heard this and tried to reroute himself.

"You can wait there, Mr. DeVito. Until I see what Mr. Diderrick has in his pocket and what it has to do with you."

Tony, awkwardly digging his hands into his pants pockets, said, "What does he have to do with anything in my pockets? I don't even know this guy."

Shmidt gave him a smug smile and a "Harummmpf."

"Breast pocket. That piece of paper sticking out. Would you mind showing it to me?" She locked eyes with him and waited.

Tony hesitated half a click, reached in the pocket, and handed over the crib sheet.

"These are my study notes, and that's all they are. I make a set of these for every exam in every class. It cuts down on the things I need to carry with me and lets me study right up to the last minute."

This lie was delivered so smoothly and quickly, Syd actually thought for a moment it was true. Shmidt, however, was having none of it.

"I saw you take it out and look at it while you were sitting and taking the exam, Diderrick. I also heard Mr. DeVito here half choking himself trying to get your attention. You think I'm stupid?"

Unfolding the sheet and fingering it she said, "Tell you what. You admit to me right now this is actually for him,"—she nodded in Syd's direction—"and I'll drop it. I know you don't need the help."

Syd froze. This was going very badly very quickly. Before he could say or do anything, Tony Diderrick glanced over his shoulder as if till now he'd been unaware of Syd's very existence.

He said, "You're wrong. Not for him, for me. And I don't cheat." He added, "You're right about one thing. I don't need the help."

Shmidt fixed Tony in a stony stare. She wanted DeVito to squirm, and worse, she wanted to put him in his place. Tony Diderrick wasn't cheating.

She didn't want to catch him up in the net she set for DeVito, but there it was. She couldn't back down now. The accusation of cheating was in the air. The code. See it, report it, or be complicit in it. Ingrained in academia.

Unyielding. Again she fingered the crib sheet, flicking it back and forth, thinking.

Looking past Tony at Syd DeVito, she said, "I'm sorry, Mr. Diderrick, but I'm going to report this to the Honors Council and let them investigate it. You know the likely outcome will be expulsion from this school."

She shifted her gaze from DeVito to Diderrick; neither changed expression.

"You can go now, Mr. Diderrick. And you, Mr. DeVito, are you ready to turn in your exam also? Or do you still have work to do on it?"

The last phrase was delivered with as much sarcasm as she could stuff into it.

Chapter 2 - Welcome to the Family

Syd failed the midterm spectacularly. It was a watershed moment for him. He saw two things at once: business, at least the way it was taught at a university, had next to nothing to do with business in the real world—his real world, and it was a waste of time and energy to get someone to tutor him to do things he would never be good at; why not just hire them straight up to do the work?

Cut the middle out.

He dropped his business major and charted out the path of least resistance to an ODU bachelor's degree; the major didn't matter anymore.

He was going to major in the family business. The family business came down to one thing and one thing only at base: money.

Making it, moving it, using it to make more of it, and, he realized, hiding it. That last part needed a specialist; a person with a very particular set of skills they would not learn in accounting class.

7

The Face in the Grave

He thought Tony Diderrick might be that person. There was no compunction on his part that Diderrick was going up in front of the Honors Counsil because of their dealings. That didn't enter his mind. Price of doing business.

Someone was always taking a pinch or at risk of taking one.

No. His interest in Diderrick was not to help Diderrick, it was to help himself. The dude showed him something in the run-in with the old bitch professor.

Cool in the moment. No hint of breaking. If he was that kind of guy through and through, he might be the guy to help Syd handle family business.

When the Honor Council convened—a panel of three upperclassmen and two professors—Syd made it his business to find the soft spot in the group. It was a technique he learned from his uncle in Jersey.

How to handle juries.

His uncle said, "Juries are like an apple; give it a little bruise and before long, the whole thing gets squishy."

The Honors Council required a unanimous vote to convict a student of a code violation. All he needed was one.

He identified his soft spot easily enough, an outspoken sixty-something political science prof who made noises like a thorough-going, card-carrying liberal, but secretly donated large sums of money to nothing but conservatives.

Finding this out had been simple, and he'd gotten a few screenshots of candidate web sites with the prof's donations clearly laid out. Then he waited. He wanted to see Tony Diderrick under the heat lamp. See whether or not the performance in front of Shmidt was a one-off or the real deal.

The Honors Council convened publicly to add to the gravity of honors code violations and to discourage anyone from falling into one themselves.

They were not normally well attended, perhaps because no one liked to be reminded of their own undetected cheating, or perhaps it was because no one wanted to be found guilty by association. There were always the few, the same kind who slow down for traffic accidents and sit in the back of courtrooms, who showed.

Syd found an inconspicuous spot and waited for Diderrick's case to come up. Shmidt was there, sour-faced and stout as ever. She did not look pleased to be there and monotoned her way through a recitation of the facts of the midterm cheating incident.

She produced the crib sheet and presented it to the members of the Council, each of whom gave it a cursory glance before handing it down the line.

The president, a fat red-faced junior—Syd recognized him from his dealings with student government—thanked Shmidt gravely for guarding the integrity of the academic process and intoned some blather about how cheating diminished the value of the work all the honest students were doing.

It sounded to Syd as if it were a foregone conclusion that Diderrick was guilty and the whole show was a check-in-the-box formality.

He began to wonder if the accused was going to get his chance to speak at all.

Red-face lolled to a halt, though, and said in an over-officious tone, "Tony Diderrick, you are here to dispute Professor Shmidt's accusation?"

He managed to say this with a hint of surprise in his voice, as if Shmidt's words on the matter had come down from Sinai.

Tony, who had been sitting complacently in a chair in front of the Council table, stood up deliberately and said, "This is a mistake. Professor Shmidt knows I'm not a cheater. She said it the day of the incident. Ask her yourself directly."

He gave the woman a side-wise glance and swung an arm her way.

"When I turned in my test she offered me the opportunity to accuse another student as the person who was supposed to use that,"—he pointed at the folded up piece of paper before the members and scanned their faces with his own accusation—"which are my condensed notes."

He paused.

"And you can ask her about that too."

The two other student members of the Council sat up with arched eyebrows at this twist. Syd's Poly Sci professor cleared his throat as if getting ready to speak.

Red-face, whose face was reddening considerably, beat him to it.

The Face in the Grave

"You're telling us the crib sheet that Professor Shmidt saw you take out of your own pocket during the exam is nothing more than a study guide, and that she wanted you to say it belonged to someone else? Why would she do that?! You're accusing a tenured professor of an honors code violation herself?"

He looked from Diderrick to Shmidt incredulously. Shmidt did not look up but squirmed uncomfortably in her seat.

Diderrick said, "Because she has something in for this student. I don't know what it is. Not my business. You can ask her."

The smattering of students in attendance began murmuring. Sometimes the most mundane proceedings got interesting. They'd picked a good day to rubberneck the Honors Council meeting.

Again the Poly Sci professor cleared his throat to speak. Again Red-face beat him to the punch.

"Diderrick, that's ridiculous and might be a separate code violation all on its own unless you can prove it. You have a witness?"

Syd leaned in. He had heard the exchange between Diderrick and Shmidt but no one else could have.

"No. No one but myself. She knows what she said," was Diderrick's reply.

"No witness. Hmm? Well, who was the other student? Tell us that and we can ask him."

Syd leaned further in. This was the crux of it. He knew the family code. You never, never, added a name for anyone in authority.

The only exception: give them the name of someone dead or someone who didn't exist. He wondered if this quiet accounting student knew the code too, if he was quiet when it counted.

Diderrick didn't hesitate and didn't waste words. "No," was his reply.

Red-face lost all pretense of equanimity. He sneered.

"No? No, what?"

He looked up and down the table at the Council members; chief priest presiding over the trial of an academic heretic.

"You won't tell us the name or you don't know the name or the student doesn't have a name?"

Diderrick didn't blink or squirm, or seem to notice the escalation from 'probably guilty' to 'must-be-shown-a-lesson' in the tone of the proceedings. He repeated his response. Same tone. Same volume.

"No."

Syd pulled out his phone and sent three texts in rapid fire as he got up and made his way slowly toward the exit, careful to make sure two people in the room saw him; Professor Poly Sci, and Shmidt.

Halfway to the door he feigned a stumble that disrupted the board president, who was just winding up for his final screed on the need to vote "yes" to convict Diderrick of an honors code violation.

Syd held up both hands in apology and said too loudly, "Sorry! Sorry, Mr. President! Please. Proceed. Just have to make an important phone call."

Red-face shot daggers at him with his eyes. Syd smiled and continued to the exit, shooting his own dagger at Shmidt who had not noticed his presence until this moment.

He relished the mixture of anger and confusion on the woman's face, knowing it would take on full bloom in a few minutes, after Tony Diderrick walked, which he would as soon as Poly Sci checked his phone and decided how he should vote.

The bruise on the apple.

Chapter 3 - Frights and First Wives

Tony Diderrick sighed. He guessed every accountant in the world had these kinds of conversations with their clients.

Conversations that went like this:

"I didn't know I couldn't spend company money to..." Fill in the blank.

From the mundane blank fillers—upgrade my plane ticket, get a new computer, spend an extra few days in the hotel—to the more imaginative—pay off my student loans, buy my wife a diamond tennis bracelet, make a down payment on a beach bungalow—to the outliers, like—pay for hookers, cocaine, or bribes.

There were always blurred lines at the edge of the nice tight columns and rows of numbers. That's why accounting mattered, after all. If it were just math, anyone could do the job. It took an artist to make the numbers work in any business.

The Face in the Grave

Tony was an artist, a true paint-by-the-numbers maestro.

It was five years since Syd DeVito saved him from being expelled from Old Dominion University and introduced him to Syd's family business.

Now DeVito was chief of staff of the governor of North Carolina; legit, by all appearances a law-abiding citizen at the right hand of power.

And Tony? Tony did not exist in any legal sense of the word. No social security number, no birth certificate, no driver's license.

Not that he didn't possess all of these things, just that none of them were authentic. It made him snigger to himself thinking how cloak-and-dagger his life as an accountant was.

Secret agents? He guessed they needed anonymity to do their thing; no government wanted anyone following their agents. But the Fratellis? They were insanely keen on keeping anyone from tracking their money.

So Tony disappeared into the Family while he lived with first one, then another, family of his own.

It wasn't the plan, he said to himself many days as he trekked between the two. It wasn't his plan to do what? Become a bigamist? He would not have used that word to describe his unique domestic situation.

In his mind a bigamist had two wives at the same time. He never did that. He had one wife when he was in one home and another when he was in another home.

He was… what? Legally speaking, neither woman was married to Tony Diderrick, although it would have taken either of them a goodly amount of detective work to get to the dead end of their husband's identity.

And he was true to them. He didn't sleep around like the rest of the men in the Fratelli crime family. He was actually proud of that.

No, the only other woman he'd slept with since he got married to his first wife was his second wife. It was complicated, but he made it add up.

That's what Tony Diderrick always did. Always could do. Make it add up.

He'd been a bit of a man-whore in college and in the early days working for the Fratellis, days when the ridiculously large amount of money that went with being a mob accountant began flowing.

He had a hard time saying no to women who had a hard time saying no to him. It got him into some very tough spots, like when he slept with Stick Gordon's two daughters on back-to-back nights during a big family confab out in Tempe.

How was he supposed to know Gordon brought his girls with him to the meet-up? And how was he supposed to say no when they said yes so easily? Always the eyes. He could use them.

ZZ Top could sing all they wanted about a woman using her legs, but Tony, who couldn't talk worth shit, bedded the girls with one look.

And he did. Alot. Right up until Gordon and a few of his guys held him upside down over the edge of the Grand Canyon and he saw his life hanging by one fat Italian paw.

It took a last second phone call from Richie Fratelli himself to convince Gordon that dropping the gigolo accountant would cost more money than he could afford to pay and that if he conveniently "slipped" right now, Gordon and his daughters might follow the accountant over the edge.

Saved by the boss, and for all intents and purposes marked as untouchable—basically unheard of for an unmade man—many guys would have become unmanageable.

Tony became the opposite.

He became a model citizen and the most careful of all members of the family. He stayed so careful with his contacts that most outside the big three bosses knew him more as a rumor than a real person.

But Gordon kept tabs on him. And waited. And, for the time being, he satisfied himself by doing unto others the gruesome things he wanted to do unto Tony Diderrick.

Tony met his first wife on a plane ride to Jacksonville, Florida, on his way to a long weekend on Amelia Island.

She was from Fernandina Beach and sat next to him. Never one to initiate a conversation, it was Shirley who asked him about his plans and it was Shirley who filled up the hour-and-a-half flight with words; Tony's contribution to the conversation was nods and grunts at strategic moments, showing he was interested.

The Face in the Grave

And he was, but not so much in Shirley's words as the button on her blouse between her breasts which was straining to keep them in check and doing a half-ass job of it.

When the woman paused for breath to reload her words, the shirt gapped in the most tantalizing manner, giving him a glimpse of a second base he wanted to tag.

Without knowing it, Tony nodded and grunted his way into a shared ride with Shirley from the airport to Amelia Island and to dinner with her that night at the Salty Pelican on the riverfront.

Dinner turned into a weekend together where he touched all the bases multiple times and listened to Shirley more than he ever actually listened to any woman.

The flood of words that threatened to drown him eventually ebbed.

He had the feeling she wasn't used to a man who could just listen. He knew he was a man who liked to listen and didn't need to talk.

It was Jack Sprat and his wife. It made sense.

And the words were not penetrating words, not things seeking access. She was content to shower Tony or bathe him in her words, not scrub him down and get anything off him or out of him. This was good.

The one thing he couldn't have was an inquisitive girlfriend. It was the one thing no one in the family could afford.

Amelia turned out to be an ideal place for him, too. Just the right mixture of locals, seasonals, and vacationers to keep relationships vague. People came and went all the time. He could do the same.

And there was the beach. To Tony there were only two kinds of beaches: the kind where you find shark teeth and the kind where you don't.

He had no use for the second kind but he could disappear into the first and emerge from a time warp with a handful of the pointy enameled treasures without a clue how long he'd roamed. Stress busted. Cost? Zero.

His second visit to the island he stayed with Shirley, his third he asked her to marry him, his fourth they signed the marriage certificate at the Fernandina Courthouse with her high school bestie and the Justice of the Peace's secretary for witnesses.

He used the name Tony Anderson—he used his real first name with all his aliases because it was too hard to get used to answering to any other name—and the former Miss Shirley Laughton became Mrs. Shirley Anderson.

They bought one of Fernandina's classic old houses with a wrap-around porch and a view of the river, big but not too big, nice but not too nice.

He'd seen too many guys put too much on display and invite too much attention—from the family and from the heat. He knew the right temperature to keep his lifestyle.

It helped that Shirley was a simple woman who thought the house was perfect and liked driving her ten-year-old Ford Taurus.

Things were nice. The honeymoon in Panama coincided perfectly with a month-long hole in his schedule where the big three were themselves out of the country visiting with family in Italy.

So Tony and Shirley Anderson of Amelia Island and Fernandina Beach, Florida established a home known only to themselves and their little community.

Chapter 4 - Shirley's Words

Sandy

My mother was what *The Sound of Music* called a flibbertigibbet. Remember that? How do you find a word that means Maria?

Shirley? She could talk. She could talk for such a long time it would become a thing itself. The sound of her voice formed a wall and became a sound barrier all its own. You couldn't hear the words for the volume of words.

But she was sweet as honey butter. She really was.

Growing up with her as an only child was challenging. Especially with a father who was away a lot and who had as few words as she had many.

I became the conduit through which all those words flowed. It had its advantages. My vocabulary is pretty big, and from a young age it never bothered me to talk in front of people.

The Face in the Grave

And I guess in a way all her words were an education in themselves.

Mom liked to read. It was the only sure way to stop up the words. Get her interested in an Agatha Christie mystery, or even better, get her hooked into a nice long James Michener novel, and suddenly there would be long swaths of silence in the house.

She loved books. She lived in them. There were stacks of paperbacks on the bookshelves. I should mention the bookshelves.

The main living room of the old house featured built-in bookcases, the kind that would normally house fancy leather bound books or at the very least nice hardbackers.

They framed a huge old rarely-used fireplace, and extended from three feet above the floor all the way to the ceiling, and to the wall six feet on each side.

The shelves were three feet tall, and if they had been used the way they were intended, would have housed around two hundred books.

Not in Shirley's house.

She piled her paperbacks into the allotted space as if on a mission to fit as many books as possible into the space. They were stacked on their sides, three rows deep, ten wide and eight to ten high.

My mother loved books so much she had a relationship with them. Once she owned one it was an intimate friend.

She personalized every one of them. She had stickers, each about the size of two baseball cards, that had a picture of a black cat standing on top of a stack of books and the words "Ex Libris" (from the library of) with a blank spot.

She wrote her name on them and put them in the front of every book she owned. She also underlined the parts of books that spoke to her. She circled words and phrases. When something about a volume particularly delighted her, she drew five-pointed stars, exclamation marks, and my favorite, little tornadoes, as if the prose were running through her heart and mind like a Kansas twister.

There was no Dewey Decimal System, no discernable order to Shirley's library, but if asked, she could put her hands on any title in her collection within minutes.

She could also tell you if a book was missing because it was "out on loan," who had it, and how long they'd kept it. It was the one thing as sure to get her "peeved"—a strong word from Shirley—as a book was to keep her silent.

It was a missing book that led me to my father's grave, but we'll get to that in a bit. I want you to see who my mom was. That she was a nice woman before all this. That she was maybe a little eccentric and talkative, but not a basket case or a loon. Before.

Before her relationship with my father turned her inside out. I love my mom. I love her words. I love her books. You understand? Not the books, but I love that they are hers and part of her. She was always a great mom.

The best. Sweet. Like honey butter.

I loved my father too, I guess. But that gets complicated. He was so… opposite.

My mom was words and motion and presence. My father was silence and stillness and absence. I felt his absence and silence.

I felt it the same way I felt the wall of words that built around my mother when she got going. It was between us when he was there and when he was gone.

I know that's hard to understand, how I could feel his absence even when he was there with us, but I bet you've known people who made you feel it; like they weren't really with you even when they were sitting at a table looking straight at you.

He was there. He didn't miss a handful of my games and never an important one. That's not what I mean.

He was present and accounted for at every significant event. But he was always coming from somewhere and headed to somewhere else that was a mystery to me and evidently not important to Shirley.

She never asked. That's why the truth did what it did to her. It was a sucker punch; one she may never get over, but at least she got up off the mat.

That's something, right?

Chapter 5 - Making an Unmade Man

How Tony Diderrick got to be the most powerful unmade man in the Fratelli crime family shouldn't be a mystery to anyone with half a brain, or anyone who ever saw The Untouchables. It's all about the money. Always. Follow the money.

How to get Capone? Murder? No. Income taxes.

Gambino. Murder? No. Racketeering.

Always. Follow. The. Money.

What if you can make your illegal money trails disappear into nothing and reappear in legitimate financial institutions as pure as the driven snow?

That's a particular kind of magic, and there was never a magician better at it than Tony Diderrick.

He was the family's Criss Angel, and he regularly did a mind freak on the FBI, the ATF, the DEA, the IRS, and all the other alphabet-soup agencies that tried to follow the money the Fratellis entrusted to him.

The Face in the Grave

He was a man ahead of his time and it translated into staying ahead of the dollar bill-sniffing bureaucrats with their unimaginative ways, means, and methods.

How did he do it?

At first he did it by being faster than the hounds. Early on he understood what the internet meant to the speed of financial transactions.

He moved money in and out of accounts and in and out of the country so quickly the authorities were perpetually shooting at a moving target, never able to get their ducks in a row before the particular piggy bank they'd targeted was empty.

It took a broad knowledge of finances and an innovator's passion for pushing the limits of the intersection of new technology and business. Tony possessed both in spades.

The next limit he pushed was something he learned about from the family's contacts with, of all places, the US military.

He heard that some agencies had networks of computers that were not connected to the rest of the World Wide Web; they were completely contained within an agency.

Immediately seeing the value of this kind of privacy in communicating family business, he built an air-gapped internet for the family before most of the family knew what the internet was at all.

Their machines connected with their machines over their own lines. It was easy enough to accomplish. The Fratellis had their fingers in tons of new construction and in cable installations, and had for years.

Tony convinced them to spring for cable runs that were placed next to the commercial lines but only terminated in family-owned places of business and computers.

Voila. Mobnet.

Communication off the grid before off-the-grid was a thing. Moving money became a thousand times easier because of the simple ability to connect to family members instantly.

The one thing that had always slowed money movement down was the most human thing of all: trust.

With Tony's instant connectivity, family members could verify moves in real time and see for themselves what was happening. Is anyone moving money without permission? Was someone making an unauthorized move?

Now it could be sorted out in minutes without bothering to go for long walks in parks away from the ever-present prying eyes and ears of the authorities.

Once Tony got the family communications air gapped, he could take full advantage of digital finance. He had the speed advantage, and the privacy advantage, but the next step he took cemented his place in the family; he took the mob into cryptocurrency.

He saw the advantages of crypto almost immediately.

Decentralized. Untraceable. Borderless.

Once he poured money into the crypto downspout, it became pure as the driven snow. He worked tirelessly to educate the big bosses and their lieutenants about what he saw coming.

The result was that Tony Diderrick had eighty percent of the Fratellis money in Bitcoin when it was less than one hundred dollars per coin.

The bosses accepted it as payment for all goods and services within the first three years after Tony implemented his campaign.

The result was that in the vast majority of the family businesses he no longer needed to deal with legacy financial institutions.

All mobsters in his family used Bitcoin. Effectively this did for family finances what the cable project did for communications; it created an air gap between mob money and the rest of the world.

Their money became untouchable. They bought and sold in their own digital economy, an economy that grew by itself without any new enterprises, or risk, as the value of Bitcoin grew.

They had money that made money just by existing. And when Bitcoin bounced to twenty thousand dollars per coin, they had more money than they knew what to do with.

The bosses, the lieutenants, the foot soldiers… the Fratelli crime family was the wealthiest family in the history of the mob.

There was no need for any made man in the family to continue working, or for that matter to worry about their son's son's sons being obscenely wealthy.

The Face in the Grave

Tony calculated that the wealth generated in moving all the family liquid assists into the crypto world had made the three Fratelli brothers—Richie, Frankie, and AJ—three of the wealthiest men in the world

Chapter 6 - Touching Off a War

Tony brought up the implications of their immense wealth in a rare meeting of all three of the brothers in Aversa, Italy in 2017. Why not, he asked, reduce risk?

The family, as a company, was in an almost impregnable position. Why not withdraw from some of the more unsavory criminal operations which carried the possibility of legal troubles?

He outlined several enterprises which regularly ran afoul of the authorities or which required a certain amount of heavy handedness—from actual leg breaking to making people disappear.

All of these, he said, made little money compared to the income the family received from its crypto holdings and assets acquired with their untraceable crypto; it made no sense to continue pursuing them.

None of the brothers appeared to be unsettled by Tony Diderrick's suggestion. He was accustomed to being the odd man out in every family meeting and knew at best, even after all he'd done and all the years he'd worked for the family, he was only a pet dog who brought home a bone.

It didn't matter if it was a golden bone that made them unimaginably rich. It didn't matter that he'd had to talk them into believing in the bone. A dog.

Dogs are useful until they're not, then you can put them down or let them get old on a chain.

His suggestion was selfish. He was getting tired. He could see how retiring was going to be more complex for him than most as he would need to do it with two different families.

He was beginning to look for a way out of his already complicated day-to-day life.

What he didn't see was how much more complicated he was making his life by telling a room full of mobsters they were wealthy enough to retire from the crime business.

He believed he'd simply given them sound business advice. It made sense. How much money did they need?

He did not see that organized crime and organized religion are mirror images of each other, the two sides of the tree of the knowledge of good and evil, neither existing for their purported purpose of obtaining wealth (the criminals) or good behavior (the church), but actually to accumulate power and control.

Nor did he see that, because of this, organized crime, like organized religion, had no natural ending point and therefore would grow until meeting a force violent enough to stop it, that the thirst for power and control in these men, as it was with all men since Eden, was unslakable with anything so petty as wealth.

The meeting in Aversa set off a series of events Tony never anticipated.

Richie Fratelli, the youngest of the three ruling brothers, left Aversa with one thing in mind, and it wasn't a plan to become less criminal but more murderous.

He started with his oldest brother, who Richie had whacked in spectacular gangland style outside a family owned nightclub in Philly.

When Richie's second brother got blown up in his car, it became evident a war was on, but who was fighting who and why they were fighting, was not.

Tony, always out in front of the money, was clueless as to why anyone would declare war on the Fratellis. It made no business sense at all.

Nevertheless, when Richie Fratelli summoned Tony to his nondescript family home in the Jersey City suburbs, Tony went expecting to hear about a rival family attempting to supplant the Fratellis—something which would not make sense given the way the family punctiliously remained in their long-established territories and paid respects to all the other established families.

But it made the most sense of anything he could come up with to explain why there was war.

It shocked him to find out that he was the cause of the war.

Richie told him so. The Aversa meeting. Why should his brothers think they were Richie's equal? Those stupid fucks had gotten soft years ago. They thought they could talk to him like he was still pissing in his pants when it was him that really ran everything.

Wasn't it Richie's idea to hire the accountant? Him who had pushed for all Tony's innovations leading to the family's success?

And these cheese heads sit at the same table as Richie and think they were his equal? No fucking way. And isn't that what Tony implied at Aversa?

"You said the three of us were some of the richest men in the world. Each of us as rich as anyone, including each other," Richie said in his thick Jersey accent.

"It's what I heard you say, Tony. It's what all of us heard."

Tony had lived a long time amongst these men. His natural taciturnity had attracted Syd DeVito, his practiced taciturnity had kept him alive. He'd seen many—more than he cared to recall—men say one word too many and often a single word meant getting whacked.

He said nothing now; he only met Richie's gaze evenly and waited.

He felt as if he were hanging by his feet again, dangling over the Grand Canyon. He fought to keep the feeling off his face. He had no idea

The Face in the Grave

how Richie could interpret what he'd told the bosses as a declaration of war on each other.

He was the accountant. "The." Singular. There had been three bosses... now there was one.

War was bad for business. An internal war was terrible for business. It attracted unwanted attention. It showed enemies there was weakness. And there were plenty of enemies.

There was no guarantee Richie would still be standing up when the dust settled. Funny thing was, no matter who "won" the war, all of them needed Tony, or more correctly, all of them needed what he knew.

In an all-out war, Tony Diderrick would become a wishbone many hands would try to grasp. They'd pull him to bits.

The look in Richie's eyes—and the murder of his brothers—told Tony the man was thinking in ways that didn't make sense on a normal playing field.

Richie might—no, Richie would—pull the entire family down on his own head rather than let anyone else rule it. He'd do a Samson in the temple of the Philistines.

That was Richie, the youngest brother of three old men.

And that meant Tony had one goal in this meeting; get out alive and make it to either of his homes unobserved.

While he had air-gapped the Fratelli family communications and finances, he had done this and more for his own families. They were air gapped from his true identity and from each other to such an extent he was sure they could not be found or find each other.

He himself was the only trail anyone could follow and he used a sizable annual sum of money on a self-surveillance team and technology no one could access except through his phone—an iPhone he hacked so that it would not, could not, be opened with anything other than facial recognition.

All of this flashed through Tony's mind at what he liked to call "survival speed."

Life around the mob had taught him many lessons over the years, none of which was more valuable than this: never under any circumstances let a boss or anyone of any importance catch you thinking.

He'd seen guys get whacked for taking an extra three seconds to answer a question.

Nature may abhor a vacuum, but a mob boss had a single answer for vacuums: suspicion. Suspicion had a solution as obvious and routine as turning out the lights at bedtime; cut it off.

For half a beat, Tony thought he'd gone past the suspicion stopwatch he had learned to keep in his head like a quarterback dropping back to pass. Richie was looking at him closely.

He was surprised at the steadiness in his voice.

"Richie, I never make family policy. I never tell anyone anything but the facts. Aversa was no different."

He stopped. Let Richie fill in his own blanks.

When the boss spoke, it was low and clear and tinged with sadness.

"You're a good man, Tony. Syd did good when he picked you. Better lie low for a bit. These things,"—he gestured randomly with one fat hand—"can get ugly… collateral damage is unavoidable."

He paused and held Tony in his gaze, making sure he got the message. Tony nodded.

It was the last time either of them would see the other alive.

Chapter 7 - Daddy Issues and DNA

Carla

I'm a great actress. Did I tell you that already? I'm "undiscovered" but I'm great. My high school English teacher and drama coach, Mrs. Bryant, told me I'm great.

She cast me in the lead female role in every play since freshman year and put up with all the crap from parents about that not being fair.

"What does 'fair' have to do with talent?" she told me. "It's in your genes."

Rita wasn't so psyched about me being an actress, but Tony was. He loved it. I guess that makes sense. He was a great actor himself. It must have rubbed off even though there weren't any genetics.

The Face in the Grave

Have you ever done the 23andMe thing? It's supposed to tell you about where your family came from. I guess maybe that's more important to some folks than others.

If I'm honest, it kind of sucked growing up knowing my natural father didn't want to be around. I mean, you can't really say I had a classic case of "daddy" issues. I don't hate men and I didn't go sleeping around either, but I think it's true that everyone has daddy issues.

The pastor at our church taught about this a few weeks before my stepdad died. He said you have to start with some idea of what God is like and the way you feel about God comes from your dad, how you relate to him.

If all that is true, how could any of us not have daddy issues?

My stepdad was a good man, as far as I knew, and as far as I understood "goodness"—he'd been our knight in shining armor—but he was also a mystery and a man who never uttered two complete paragraphs to me in his life.

On top of that my natural dad got me started, so to speak, and took off never to be seen again. So this is God?! Maybe I've got it backwards. Maybe we all have God issues that we call daddy issues.

Anyway, you have to admit it's confusing growing up in this old world no matter what your family situation. And mine has only gotten more confusing the more I find out. That's why I did the 23andMe thing,

Is it a rule of the universe that answering one question leads to three more questions? I got the report from 23andMe. My report wasn't shocking. I had a pretty good idea about my heritage even though I never met my natural father.

From pictures I guessed he would be standard stock for our part of the Valley. The settlers of which I'd learned about in my seventh grade Virginia History class. That means a mix of German and Scotch-Irish blood. My mother had a touch of Swedish blood thrown in, which accounts for the blonde hair and blue eyes we both have.

On a whim, I decided to test Tony's DNA. I knew we didn't share any blood, but I thought it would be interesting to know about the taciturn man who rescued us from the side of the road.

I was sure he wouldn't approve; I mean, the man was insane about any personal information. Ruthless. Absolutely no pictures of him on any social media, ever.

He shredded every piece of mail that came to our house, including junk mail. The only personal pictures we had of him were hard copy photos taken with a Polaroid camera.

I found a brush in a box full of odds and ends and asked my mom if it was Dad's. She said she thought it was so I took a chance and sent it off. Then the real shocker came. The last line of the report said my dad had a first-level relative in North Florida.

I looked at that and shook my head like a cartoon character. I compared the data to the report on me to see if I was reading it right. I was. My level of relationship to my mother and natural father showed the same as my stepfather and whoever was in North Florida.

I thought about showing this to my mother and getting her thoughts on it. But I stopped short. What if she already knew Dad had other children? What if I wasn't supposed to know?

Like I said before, do we really know our parents when we are growing up? All we know is what they want us to know.

I decided to keep the information to myself and to see what else I could find out.

I found out a lot.

More than I wanted to know.

Chapter 8 - Shirley Checks Out

Sandy

When my dad didn't come home from his latest business trip, it wasn't a worry. He never really ran on a schedule; at least not a schedule we knew about.

When he was gone he never communicated. Ever. Not a phone call, not an email, not a text. Nothing. This was his normal, so it was our normal. He was never gone more than three weeks and usually only seven to ten days.

I don't think my mother knew his exact schedule herself. His homecomings always carried an air of surprise, which made it fun.

I'd be sitting at the kitchen table working on homework, the front door opened, and in stepped my dad.

The Face in the Grave

When I was young, up till around eighth or ninth grade, he brought little gifts. These things were never much and never gave an indication of where he'd been—just Dollar Tree junk that was broken before the next trip, but to a kid, exciting enough. It made me feel special, like I mattered.

Like he saw me, you know?

There's a saying adults use: children are to be seen and not heard. I know you're not asking for my opinion but I think the wave of kids who grew up in the same time I did and got labeled as ADD and ADHD are misdiagnosed.

I think it's the adults who have the attention deficit—the parents of those kids. They don't really want to see or hear their kids. Makes you wonder why they had them in the first place.

Seriously. Think about it. Two people have a kid and as soon as they can, they put it in someone else's hands for eight to ten hours a day while they go off to work or some other activity. Maybe I'm biased because my mom never did that but isn't it worth thinking about?

I felt seen by my mom and I felt seen by my dad and it was good for me. I know most people who read this will think I'm crazy to say I had a good upbringing when I was raised by an accountant for the mafia who had another family in another state, but those were facts that were opaque to me as a child and don't outweigh the truth that my mother and father loved me and paid attention to me.

Love is real, more real than anything if you listen to the great thinkers of the ages, and it can't be diminished even when it passes through the hands of thoroughly flawed people.

In fact, that may be why love persists and prevails in our hearts and minds as the high thing, the only necessary thing even in our science-driven, skeptical culture. Our flaws and our doubts do not kill it even when we have no empirical evidence it exists at all.

Wow. That got off on a philosophical bent, didn't it? Well, this is my story and I get to tell it my way here. Lord knows there have been enough 48 Hours mystery and Netflix true crime docu-series about me and my family.

This is my chance to tell it my own way.

Where was I? My father not coming home from his last business trip. It wasn't until four weeks had passed—the longest he'd ever been gone—that I saw my mother was worried.

It was another week before I asked her where my father was. This was not a conversation I had ever had with my mother. You grow up in your own normal and my normal was a dad who dropped off the face of the earth on a semi-regular schedule and returned the same way, like a Star Trek teleporter existed somewhere near my home.

I guess I always assumed my mother knew where he was and could reach him in an emergency.

Turns out that this, along with many other assumptions, was not true. Mother told me she had no idea where my father was. She never did. The only time she asked him, he told her his business was always fluid and he couldn't say exactly when he would be home. He did not like being contacted when he was away.

He said, "Shirley, other women have husbands who go to work and come home every evening but aren't home when they're home. You have a husband who is away from home a lot but when he's home, he's home. Let me take care of my business when I'm gone and you and our family when I'm here."

That settled it for her. He had never given her a reason to worry in all these years, she said. Right up till now. Now she had called and texted a hundred times a day for a week, and nothing.

She didn't cry, but she stopped talking and she stopped reading her books. I came home from school and found her at the kitchen table, the blinds drawn and the lights out, a full cup of cold coffee between her hands. She stared into nothing.

I managed to get her up and to the doctor's office.

The doctor said nothing was wrong with her. All her vitals were fine, no sign of a stroke or heart attack or aneurysm or anything like that, but she was gone.

It was like my mother walked out of her house, locked the doors behind her, and was gone. She decided she didn't want to live there anymore so she left this present darkness even as the heat dissipated from her last cup of coffee.

The Face in the Grave

I went from being a normal high school senior with a stable home, thinking about girls, colleges, and SAT scores, to a person with no mom or dad and no idea how to navigate the next week much less the next four years alone.

The daily mail coming to the house was more than I could manage. I hated the sight of it. I added it to the stack of notices and bills growing on the table in the foyer, each time murmuring a half-hearted trope about another thing for mother to do when she got better or father when he came home.

But six weeks since she took that last sip of coffee, and still no sign of Tony. I began to see I was on my own for good.

The report on my mother was no report at all. She was just as gone as her husband, my dad.

I received a letter from a school in Virginia around that time. Old Dominion University. It was a school both Tony and Shirley thought was a good fit for me; not too far away and not too expensive.

I cried a little when I opened it, remembering when, in my not-too-distant-past, there were normal conversations about normal life at this kitchen table. It seemed so far away.

My tears and my mood blurred the "we are happy to inform you." Accepted.

How can you feel accepted when your whole life has tossed you out on your head?

It did not occur to me then and there, reading in my sunlit kitchen at the table where my mother decided to close the door on the land of the living, that the piece of paper in my hand was opening a door for a completely new life for me, a life that has taken me places I never dreamed of.

Chapter 9 - Precautions

    Tony Diderrick left the Fratelli house the same way he always did; he took the same cab company cab to the same gate in the filthy dung heap of an airport in Newark and took the same direct American Airlines flight direct to Omaha.

    He spent the night in the same hotel in the airport and took the earliest flight on Delta direct to Charlotte, again the same as his usual routine.

    To anyone following him, it would appear he was a businessman making stops along a route of cities serviced by his company.

    It would have taken a careful observer to follow the intricate dance steps he'd developed to detect and lose anyone tailing him.

    In Newark, the cab driver who picked Tony up was a mob man. He knew this to be the case because Tony hired his own man to follow the cab

The Face in the Grave

driver and report back using an anonymous Gmail account Tony monitored with the phone he used for family business.

The man did not know who paid him and Tony replaced him at irregular intervals through a third party. Payment for all his business was in Bitcoin and always ten percent more than the agreed-upon price.

He understood the first rule of counter-surveillance was simple: make your first move so predictable and plain that any surveillance asset would be bored.

The first real tricky move was what happened next.

Tony handled a great deal of correspondence for the legitimate family businesses and normally left family meetings with envelopes and the odd package here and there.

Part of his Newark routine included dropping off the mail. In a calculated risk, each time he flew, his business cell phone went into a prepaid first class mailer addressed to a PO Box in the little post office the family used in the suburbs of Jersey city.

He maintained seven such boxes and randomly switched between them on each trip. No other mail ever went to these boxes, only the phone, which he powered down, removing the SIM card before mailing it.

On arriving in Omaha, another private security guy trailed him from the time he left the gate area.

This person never came from the same private security company twice in a row and no one in the loop knew who they were trailing. All payments to all companies were in crypto and paid for three years in advance.

Tony activated the trail with an email sent from an anonymous Gmail account on a Chromebook he destroyed after every trip.

By the time he arrived in Charlotte, he had a good idea if he was being followed.

He depended on two things: the real time feedback of his private security and his gut. Charlotte was the first decision point. If either his security or his gut left a shadow of a doubt about a tail, the next flight was a red-eye to LAX or NYC, depending on the nature of the threat.

If he thought it was the family, he flew West; if it could be the feds or any other law enforcement, East.

In either case he could activate further private security and check for tails again.

In the early days setting up this system, he had done this regularly, but it proved unnecessary and time consuming.

He'd done it only once in recent memory, following a family confab when his Omaha team thought he had a tail that smelled like the Law.

After spending an extra week in New York letting things cool, he'd gotten an embarrassed email from Omaha explaining they'd put two guys on "the target" who were not aware of each other.

The one had tipped on seeing the other. Tony made a note to never again use the company, wrote off the loss of two year's pay as information well paid for, and made it home to Florida in three weeks on a trip that should have been no more than two.

It was a time of year he could afford the extra time away, but not by much. Keeping two families going and being present where his own worthless drunk of an old man had never been was a constant strain and something he took as seriously as keeping all the numbers in all the columns lined up.

This trip he never thought twice about where he would fly once he hit Charlotte. This was the last trip and no matter what his security said, he would fly west for a week in LA.

It was a necessity because this time he was cutting his three families down to two and he intended to sever more than just his ties to the Fratellis; he was going to sever the Fratellis ties to their money.

He knew it was a move that would bring the house down, but unlike Richie Fratelli, he was no Samson and had no intention of being in the temple when it caved in.

No. Tony Diderrick would be hiding in plain sight, the business guy from Brand's Flat and/or Amelia Island.

The difference now would be his only business would be running his two families. All he had to do was make this a clean break and implement his exit protocol.

The precautions he took to shake free of tails had not begun because he was fearful of the Fratelli family, but because he was afraid of the feds.

The Face in the Grave

As far as he knew, the feds had no idea of who he was or what he did. He wanted to keep it that way. He'd seen The Untouchables.

But when his counter surveillance team reported that someone other than law enforcement was tailing him—this was a few years prior to meeting his first wife—he decided his trust for the family wasn't mutual.

He began to think of the famous line from The Godfather, and how he would ever get out if they always knew they could find him and pull him back in. He didn't want to live the mob life forever.

After meeting and marrying Shirley, and especially after she became pregnant, he started planning for the day he would leave the family for his family. It wasn't a pleasant thought. He'd had no family before Syd DeVito brought him into the fold. Only the drunk and a mother who left long before he could remember. He never grudged her that decision. He thought she was smart to go and stay gone.

Richie, his older brothers AJ and Frank, and their wives, became his family.

Frank, the oldest by fifteen years, became Tony's surrogate father; AJ, the middle brother, his uncle; and Richie, the youngest, his brother.

He went from feeling alone in the world to being a vital part of a big, loud Italian family. They treated him like family and protected him as much as a non-made man could be protected.

He loved them. But Tony watched the effect great wealth had on his adopted family and their kids.

Long before his moves to crypto paid off, there was so much money amongst the brothers they each could have purchased small islands and lived out their lives in ease. Then the crypto boom hit.

The amount of money flowing through the family quadrupled. It was like a cocaine addict getting a taste of crack—same stuff with a quicker, nastier high that didn't last as long.

Their children's children's children would never have had to work a day in their lives.

He saw the pettiness between these sons and grandsons, daughters and granddaughters of means; the abuses, the drugs, the "I can buy my way into or out of anything" mentality oozing off them like cheap perfume.

Of the three brothers' eleven children, only one reached her late teens with anything resembling humility and common sense. Being a girl excluded her from any chance of becoming part of the family's leadership, but she never seemed interested in that anyway, which in Tony's eyes proved she had more common sense than her siblings and cousins.

The rest of those jerkweeds spent their time pouring money down drains or snorting it up their noses at a rate that strained the imagination.

Tony had not set out to take any of the family's money. It never entered his mind. He was well paid. Ridiculously well paid. He never asked for a raise.

Richie and the brothers took care of him from the start. He had plenty of money to keep both his families comfortable and to keep them well insulated from one another.

It was the intersection of his Fratelli family and his Virginia family that led to Tony Diderrick taking half a billion dollars from the mob.

Chapter 10 - Parable for a Mobster

Tony attended a small country church with his Virginia family, a fact he found equally amusing when he sat in the church looking around at the congregation and when he sat in the Fratelli board room looking around at the Fratellis. You never knew who might be sitting next to you, did you?

Tony had no use for God or any of his trappings. If there was a God, where had He been when Tony's old man drank away their grocery money and then beat his only son's ass when Tony asked for lunch money?

He settled that account a long time ago.

Now, as a grown man, a member of the most notorious crime family on the planet, and a polygamist, he thought God, if he existed, had no use for a guy like him, and he was fine with that too.

His Virginia wife was a sweet, church-going woman. He went to church with her for the same reason he went grocery shopping with her; he liked her company.

The Face in the Grave

Usually during church services he sat playing with accounting figures in his head for an hour, letting the preacher's words wash over him much the same way he let Shirley's words wash over him when he was with that wife, no intention of letting those words erode his beliefs or affect his decisions.

But his input during the fateful meeting in Aversa had been the result of a sermon making its way through his normal detachment and connecting the dots he'd seen appearing in the family.

The church voted in a youth pastor who liked to emphasize sermon points with a loud "whoop!" sprinkled in randomly.

Tony had to admit the annoying speaking style had the tactical advantage of keeping hearers more engaged than the old war horse of a minister who preached most of the time, a man who droned through thirty minute monologues with little to no variation in pitch or tone.

The new priest—Tony never could get used to the Protestant "pastor" moniker favored by his co-congregants—whooped him into hearing a fragment of a sermon about Jesus and a rich man who died.

The rich man had five brothers while the Fratellis were only three, but the similarities between the guy in the story and the Fratelli brothers were too clear to ignore.

The priest pointed out that even hell was not enough to get the rich man's attention. He said here's a guy who is dead and in hell and yet thinks he can order around this bum named Lazarus who is in the good place. Why did the rich man think that way? How could he look around him and still not see he was done?

The priest let a long pause rest over the congregation. Tony knew what he was going to say next before he said it. He knew it because he had watched filthy rich men up close for thirty years.

The priest said the clue was in the first two lines of the story: there was a rich man and there was a beggar named Lazarus. That's it.

The bum had nothing at all, but he had a name. The rich man had everything but he had no name. He was not a person anymore. He lost his name somewhere along the way and he became his money.

He was nothing but his money.

Rich man. Rich men thought they could tell anyone to do anything. Get me a drink of water? Right away, sir. Whack that guy who's mouthing off too much? Right away, sir. Send a man with a message to my brothers? Of course, sir.

That last bit made Tony clench his teeth. The priest asked the people to take an honest look at their wealth and see how much of their lives it owned. How free were they to give it away? Then he asked them to pray.

Everyone bowed their heads. Tony stared straight ahead. He realized he had moved to the edge of the pew as the sermon unwound.

Rita squeezed his hand and gave him a side eye questioningly without raising her bowed head. Alright?

He nodded slightly and scooted back against the pew. It was then that Tony began thinking of a way to save these people from themselves and spring himself from the mob life at the same time.

Chapter 11 - No Reason

Tony had gone to Aversa with the idea of helping the men he loved to see they were in danger of losing their names. He knew better than to think he could do this all at once. The suggestion to dial back discreetly criminal activity was his opening bid in what he hoped would be a change in direction.

Reason.

Could they hear something reasonable? Could they see the truth of how much wealth they had and what it was doing to their family?

No. The Aversa meeting blew up in his face. Frank and AJ were dead. Tony was scared. And sad. He decided to use a different tack. Subtle wasn't going to work. Of course it wasn't! The dead guy in hell didn't get the message.

How do you get a rich man's attention? Make him poor. That's when Tony Diderrick decided to take the mob's money.

The Face in the Grave

It was insane. How could someone hope to steal the mob's money and get away with it? How could you hide from an organization with unlimited resources they could use to find you?

Well, Tony told himself, I'm not stealing their money. I have no intention of spending it, I'm just going to put it in a place that will stop them from using it to make their names out of it.

And that might answer the big question.

If Tony controlled all that money, they couldn't use it to find him. He already had a well-developed counter-surveillance scheme. He would beef it up with some of the funds, pay himself a reasonable retirement, and make the rest disappear.

He had all the pieces in place.

All he was really doing was moving his retirement up a couple of years… and making three quarters of a billion dollars disappear without a trace.

The last part would actually be the simplest.

Each of the three bosses controlled fifteen to twenty crypto wallets they used for various purposes.

Tony set this up to make his accounting work easier although there was always a great deal of slippage between the intended use of a wallet and where the funds actually went.

None of the fat cats ever took the time to fully understand crypto; if they had, they would have insisted on knowing what only he knew: the seed phrases for each and every one of the family crypto accounts.

Chapter 12 - Tony's Funeral

Carla

My dad's funeral wasn't a big event.

Mom was so shocked by his passing that all the planning fell to me. Not that I was any less shocked. I've since come to know that each of us deals with death in our own way.

Some folks go into their own head and work it out; others—and this is the way I'm wired—go and work it out by working it out; staying in motion. I'm no psychologist but maybe it's a response to the stillness of death.

The Face in the Grave

The first time I saw a dead body, that's what shocked me. It's so plain, so sharply obvious that this person is gone. People use the euphemism that someone "fell asleep" when they died, but I've never thought that was right.

Death is nothing like sleep. Animation is the word. A dead body is inanimate. You see it from a distance. You don't have to even get that close. They're gone. Still. Inanimate.

So the reaction—my reaction—is to get moving and stay moving. If still equals dead, I will not be still. That might sound stupid to some of you, but that's because you're not wired like me.

So it didn't bother me to be in charge while my mom did grief in her own way. Not that she didn't have some input. I was planning on cremating my dad. Had it all lined up.

Mom heard me on the phone with the funeral director and she flipped. No, we don't do that, she told me. That's no way to do a funeral. Even when I said we could do a viewing with a casket and then do the cremation she told me no.

Her husband was going to have a "proper" burial, and she didn't care how much it cost.

In the end, the only concession I got out of her was to put Dad in a vault in a mausoleum at the Mount Solon cemetery instead of putting him in the ground.

I don't want anyone to think I was being cheap about my dad. That's the way they get you, right? That's the line. "Of course you want the best for your loved one."

Actually, that translates as "we will be the first people to judge you if you tell us to find a way to get rid of your loved one's inanimate, lifeless, no-longer-useful-to-them-or-anyone-else body."

It's a skill the funeral director people have that you can't measure without a micrometer for the change in the lift in the eyebrow or an audiogram to detect the change in pitch of their voice.

The truth was simple: my mom was no longer working and my dad was our only source of income. We didn't know anything about our finances—didn't know he had a nice little insurance policy that would keep Mom comfortable and get me through any in-state college I wanted to attend.

That came later.

Right then, in the week after he passed, Mom mostly stayed in bed and I mostly stayed on the phone with the pastor, the funeral home, and church members lining up to bring us dinners we politely thanked them for and then froze because no one was interested in good food; we were interested in comfort food: Chick-fil-A waffle fries and Ciro's pizza.

The mausoleum compromise saved us a pretty penny at the time, and not cremating Tony turned out to have saved more pretty pennies than could be counted in a lifetime.

We buried him on a Tuesday—is it right to say buried when there's no hole in the ground?—because there was no reason to wait for anyone to come from out of town.

Everyone we knew who knew him was us and the people in our community. I did ask Mom if we should try to get Dad's work people involved but she told me she wouldn't know where to start to contact his work.

There was a good turnout for eleven o'clock on a weekday. Our church people all came, and a few family friends. The pastor did a good job preaching a funeral for a person he didn't know. It was vanilla. No blaming him for that.

A lot of the folks came back to the house afterward but that was just weird. It drove home to me how my dad was not only an unknown quantity to the preacher, he was an unknown quantity to all the people milling around our house quietly consuming deviled eggs and slices of sugar-cured ham.

A man of few words. That was the way the preacher described my dad. But that wasn't all the story.

He didn't just have few words, he had few connections, few real connections. In fact, it seemed, sitting there in our living room, that his wordlessness infected the people trying to comfort my mom and myself.

It was as if he'd made silence normal. He was good at it. And you have to ask yourself, how many people do you know who aren't awkward in an awkward silence? My dad never had an awkward silence; at least if he did I never saw it.

I know you've been to funerals and wakes where pockets of people pool together and share little laughs. That didn't happen at my dad's funeral.

The Face in the Grave

He was silent and they held suit.

Even old Maude Smithson, who could fill up the airwaves with endless chatter, sat quietly at the dining room table.

Soon groups of two or three broke off and left. The crowd dribbled out and we were alone.

Mom went to her room and came out stretching both arms over her head, wearing her favorite gray sweatshirt and a pair of Adidas running shorts showing her already-thin legs grown stick-like for lack of eating. She yawned and came to me.

Hugging me hard, she said, "It's quiet as fuck in here."

Hearing the "f" word come out of my mom's mouth would have been shocking enough; I can't say I'd ever heard her curse before or since, but she slurred the middle of the expletive so it came out like a Boston street vendor, or Bill Burr getting warmed up for a set.

So my tiny, southern, church-lady Momma breaks the silence of the funereal atmosphere in our home like this: it's quiet as fawwwk in here.

I looked at her, thinking she'd cracked, but she was smiling. A real smile that took in both the sorrow and the hope; a smile that said we were going to go on.

That's how, fifteen minutes after the last of the official mourners departed, our house was filled with howls of laughter. My mom.

It was like she went into that bedroom, took off the black dress, hung it up neatly, and came back out alive and determined that we weren't going to live in the mausoleum she's just put her husband in.

Chapter 13 - Dynomark

Tony's plan to disappear had always been contemplated and provided for; his plan to disappear and make the Fratellis money disappear at the same time had not.

He assumed it would not take Richie long to trace the loss of the money to the loss of the family accountant and that would ignite a shit storm.

All the muscle would be alerted, every string they had would be pulled, every favor called in. No one could move money without him knowing about it, and no one could cut off his access to the money, even if they thought to do so.

He had time to get home to both his homes and see both his families while he implemented new security measures and picked the perfect moment to turn off the mob's cryptocurrency spigot. And while he had time to turn on and co-opt Dynomark.

The Face in the Grave

After a quick visit to Amelia Island, Shirley and Sandy, he headed north to Virginia.

He tripled the conventional security measures he had planned for his retirement. The people of Brand's Flat and Amelia Island would have been amazed to know their communities were guarded 24/7/365 by redundant teams of private security, all of which unknowingly worked for and reported to Tony.

Every person who came within ten miles of either of his homes via normal travel was documented. This was a good system he'd had in place for fifteen years, and he was confident it worked well, but it was conventional.

He needed something more, and being the kind of man to plan for rainy days that might turn into monsoons, Tony Diderrick had a very unconventional level of security he had readied for this storm.

Tony's familiarity with family operations made it simple for him to keep tabs on the two dozen or so contract killers (i.e. "muscle) likely to be dispatched to whack him and recover the family's money, but he knew something none of the hit men knew about themselves.

In early 2011, Richie got wind of a new technology developed by the defense contractor Dynomark.

In principle, the system was this: Navy Seals would consume edible geo-trackers before missions, allowing commanders to locate them at any time.

After a mission was over, the tracker would find its way out of the Seal through natural processes. Navy brass was in love with the idea. The government spent an obscene amount of taxpayer dollars bringing the Dynomark trackers online.

Two things stopped the project from making it to the field in the colon of elite special warfare troops.

First, the contractor guarantee that the technology would pass through Seal's long and winding road in no more than a week proved to be untrue—the three men and two women who swallowed the prototypes in a blind trial were trackable after six months, and at the two-year mark, four of five were still traceable.

The second reason was simple enough; the Seals revolted and threatened to quit en masse if the brass tried to force them to take the tracker pill.

According to the contractor, there had been discussions at the highest levels of the military about surreptitiously feeding the trackers to the troops.

After all, they reasoned, it had cost a lot of money to develop.

But in the end, the Chairman of the Joint Chiefs vetoed the idea and ordered Dynomark to be paid off, the proprietary rights to the technology becoming the property of the Government.

The technology was classified top secret and mothballed.

Richie Fratelli took it out of mothballs. Nothing secret is ever very secret. Especially when you've given ten years of your life to perfect an amazing technology.

The team of contractors was threatened with the usual stuff: non-disclosure agreements, a one-hundred-thousand dollar fine and fifty years in prison if they squawked.

The DoD has always been leaky and always for the same reason: people are not as motivated by negative consequences as they are by positive possibilities. And pride outweighs fear.

Add to the disappointment of having their pet project deep-sixed the relative pittance the government paid them to close out the deal, and you had a situation tailor-made for a leak.

The Dynomark tracker project lead had a wife who liked to shop in the garment district in the city. When she did, she liked to have dinner at Cristaldo's, a restaurant in Little Italy that Richie owned and used as a kind of office to do low-level business.

The wife talked a lot when she drank, and the night the feds bought out and shut down Dynomark's tracker project, she was in the city, dined at Cristaldo's, and talked a lot.

Her waiter thought the story she told about her husband being an inventor and electronic bugs people swallowed sounded like drunken babble. He repeated it to a few of the other waiters that night as a joke and one of them repeated it to Richie the next time he came for dinner.

The Face in the Grave

That's how the existence of a top secret pentagon project came to Richie Fratellis ear. He didn't think it was a joke. He wanted to know who the lady was.

A check of the credit card receipts gave him a name. A week later, the Dynomark project leader was having dinner with a man who knew all about his dead project, only the man didn't talk about it like it was dead. He talked about it like it was very much alive.

The cloak and dagger of the government confused the project lead. He knew the JCS had shut them down, but maybe another of the alphabet soup agencies was ready to go forward with it. CIA? ATF? FBI? He didn't care. He didn't want to know. Didn't need to know.

All that was important to him was the revival and deployment of his project… and the resurrection of his company.

He never knew he was meeting with Tony Diderrick, the accountant for the Fratelli crime family.

And no one in the Fratelli crime family except Richie Fratelli and Tony knew that for ten years now, every major player in the family had been fed edible GPS trackers.

They started small and practical, and staying true to the basic paranoia of avoiding getting whacked, Richie got every family hitman tagged. He had his own top secret secrets and the hitman GPS program was the top of that top. Tony and Richie alone knew.

As the program expanded and the technology improved through field testing, the Dynomark company reps only met with Tony, who reported only to Richie.

When Dynomark developed an app that interfaced with all the major map apps on any cell phone, Richie had a live picture at his fingertips. He expanded the program to include all family members.

Eventually he could see where everyone was at any given time, like a soccer mom tracking her teenagers. It became a byword amongst the crews that Richie was some kind of freak who had the ability to find anyone anytime he wanted or to know where you had been.

It suited Richie to have his people think he was supernatural or in league with the devil. Good. Let 'em think that way. Keep them on their toes.

What he didn't know was that Tony fed him a tracker too. Tony didn't decide to do this on his own. It happened when the Dynomark techs showed him a nifty back door that the master account on the app could use to block individual trackers from showing up on the subordinate maps.

The techs were operating under the assumption the government agency they thought they supplied would have many areas of responsibility and no one would need or want to clutter their maps with hundreds of geolocations.

Tony tucked this information away. Then two things happened—actually, three.

Six months before the fateful Aversa meeting, three new trackers showed up on the maps app Tony regularly checked. It took some calculations and time to sort out, but the three trackers:

dm2603376

dm0290086

and dm 0328660

were definitely himself (easy enough to figure out), AJ Fratelli, and Frankie Fratelli.

This had been concerning when it happened. It had also been another one of the high stakes moments he'd navigated over his years in the family.

Obviously Richie knew Tony would see the new trackers. He and Tony were the only people with access.

If Tony questioned Richie, it could lead to discussions he did not want to have with a mob boss; discussions about words like "trust" and "confidence." Deadly words in mobster life.

On the other hand, if either of the two older brothers got wind of what was going on, he couldn't see any way he didn't get whacked for not telling them.

As he had done so many times, and as suited his approach to life, adapted and perfected in the presence of his explosively abusive father, he kept his mouth shut.

A few weeks into keeping his mouth shut, he got an idea. If Richie wanted to track everyone in the family, why should he be the exception? The more Tony thought about it, the more it made sense.

The Face in the Grave

If Richie had a tracker, Tony could keep tabs on him too and if it ever got out that the other brothers had trackers, Tony could point out that everyone had one, including himself.

That might keep him from getting whacked.

Accordingly, Tony fed Richie a tracker during dinner at that same meeting in Italy. It was simple enough to do; the equivalent of a grain of pepper in a bowl of salad.

He excused himself after the main course, and before dessert the tracker was actively pinging and he had excluded its location from going to Richie's version of the tracker app.

Now Tony Diderrick was the only person on earth who knew where every member of the Fratelli crime family was at any given moment. He was only one of two people on earth who knew the tracker existed.

Being the accountant and seeing the value of things, he could not help but wonder what the market value of such information might be; to the family, to competitors, to the feds. He thought it might be worth quite a bit.

When Tony "retired" upon leaving Richie Fratellis home in New Jersey, he implemented another piece of Dynomark information he alone knew about: a particular chemical cleanse regimen guaranteed to disable and/or rid a person of one of the geotrackers if they'd swallowed it.

He did this during the LA leg of his journey home. Always looking for layers of added protection, he reasoned that Richie might have discovered his own work-around in the Dynomark tracking system.

He figured if Richie had managed this and was tracking him, the trail would go cold as far from his true destination as possible. It only cost him an extremely sour stomach and three extra visits to the airplane bathroom on the flight west.

So it was that Tony Diderrick walked away from a thirty-year career as the accountant to the Fratelli crime family. He was fifty-seven years old. He was not on the map. Not the family's or the Fed's. He did not exist. He was not real.

But the 750 million dollars-plus that dropped off the map with him was real.

When the Fratellis discovered their money and their accountant were gone, it wasn't the accountant they tried to find. They assumed, as Tony anticipated, he was in a concrete-filled barrel in the Hudson.

In their thinking, he wouldn't turn up again alive, but the money... no one stole that kind of money with no intention of spending it. They waited for one of their number to show up with a new beach house or a fleet of Lamborghinis or a casino named after their mother.

The knowledge that extravagant spending might bring them under suspicion actually had the effect Tony had been looking for at Aversa; everyone got real conservative with their money. They thought twice before shelling out sums which they'd never hesitated to spend before.

It would have made him smile. And he did smile, in his living rooms in Amelia Island and Brand's Flat, but it had nothing to do with money the mob spent or he spent.

He smiled at his wives and his children who he fully intended to continue living their simple lives.

As for the money, well, his intention was to take it to his grave.

And he did.

Part II

Chapter 14 - The Bubble of Normal Breaking

The coffee was good; the smell as invigorating as the taste.

Sandy Anderson took small sips of the steaming hot liquid even though it burned his tongue a little. Waiting for coffee to cool was just wrong. You took it as it came to you and that was that.

He was in Amelia Island Coffee on the main drag in Fernandina Beach. Marcy, the pretty, utterly unattainable college girl barista, zipped along solo with the light morning rush.

It was just past six a.m. on a Tuesday morning. He admired Marcy's efficiency almost as much as her lithe body. It was like watching a dancer as she moved between the register and the espresso machine.

She caught him staring and smiled when he tried to act like he wasn't. Too late. He smiled too.

The Face in the Grave

His routine was to come to the coffee shop and sit for twenty or thirty minutes on the mornings he took the trek down to Jacksonville to visit Shirley in the psychiatric hospital.

If he timed it right and took Route 200 out to Yulee, he could make it there in less than an hour and a half.

Sometimes, on weekends, he drove down A1A to Fort George Island and took the ferry across the river to Mayport. It was expensive and took time, but money wasn't everything and time on the ferry was not wasted. It was a good place to think.

He was pleasantly surprised to find, after the dust settled from his father's disappearance and his mother's mental break, that finances were not going to be a crisis.

The bank accounts the family lawyer helped him gain access to easily covered expenses for the foreseeable future and there was even a savings account designated "college fund" with enough money for him to attend any reasonably priced school for two to three years without needing to work.

It took him a couple months to get a handle on bills but most expenses were auto-draft and didn't need his attention.

Sitting in the coffee shop, he felt a sense of normalcy returning and pride in himself for "adulting" enough to keep the state from giving him a guardian.

Normalcy. Was that what this was? A father gone without a trace and a mother just as gone?

Well, it proved you could get used to almost anything.

He drained the last of his black coffee from the heavy thick-lipped white ceramic mug and pushed back his chair. Returning the mug to the bar, Marcy met him at the black bus tub.

"I'm sorry about your mom," she said. "I don't think I ever told you."

"Ah… thanks," he said.

"Everyone thinks you're doing great, all things considered."

She looked at him. It took him an extra beat to pick up on the question in the statement and in the barista's eyes.

"Oh, well, everyone… that's good. I'm doing pretty good." He faded off awkwardly.

Marcy didn't look away, didn't let him hang up on her. She was listening. And seeing. Sandy hung up first. The moment reverted to "normal."

Marcy cast one last line his way, fishing for reality.

"Any news about your dad?"

He smiled thinly and backed away. "No. But thanks for asking."

Exiting the coffee shop and starting up his old beater F-150, he sighed deeply. Everyone thought he was doing pretty good. He had not had the time to think about how he was doing.

The barista unknowingly poked the balloon around his emotions with her innocent question. No one had spoken directly since his world broke into pieces.

"Everyone" spoke to "everyone" about his situation but no one asked him how he was doing. At least not anyone who mattered.

The state-appointed counselors and social workers asked their perfunctory checklist questions but they didn't know him. The people who mattered—his friends or the people he counted in that category—were nice and around but stayed at a safe distance.

He saw it in their eyes when they said, "How're you doing man?"

It was in that last word; man. Like the difference between "I love you" and "love you" in a text message. Man.

"How're you doing, man?" Not "How're you doing, Sandy?"

And it was in their eyes.

Their eyes said, "I don't really want to know how you're doing and if you're gonna crack up please do it with someone else."

But just now Marcy, his ballerina barista, saw him, and he knew it. She wanted a real answer. She was asking.

Whether it was the shock of his fantasy girl speaking or that she actually wanted to know how he was doing, or both, the balloon broke there in the truck as it sat throaty, idling, adding a bassline and rocking him gently.

He cried for the first time since his life and home went silent.

Salty tears dropped into the edges of his mouth and mingled with the lingering taste of coffee. He made no attempt to wipe them away. Let them

The Face in the Grave

fall. Let it go. Come and wash away this fake skin I've been wearing. Wash it away like an afternoon Florida thunderstorm.

    He threw the truck into drive and eased on to Centre Street, headed for Jacksonville and his broken mother.

Chapter 15 - The Book

Carla Dyson followed her daily routine. Routine. There was a word. What was routine?

When death visits a home, especially in the stealthy way it had come to the Dyson home, it rattled every rung on the ladder of routine. Step, step, step, and then there's no place to put hands or feet, only the long drop into eternity.

She pondered that. Would there be a routine in heaven? Some kind of rhythm? God created seasons; daytime and night. There must be something to that.

Finishing her breakfast of two over-medium eggs and a bowl of grits, she rinsed off her dishes and put them in the dishwasher. She grabbed a bottled water from a plastic-wrapped eight-pack on the kitchen counter. It was getting hot out now that school was over and June was almost spent.

The Face in the Grave

The door to her dad's office was cracked. She had not been in the office since the day he died. The thought of going in there gave her chills but she didn't know why. A cracked door is not a closed door. It's inviting rather than forbidding.

She could see the morning sunlight spilling into the room. That would be from the window behind his desk that looked out to the west where you could see the twin little mountains, Betsy Belle and Mary Grey.

And closer, the backyard leaning off into the small valley where the train tracks ran. There were redbuds sprinkled in amongst the hardwood trees. They were colorless now, but in springtime their fuchsia flowers always made her feel like she and they knew a subtle secret the other trees didn't know.

It made her heart full when she saw them bloom again each year.

She went to the door and stood outside his office, momentarily frozen by melancholy, then she pushed the door open and went in.

The smell of the room immediately overwhelmed her. Her knees buckled. Her dad's pipe sat in a brass ashtray on the desk, ready for filling and the strike of a match.

He only smoked it in the backyard, but the scent of cheap cherry-blend tobacco lingered here on the hoodie and hat he wore while he smoked. They hung on a hall tree in the corner of the room, abandoned like the pipe on the desk by the smoker.

As much as the tobacco smell created a rift in Carla's emotions, it was the smell of his old everyday Aramis cologne that bent her over double with memories and sadness.

The key to wearing a cologne, he told her, was to find your own scent, never share its name with anyone who commented on it, and use just enough that people knew there was something there but also let you deny you wore anything.

He said if he ever had a son, that would be the only person he'd pass on the Aramis secret to.

Like the hint of pipe tobacco, the Aramis was barely here—a suggestion—but it was strong enough in memory to put her on the ground and release a torrent of as-yet-uncried tears.

The sobs wracked her body for a quarter hour. Their intensity surprised her. She was glad no one else was home. She let her voice join her tears, feeling free in the way only an empty house invites full emotion.

When the storm began to subside, she half crawled, half scooted to a bookshelf where a box of tissues sat between volumes of her father's mostly nonfiction books.

Tony was obsessed with World War Two and never tired of reading the latest take on a battle or leading character from that era.

His tastes in fiction ran mostly to Herman Wouk and Charles Dickens—he said no one could make him care about people who seemed to do so little for so long like Dickens and Wouk. This type of storytelling made sense to him. The words fit together and lined up and eventually brought you to a bottom line that added up and paid off.

His favorite was A Tale of Two Cities, which he read and reread. The copy on his shelf showed the velveteen wear of being well loved.

From where Carla sat wiping her nose she saw the book was not set all the way in its place. It stuck out half an inch as if her dad had just been about to pull it out and read it before being interrupted.

The thought of leaving it like this disturbed something in her. Too much like everything else about her dad leaving so suddenly.

She stood up and gave it a push to put it back in its place. It didn't move. She pushed again. Again it didn't move.

She pulled it from its slot and discovered the problem; a paperback book from the shelf above had fallen down and lodged behind Dickens' master work.

She reached in and pulled it out. Now her dad's favorite went easily back into place.

She scanned the paperback shelf, looking for the proper place for the fallen book. There was no place, no slot for it. No books were out of place. Curious.

She pulled the Dickens volume back out and ran her fingers over the back of the bookshelf trying to discover how the paperback got there. There was no gap, no way it could have gotten back there accidentally.

She looked it over more closely now. Who hides a book on a bookshelf? And why?

The Face in the Grave

Tunnel in the Sky by Robert Heinlein. It was slightly dog-eared. It smelled like old paperback and the edges of the pages had the brownish yellow of age. The cover was black with a cheesy Illustration of a fifties-looking guy in a fifties-looking space suit standing in a doorway opening through planet earth.

She turned it over and scanned the back cover blurb. A story about survivalists and interstellar portals?

This was not one of Tony's books.

Couldn't be, could it? It was so far from the books he normally read it couldn't be his. But here it was. And here it was hidden. She turned it back over and flipped open the front cover. There was a premade label with a picture of a cat standing on a stack of books. It said:

Ex libris
Shirley Laughton
Amelia Island, FL
#335

Although she'd never seen a label like this before, Carla knew her Latin—it was her favorite class three years running with Ms. Sheffield at Wilson Memorial High School.

Ex = out of or from.

Libris = books/library.

So she was holding in her hands a book from the library of one Shirley Laughton of Amelia Island Florida. 335 couldn't be an address. It must be the book number. Lots of books.

She wondered who Shirley Laughton might be and if she would be missing one book out of such a big library or if this might be a book from a used bookstore; Shirley Laughton gone and her libris scattered to the wind. Another melancholy thought.

Carla pulled out her phone and googled the name and the city. Nothing. She opened the Facebook app and searched there, again nothing. Oh well, not everyone was online.

She thought about taking the mystery to her mom but decided against it. A slight uneasiness made her stop.

Her mom might know who Shirley Laughton was and then again maybe not. For that matter, her dad may or may not have known the woman.

Possession of the book didn't mean anything did it? Mom didn't need any bad news right now.

And what if it turned out Ms. Laughton was someone her dad wanted to keep hidden away like this book? That would not be good for anyone right now. Better see what she could find out on her own.

She closed the cover and walked to her dad's desk, running her hand over its smooth dark wood surface. It was cold to her touch. Room temperature. That's what the desk was.

That's what her dad felt like the last time she touched him. She shivered in spite of the summer sunshine flooding into the office windows.

Chapter 16 - Shirley Comes Home

Sandy was shocked to find his mother sitting up in bed eating jiggling cubes of alien-green Jell-O. One glance and he knew she was really present. She gave him a weak smile and tried to speak. The Jell-o and several comatose months kept her from saying it clearly but he got it. "I love you."

He stooped down and hugged her tightly, realizing for the first time in his life how small she was in body and simultaneously how large she was in his life; how empty life had been without her, how full he felt right now. He blubbered into her neck, "I love you, Momma."

His trips to the hospital became all-day affairs. Now that she was back, he was not going to let her go again. Every time he opened the door to her room he felt a little roller coaster ride go off in his belly. Every time she looked up and met his eyes the ride came to a smooth stop.

Sandy took over his mother's social rehab and closely monitored her physical therapy. Shirley made great progress, much ahead of the prognosis

The Face in the Grave

of the medical staff. Two weeks after coming "back from La La Land," as she called her mental break, she and Sandy ganged up on the attending psychiatrist and made their case: let her go home.

Familiar surroundings would help her complete her recovery faster than staying here. They won the doctor over and the next day, a Saturday, Sandy took his regular cup of coffee and his beater pickup truck to Jacksonville to bring his mother home.

It was a good day and a hard day all at once.

Shirley smiled a lot and cried a lot. Sandy assiduously avoided talking about the elephant in the room. This landed the two of them in periods of awkward silence that grew as large as the elephant itself.

Tony was gone. Sandy was going. What would Shirley do all alone in this house? Toward the end of July, after the two had settled into a routine and Sandy no longer entered the kitchen expecting to find his mother once again catatonic at the kitchen table, he came out with it.

"Mom, do you think we should sell this place? Isn't it going to be too much, you know, for just you?"

Shirley, sitting in the same chair at the same kitchen table where he'd found her, didn't meet his eyes. She stared through the refrigerator. For half a beat, Sandy thought he pulled the wrong lever in his mother's brain. Then she smiled a tight-lipped smile.

"Sandy, we can't leave this house. Where will your father go when he comes home? He'll come here. And if we're not here, how will he find us?"

Sandy searched her eyes to see if this was a joke or a delusion or something in between. He started to probe her with a question but she cut him off.

"I know it's not likely, Sandy. And I know he could find us even if we moved. But something bad happened to me and you took care of me. You waited. You gave me a place to come home to. Something bad happened to your father or he'd be here. I can wait for him like you waited for me."

Sandy let out a long breath he hadn't realized he was holding in.

Shirley continued.

"Besides, I've got my books to keep me company. They've always been good for that. A book is a faithful friend. A good book is better than a best friend. You can have more than one of them and they don't get jealous of each other. I've got lots of them. Where would I put them if we moved into some little place?"

Sandy smiled at his mother's old adages about books. This was Shirley for true and for real, talking like his mom again. A little cracked maybe, but only in the normal way. She got up.

"In fact," she said, "I think I'm going to have coffee with one of my besties right now."

She walked into the den to the bookshelves and stopped at the far right row of books on a shelf level with her eyes. She stood there with one hand on her hip and the other to her face, tapping her lips with a forefinger.

"Hmmm," she murmured. "Sandy? Have you moved any of my books? Has anyone borrowed one?"

Sandy got up and followed her into the room. A sick feeling rose in his stomach—a feeling triggered from a thousand such interactions with his mother and her books from earliest memory.

A missing or misplaced book wasn't a misdemeanor in the Anderson home, it was a felony. Book-napping brought about swift trials and convictions without an opportunity to present a defense.

"No, Mom."

He started to add that he'd long ago decided he'd rather walk the mile and a half to the library than hassle with her about borrowing one of her "best friends."

But the look on her face told him it wasn't the time. She ran her finger down the row of books, letting it flick along the spines. He knew this shelf. This was where she kept the best of her best friends.

This shelf was the closest thing to an altar that existed in the Anderson's non-religious home.

The twenty or so volumes enshrined here could only be handled by the high priestess herself.

Even in his childish hubris he'd never once thought of violating the sanctity of the Shelf. No one but Shirley Anderson could account for the canon of the holy shelf.

The Face in the Grave

Like scripture, a book made it to its place there by virtue of its belonging there. And like the books of the Bible, it contained books with many and diverse authors from many eras and genres.

Tunnel in the Sky by Heinlein sat next to *To Kill a Mockingbird* by Lee. *The Caine Mutiny* by Herman Wouk nestled up to *The Count of Monte Cristo* by Dumas.

And there were Dickens and L'Amour and Stephen King.

Shirley's finger stopped at the far right end of the row of books.

"Missing," she said to the bookshelf.

Chapter 17 - Surfing Safari

Life is stranger than fiction, they say, and it is. Carla Dyson and Sandy Anderson would testify to it. It was certainly a strange day when they met each other that fall at Webb Center on the campus of Old Dominion University.

For Carla, ODU was a practical decision. She wanted to stay in-state and avoid out-of-state tuition, but she wanted to leave home too.

She told herself she could've gotten into UVA, but it was too close. Virginia Commonwealth was further, but Richmond wasn't a city that appealed to her.

Norfolk and ODU, with Virginia Beach a stone's throw away, was perfect. No one from home was going to just show up in her dorm room without warning and the beach was far enough away that she couldn't just bug out and skip classes without thinking ahead.

Sandy came north because Shirley Anderson wanted him to.

The Face in the Grave

His plan, given the recent break with reality his mother had experienced, was to attend the University of North Florida in Jacksonville and live at home.

Shirley didn't like this plan. She wanted Sandy to go to the same school his father attended. What her motives were was unclear to Sandy. It didn't seem like a good idea to go that far away.

He had a hard time believing his mother was serious about him leaving the area and pushed back to the point that the two had a row over it.

When the dust settled, Sandy saw his mother earnestly desired him to attend ODU because the school was connected to his missing father, and she'd heard Tony say he hoped his son would go there. That settled the matter. He took some of the money set aside by his missing father and went north.

It never occurred to him that he'd never seen a diploma from ODU, or a class ring, or ever met any of his father's classmates. It was enough for Sandy that Shirley wanted him to go to the school and she had Tony Anderson's word on it.

Before his first semester was three weeks old he would experience a tectonic shift that would not only change his future, it would forever alter his past.

Having been raised on a Florida beach, Sandy wasn't impressed by Virginia Beach. The waves were lame, the resort strip tried too hard, and the clientele—well, they just weren't Florida girls. They looked like people who put on bathing suits a couple of weeks a year instead of the girls he grew up with who wore bikinis like their birthday suits.

The whole scene brought him down. He told his Virginia Beach-native roommate, Dave Harman, all about it one afternoon.

"Dude, locals stay off the beach this time of year and we stay north of 85th street and south of 15th anyway. I've been to Amelia. You need to hit Sandbridge, bro. It'll be like home for you. And it's mostly locals there. Better surf too. This Saturday I'm taking some kids from our psych class out there. Meet up at Webb at eight if you want to come. Bring some beer."

So Sandy Anderson met Carla Dyson for the first time on the third Saturday of their first semester at ODU. Dave drove a monumentally dirty fifteen-passenger Ford van with the two middle rows of seats torn out, effectively turning it into both an eight seater and a party van. The top sported a rack for surfboards.

Sandy noticed Dave had successfully recruited two of the three cutest girls from Psych 101. It impressed him. Sandy was no ladies' man and no social butterfly. Despite being objectively nice looking and friendly, he depended on the Daves of the world to connect him with people in general and with women specifically.

The two girls got into the van first and took the back seat for themselves, leaving the men to sort out who would sit in the remaining seats.

The first guy in, a lanky six-foot-something dude who went by Flipper, got in and laid out lengthwise on the center bench; the other two guys took the passenger seat and the single next to Flipper.

Sandy was left to either argue with him to sit up or take the third seat next to Carla.

When he hesitated, Carla noticed. She patted the seat next to her and said, "Come on. I don't bite, and Molly here already ate this morning. Don't have to worry about her for another three hours."

She smiled with her eyes and Sandy sat down. Her friendliness prompted him to attempt a comeback.

"Didn't know I was catching a ride to the beach with cannibals."

Molly rolled her eyes at this and turned her attention out the van window to the light posts on Hampton Boulevard. Sandy felt his face flush.

Carla held his gaze and chuckled. "No. Not cannibals. Wild animals, maybe." She patted a paperback book in her lap.

"I've been reading up on them."

He glanced at the book. Carla's hand covered the title. He liked her hand. He liked her smile. His face got more red. He wanted to look away but she didn't break the moment and he was transfixed—a buck in the headlights of the girl's eyes.

She could run over him or gently apply the brakes. He wasn't going to move.

She said, "You're from Florida, right?" He cocked his head and arched his eyebrows at this unexpected question.

"What? How…?"

The Face in the Grave

"Mrs. Armentrout had us all say where we were from the first day of class, remember?"

"I do, but you… there are what, seventy-five or a hundred people in the class? You remember all that?"

Carla's smile got bigger.

"I wish! How easy would classes be if I had that kind of memory? I do know a guy back home who never forgets a name. He's the preacher though. I guess that's his job.

"No, I just have this thing for beaches. I grew up in the mountains but I loooove the beach. You said you were from Fernandina Beach, Florida." She shrugged and smiled as if this explained everything.

Sandy copied her shrug. She laughed.

"Tell me about Fernandina," she said.

Sandy did. Then Carla told him about Brand's Flat. They were just getting into family and friends when Dave pulled the Ford into the public parking lot at the north end of Sandbridge and hollered, "Let's roll, kids. Sun's out, surf's up, and sand's about!"

The troops dutifully filed out, grabbing coolers, beach bags, and chairs while Dave got the surfboards down off the roof rack. He called to Sandy, "Come and grab one of the boards, man. Show us how it's done."

"I'm not much of a surfer," Sandy said, mostly truthfully. He wasn't one of the endless summer brand of surfing existentialists. He learned to surf out of self-defense more than a desire to catch a wave and sit on top of the world. He figured it would be hard to explain—growing up on a beach and not being a surfer.

He thought it must be like growing up in Norway and not knowing how to ski. So he learned in the summer between fifth and sixth grade. It was easy for him, and like most people to whom things come naturally, he did not know he was exceptionally skilled at it.

"No, no, dude. You're surfing. Come on," Dave said.

It was a warm day but the ocean had already taken its turn toward fall temperatures.

While the two girls and two other guys set up base camp, he and Dave paddled out and caught the first rides of what turned out to be a nice set in the chilly water.

It was an hour before he rode the last wave in and jogged with the board to where the others were, the boys sitting in beach chairs surreptitiously drinking beers and the girls laying out on towels. He was cold. Carla sat up when his shadow passed over her.

"Done hanging ten, or whatever you call it?" she asked.

Teeth chattering, Sandy said, "Ya-yeah. Not used to these conditions."

"You're pretty good at that," she said, nodding toward the surfboard.

He looked embarrassed. "Not really. I'm just average."

The other girl, who had a face perpetually communicating she regretted her life choices, turned onto one elbow and said, "You're in my light."

Her breasts tried to escape their bikini top hammock as she said this and Sandy glanced at them involuntarily like a man struck in the knee by a doctor's rubber hammer.

The girl looked down at herself then back at Sandy with a "you're a disgusting pig" expression.

He looked away and tried to move his shadow at the same time, kicking sand onto Carla in the process.

She got up and dusted herself off, shaking the towel off downwind of the other girl. She handed it to Sandy with a wry smile. They began walking down the beach.

"You can't stay out of your own way can you?"

Sandy was toweling off his hair as they walked.

He stopped and said, "What?"

"What?"

"What did you just say?"

"I said, you can't stay out of your own way. Never heard that before?"

He gave her a hard look. "No. I've heard it all my life actually."

"Yeah?"

"Yeah. My father said it all the time. It was like his pet phrase. 'Sandy, you forgot to do your chores again… can't get out of your own way can you?' Or, 'Sandy, you got a D on your algebra homework… can't get out of your own way can you?'"

They started to walk again. Carla laughed.

The Face in the Grave

"That's funny. My dad said the same thing except for me it was, 'Carla, you forgot to take out the trash again, you can't get out of your own way, can you?' I'm not sure I really even know what he meant by it."

For the first time since he'd met her, Carla's smile faded to a sad expression. She looked at her feet for several paces and it appeared to Sandy she might be on the verge of tears.

"What's wrong?" he said.

She stopped walking. Her shoulder brushed his. He suddenly felt like he should put his arm around her but he didn't. Scared to do the wrong thing. When she looked up at him he wished he had.

Big tears pooled in the corners of her eyes, ready to breach the dam of her eyelids at any second. The surprised look on his face made her snort-laugh in spite of the tears.

She wiped them away and said, "Oh God. I know what you're thinking. 'I picked the crazy one to go on a walk with.'" She flicked her head back toward the others.

Sandy said, boyishly, "No I wasn't. I mean no I'm not."

Trying to keep up with the shifting emotional sands, he added, "Your friend had no trouble telling me to get out of my own way and hers too."

Carla smiled again, her cheeks colored from the almost-cry. It suited her, smiling. It made her face magnetic to Sandy's eyes.

"Friend? Her? I barely know that girl's name. She just wanted a day at the beach and she didn't want to hire an Uber."

Sandy breathed relief. He liked this girl and now he didn't have to worry about cracking the girl code of 'wherever two or more hot girls are gathered there is drama.' And he'd already eyeballed the other girl's boobs.

Carla seemed to read his mind.

"No. No need for an Uber when you can pay with cleavage. I don't blame her. The thing I never get is how they hang those things out there for anyone to see and get all huffed about it when someone looks."

They were walking again, shoulders bumping as they zig-zagged up and back with the incoming surf line. Sandy didn't know any girls who talked like this one. It made him feel almost like he could be himself. Almost.

"Why did it upset you when you talked about your dad?" he said.

"He died last spring," she said, this time without breaking stride. "I'm not used to it yet. Life without him. Which is funny because…"

"Because why?"

"Because my dad was away a lot. It was normal for him to be gone. In some ways that may be making this even harder."

She set her jaw and sucked in one cheek. "I keep expecting him to come walking in the door like he used to… but he doesn't."

"I know how that feels," Sandy said.

Carla questioned him with a look.

"Well not exactly. But expecting him to walk through the door… yeah."

"Your dad died too?"

Sandy explained the disappearance of his father and his mother's mental break. Carla listened and nodded.

They turned around at the end of his story automatically, like turning over an old LP. The second side was her turn to fill in the details of the aftermath of her dad's passing and for each of them to ask questions.

By the time they got back to the others they were bonded in shared suffering.

Angry black clouds towered in the west and the wind picked up, cutting short their beach day.

Sandy and Carla barely noticed the change of scenery from beach to campus: the car ride, the drop off, the unpacking, the dispersal of the others—the whole day—had become an unbroken conversation with someone who understood what the last six months had been like.

They camped out on a couch in Webb Center at windows overlooking the quad. The rainstorm came and went. The sun tried to make an appearance, but the day was spent by the time the clouds began dispersing.

Dinnertime rolled around. The discussion turned serious. The best pizza? Carla claimed a local place near her home was it.

"Nobody beats Ciro's," she said.

Sandy said, "It's not better than Napoli's in Jacksonville."

A student walking by overheard them and interjected, "Best pizza is Orapax, down the street in Ghent."

The Face in the Grave

A glance at each other and they were in Sandy's car letting the maps app tell them how to get to the restaurant. It turned out to be a Greek place sitting on the border between one of Norfolk's oldest neighborhoods and a sliver of industry consisting of a private shipyard and the Norfolk Southern rail yard at Lambert's Point.

They grabbed a table in a corner and ordered a pizza; Zorba's, all the way. While they waited for it to come out they were entertained by the sound of two men screaming at each other coming from the kitchen.

They couldn't understand a word of what was said in what they assumed must be Greek. When the waitress refilled their water glasses, Carla nodded toward the sound questioningly.

"Oh," she said, "That's my father and Papou. They're fine." She shrugged. "It's normal."

As if to accentuate this, one of the two males voices screeched to a crescendo and then both went silent.

The pizza came. They ate in silence, each enjoying the company, each wondering where the evening would go from here. They ended up in her dorm room sitting on her bed, kissing. He was a shy kisser, but good, gentle and decent, she thought.

He was just happy he didn't have to use any words and that she took the lead. He was never good with words or girls and never sure of his footing.

After what seemed like a long time but was really only the way new romance slows the clock, Carla leaned back on one elbow. She knocked her shoulder-sling beach bag off the bed. It fell on the floor, spilling its contents. The paperback she'd been reading in the van, before she and Sandy started conversing, tumbled on the floor.

Sandy didn't want to break the mood but his mother's book OCD took over. Can't leave a book on the ground, even when you're making out with a beautiful girl.

He picked it up. He recognized it immediately: *Tunnel in the Sky*.

Chapter 18 - The Tunnel in the Sky

Sandy saw that *Tunnel in the Sky* had not fared well in the beach bag. The front cover was folded back on itself on one corner, leaving a diagonal crease that made his mouth twitch as if he were seeing a battlefield wound that would never heal right.

He went to fold it back but noticed the black border of a book tag stuck to the inside of the mangled cover.

The unmistakable pattern of his mother's book identifiers triggered him even more.

The book felt hot in his hands. He wanted to put it down, get rid of it before he got the blame for this desecration, but he fought the feeling down long enough to see the rest of the tag, curious if the owner of this book were as meticulous as his mother, printing her name, hometown, and the serialized number of the book from her collection—a habit she'd kept from age twelve.

The Face in the Grave

He straightened the cover and flipped it open in one motion. Then he did drop the book as if it would burn his hands. It fell perfectly flat and thwacked the dorm room tile floor.

Carla, who had been observing Sandy's discomfiture over the book amusedly, sat up. The look on the boy's face was frozen between horror and curiosity.

"Sandy? What's wrong?" she said.

He pointed to the book as if it were a snake. Carla sat all the way up and looked at it. "The book?"

"How did you get my mom's book?" he said.

"What?" She got up and retrieved the paperback from the floor.

"This isn't your mom's book. It's my dad's book."

They locked eyes, each with a puzzled expression.

Sandy held out his hand for the book. "Please?" he said.

She handed it to him. He opened the front cover.

"This is my mother," he said, putting a finger on the book label.

"Shirley Laughton. Amelia Island. Except that was her maiden name. She's Shirley Anderson now. And believe me… if you grew up in my mom's house, the one thing you'd recognize is one of her books. This one's been missed. She tore through three shelves of paperbacks looking for it."

He closed the cover and handed it back to Carla, who looked at it as if it were a moon rock.

Sandy repeated himself. "Where'd you get it?"

"In my dad's office," she said, and told Sandy about finding the book hidden behind other books.

"I remember thinking it was weird at the time." She blushed.

"What?"

"This may sound stupid."

"It's already crazy, might as well give stupid a try."

Carla grinned at this and Sandy felt a twinge of regret for the interruption of their make-out session.

"I saw that label with the woman's name on it. My dad obviously did not want anyone to find it. I thought he might be having an affair. That's the last thing I wanted to think about or ask my mom about with him just dying."

Sandy said, "I guess it's possible. Anything's possible. I don't think my mom is the type to have an affair. But what do I know? She is alone a lot. My father is gone a lot…"

"I tried to look up the name on Facebook. Didn't come up with anything," Carla said.

"That's easy. My father was a social media Nazi. No accounts for him or her. Never. I had to sneak my own accounts. And he was nutso about anyone putting pictures of us in their posts," Sandy said.

"So was my dad!" Carla said.

"He wouldn't even let us take selfies with him unless we promised never to share them with anyone. And he hated it when we took his picture at all. I only have a handful of pictures of him."

Suddenly Carla teared up. Sandy hugged her spontaneously. They held each other, both thinking how strange it was to find so much comfort in another person they'd just met. Feeling the bond of shared suffering.

"I miss him," she choked out through the tears. "Nothing feels right without him. My house. My mom… nothing."

She exhaled on his chest, long and slow, releasing the sorrow onto him. He absorbed it and noticed the warmth and roundness of her breasts against him in spite of himself.

He held her, waiting for her to make a move; his own sorrow stirred alongside hers, all of this pushing his emotions close to some unseen limit.

Maybe this was what his mother got just before the emotional circuit breaker tripped and she went offline for three months. He swallowed that fear and held onto the girl.

Finally she let go of him. She went to the bathroom and washed her face. She came out rubbing her face with a towel.

"Want to see a picture of me and my dad?" she said.

"Sure," he said.

Carla took her phone from the same beach bag. She held it up to her face several times, then said, "How come this Face ID only works when you don't try to make it work?"

She made a face.

"I'm not good at remembering my number. That's another thing with Tony… he was crazy about passwords and codes. Never let us use birthdays

The Face in the Grave

or easy-to-guess things, and made us change everything every three months."

Sandy grimaced.

"What?" Carla said, still trying to get her phone unlocked.

"Tony is your dad? My father's name was… is Tony too." Sandy sighed.

"It's so weird not knowing how to talk about him."

Carla said, "Got it!" She tapped the device a few times and scrolled through her pictures. Finally she stopped on one.

It was out of focus, obviously taken in low light with the camera moving. She held it up to him. "Bad picture, but it's the most recent one."

She pinched it and enlarged it to show her dad's face.

Sandy, still lost in thought over his missing father, took the phone from her, glanced at the picture, and started to hand it back to her. As he did, the movement of the screen subtly offset the blurred image and for an instant Sandy saw a familiar face, a face that chilled his blood.

He shrank the image slightly, as much trying to get the image to go away as to bring it into focus.

This could not be.

But as the photo shrank and gave up some of its pixelation he saw the eyes, the closed-mouth smile, and the nose—the unmistakable nose.

He dropped the phone like it was suddenly the temperature of the sun.

Carla said, "Hey!" and tried to catch it. She missed.

There was a sickening "thwack" as it landed face down, perfectly flat.

"Sandy! You broke my phone!" She picked it up and showed him the screen, spider-webbed from the center out.

Sandy was standing frozen like a mannequin, his hand outstretched in the exact position from which he'd dropped the phone.

Carla felt heat rising in her cheeks. It was instantly extinguished and replaced with cold fear when she looked at Sandy's expression.

"Sandy? What's wrong? Here. Sit down."

She gently maneuvered him to the bed and sat him down. It was like posing a doll. Every joint in the man's body had gone stiff.

The fear rose. Carla shouted, "Sandy!!" She didn't know what else to do. She slapped him.

His eyes returned. Carla let out a long breath.

"What was that?!" she said as she saw his body begin to uncoil.

"Are you epileptic? Was that a seizure?"

Sandy didn't say anything. He couldn't. He took out his own phone, unlocked it, and opened his photos.

When he got to the one he had in mind he handed it to Carla.

"Here," was all he could choke out.

Carla screamed then. A sound Sandy never forgot. A sound he never wanted to hear again from anyone. Ever.

Chapter 19 - Coffee and Tsunamis

Sandy and Carla sat at a booth, each holding a white ceramic coffee mug full of cold coffee. It was two a.m.

They'd walked to the Waffle House on 49th Street and Hampton Boulevard across from campus, not wanting to be alone, not wanting to be together alone. Needing the sights and sounds of something normal to soothe the churning sea of emotion threatening to drown them.

The only other patron was a Norfolk cop intent on keeping up a stream of conversation with the lone waitress, who tossed 'umms' and 'ahhs' to him over her shoulder as she cleaned and stacked freshly washed cups and plates.

The clink of the dishes and murmur of indistinct words were hypnotic.

Sandy circled around to the phrase they kept landing on. "What should we do?"

Carla supplied the bookend reply. "I don't know."

The Face in the Grave

The pictures in their phones were evidence enough that both Tonys were "their" Tonys.

Comparing their calendars of the past year showed the pattern clearly. Whenever Tony "Anderson" was away from Amelia Island, Tony "Dyson" was in Brand's Flat, and vice versa.

There were gaps when he was absent from both places; this must be when he was working, right? Or could there be a third family with yet another "Tony" out there? And if not, what was his job?

They felt as if a tsunami coming ashore threatened to remove any familiar landmarks in their lives.

"Your mother?" Sandy asked again.

"Knows nothing about this," Carla said. "I'm not sure of much right now, but I'm not changing my mind about that. Rita knows nothing."

She paused as a thought occurred to her. She put her hand on his.

"I never said I'm sorry."

Sandy shook his head. "For what?"

"For your loss. In all the shock of this I forgot… now you know what happened to your dad. None of this changes that. I'm sorry."

Sandy sat back and tilted his head up, looking at the ceiling. The waitress started to saunter over with a fresh pot of coffee. He waved her off.

"My father… is dead," he said to the ceiling in a monotone.

"My father. Is. Dead."

Carla remained silent, staring at her coffee mug.

Sandy went on.

"My father is dead and my mother doesn't know it. My father is dead and has another family, and my mother doesn't know it." He gathered himself, looked at Carla who looked up.

"My father is dead, he has another family, and my mother just came out of a mental breakdown…"

He smiled grimly.

Carla returned the look. "What are we going to do? We can't tell one and not the other, can we? I know my mom. She's going to want to know everything. She's going to want to meet your mom. She's going to ask a million questions, and—"

Sandy cut her off.

"And we don't have the first answer."

"We... I can't keep this to myself, Sandy. I'm not made for keeping secrets."

Sandy said, "Me neither, I guess we didn't get that from his genes."

He looked away when he said this and Carla saw color come to his cheeks.

"What?" she said.

"Carla. We were just now making out in your room!" He said this in a lowered whisper, looking over at the waitress and cop to make sure they didn't hear.

His eyes were wide. Carla sat back and pursed her lips in thought; then she saw it. She suppressed a smile. A little levity wouldn't hurt. Maybe it would help.

"I don't see the problem," she said. Loud.

Sandy missed her playful undertone. His eyes got bigger and his cheeks got redder.

There was nothing funny in the world right now.

"What?! You embarrassed by me now?!! Didn't you tell me I was a great kisser just a couple of hours ago?! Kissing your sister is no crime!" Louder.

Sandy looked like his eyes might pop like soap bubbles.

"Didn't Momma always say, 'incest is best'?!" Loudest.

The waitress and cop were staring at them. Carla thought Sandy's face might actually catch fire, or melt like the Nazi in Indiana Jones.

He started to get up. He was sweating. He looked so pitiful she immediately regretted her prank.

He was out of the booth and headed for the exit before she caught him by the arm. She lowered her tone.

"Come sit down, Sandy." When he hesitated, "Please. It's okay. You don't know the whole story."

She coaxed him back to the booth. The cop and waitress went back to their non-conversation, show over.

When the two of them settled back in the booth, Carla took Sandy's hand. "I'm sorry," she said.

The Face in the Grave

"But I couldn't resist. If you could've seen your face… it was just too good to pass up."

"I don't see what's so funny," he said. "Maybe it's no big deal to you but… but…"

"But what?"

"But I'm not good with girls, okay? Not good at all. Today was… it was amazing. I thought to myself this can't be happening! Here you are, this pretty girl and we just meet and you talk to me and everything and it was so easy and good and…"—he lowered his voice again—"and you are a good kisser—a great kisser—and then I find out you're my sister!!!"

His misery was both pitiful and comical and a giggle escaped Carla despite the weight of the moment and her best efforts to suppress it. Sandy flared and started to get up again.

"I'm not your sister," Carla blurted out, throwing the words around him like a lasso.

He dropped back into his seat. The anger fading into confusion and relief. He questioned her with his eyes.

"Well, I'm not your biological sister. Tony adopted me when he married my mom so…" she paused.

"I was going to say I'm your stepsister, but that's not true either, is it? Wouldn't that mean someone got divorced?"

She blew out an exasperated breath. "I'm confusing myself."

"My head's been spinning since I first saw that picture."

"It's a lot to take in. But at least you weren't kissing your sister. And…"—she smiled at him—"you're a pretty good kisser too."

He smiled back at her. For a moment the confusion and loss went away. There were stranger couples out there, he thought. Maybe this could work.

Carla broke in on his thoughts.

"We should try to find out as much as we can before we tell anyone. I think I know where to start. Tony had a cell phone he kept pretty close. It's locked up in his office at my house. I haven't had the heart to look at it till now. I'll drive home and get it."

Sandy nodded. "Same thing at my house. My mom used to joke to him that he slept with his phone." He looked at his watch.

It was a quarter to three. "How long would it take us to get there?"

"Us?" Carla said.

"I don't want to be alone," Sandy said.

Carla couldn't blame him for that.

Chapter 20 - Meet the Parent

The drive west on Interstate 64 in Carla's car was uneventful.

They reached the top of Afton Mountain just as the sky behind them began purpling from a sun that wouldn't fully penetrate the clouds that day.

Sandy drove while Carla slept most of the way. They stopped at the Sheetz at the Tinkling Springs exit to fuel up and to give Carla's mother time to wake up and get going before they arrived.

Sandy tried to get Carla to leave him there while she retrieved the phone but she wasn't having it.

"We're in this together now. You may as well meet my mom. And…" She hesitated.

"And I think you should go to the graveyard, don't you? Show your respects?"

The Face in the Grave

Sandy had no such notion in mind when he came along on this trip, but the earnestness in Carla's tone made him feel as if he should've already thought of this.

He said, "Of course."

They drove to Brand's Flat.

"What are you going to say about us—me?" he said.

"And how are you going to explain coming home for no reason?"

It was Carla's turn to squirm.

"I hadn't thought about it. As far as coming home, well, since my dad died nothing's been normal around home. I'll just say I couldn't sleep and I missed her and I decided to come home for the day. And you?"

She gave him an up-and-down glance.

"You are my new boyfriend who didn't want me driving here alone in the middle of the night."

He arched an eyebrow at this.

"It's true enough isn't it? Once you meet my mom you'll see. I realize fully the irony of what I'm about to say… it's impossible to pull one over on Rita."

In spite of Carla's warning, Sandy almost choked on the sip of coffee he'd just taken in.

It took great effort not to spew it all over the windshield.

Carla took one look at Sandy's red face and began laughing—a deep, childlike, unpretentious belly laugh, the kind that cleanses the soul and infects anyone who hears it.

Sandy caught it and by the time they drove the remaining three miles to the Staunton exit on 64 they were gasping for breath and wiping away streams of tears.

They pulled over at Rowe's steakhouse just off the exit to pull themselves together before making their way to Carla's home.

To Sandy, newly observing the world through the lens of his father's polygamy, the house appeared to be newer and larger than his house in Fernandina Beach, but not by much.

He was trying to work out the economics of his late father's lifestyle. He guessed the home in Florida, while smaller, cost more than this one.

What kind of job supported two mortgages and two homesteads? He wasn't great with money, but his brief stint running the Anderson house while his father was missing and his mother was broken showed him the basics.

To accommodate all the expenses, if this home ran in the same modest way his own did, he worked out that the man would have to make two hundred, maybe two hundred and fifty grand a year.

He reminded himself of the travel expenses and added another fifty thousand.

Tony often came and went several times in a week on "business." Sandy wondered what that might be. There were plenty of jobs out there that paid that kind of money, he knew, but for all his father's coming and going it seemed to leave little time to do a job that would pay that handsomely.

He didn't realize how long he'd been sitting and staring at the house when Carla broke in on his thoughts.

"I'm glad you get to do this first. You can show me the way through this weirdness."

Sandy shook himself mentally.

"Yes. Weird. Carla? Did he ever hint at what he did for a living?"

"That's what's on your mind, huh? He wasn't one to talk much at all. I don't remember him saying anything about his job."

She thought for a second and added, "I know this isn't what you asked, but he was great at helping with my math problems. For some reason I always pictured him as a math teacher. He was so good with numbers and patient with me. No way that's what he did, but it's the way he felt to me."

Sandy grinned.

"I'm thinking a math teacher doesn't make enough money to run two complete households. But he always helped me with math too. Come to think of it, it was the only thing I ever saw him get talkative about."

The front door of the house opened and an attractive middle-aged redhead came out on the porch, shading her eyes from the morning sun. A look of concern pulled the edges of her mouth down.

She called, "Carla? What are you doing home? Everything okay?"

The Face in the Grave

The woman craned her neck trying to see into the car. Her look went from concern to suspicion when she saw Sandy get out of the car.

He stood still, observing his father's second wife and waiting for Carla to answer her mother.

He saw two things clearly: this woman was very pretty—no wonder her daughter was hot—and this woman could not have looked more different than his mother if you set out to find her opposite.

Not that Shirley was unattractive, not at all. It was hard to think of one's mother in these terms, but she was what you'd call "sneaky hot." More Mary Ann, less Ginger—a show Tony liked to watch when he was home.

But the second Mrs. Tony... she was a pure MILF; one hundred percent Ginger.

Sandy caught himself staring and looked down. The old man may be a lying, cheating fraud, but Sandy had to admit he had good taste.

Carla was talking.

"...couldn't sleep... needed to see you... wouldn't let me drive alone." She unfolded the story the way they'd rehearsed it.

Wife Two took this in with a doubtful look and gave Sandy the same up and down glance her daughter used on him.

Looking at the woman as he approached, he saw gauntness in her face and worry around her eyes. This woman was suffering.

Suddenly the doubt and suspicion in her expression gave way to a sad smile. Sandy saw Carla in her mother's face.

She said to Carla, "I'll take you any time I can get you, girl."

Carla hugged her mom. They cried as Sandy stood awkwardly awaiting an introduction, hopeful their cover story would hold up without interrogation. He had no desire to lie to this woman, to add to the house of cards his father built that sooner or later he and Carla would have to pull down on her head.

He flashed to his own mother and imagined this scene playing out at his home, which would inevitably happen before long.

This woman and his mom must face each other at some point. What would that look like?

He shook his head over this just as mother and daughter disengaged from their hug. Wife Two was looking straight at him with a puzzled expression.

He smiled weakly, embarrassed, unsure of what to say. Carla saved him.

"Mom, this is Sandy. Sandy, my mom, Rita Dyson. I'm sure he could use some coffee and a bite to eat. We've been up most of the night."

Sandy stuck out a hand and said, "It's very nice to meet you, Mrs. Dyson." Rita stepped through the handshake and threw an arm around him.

"We're huggers around here, Sandy," she said.

Sandy smiled and relaxed. He liked this woman already.

"And I appreciate your manners, but you can call me Rita."

"Yes, ma'am." Sandy replied.

In the wonderful manner of country cooks, Rita Dyson made a breakfast of ham and eggs with slices of fresh tomatoes appear on the table like a magic trick.

Sandy and Carla sipped coffee from mismatched mugs bearing sayings about the effectiveness of prayer and the value of faith.

When Sandy began to fall to on the delicious-smelling food, his fork was halfway to his mouth before he realized Rita and Carla were pausing to give thanks.

He lowered the utensil slowly and gave Carla a sheepish look. Obviously this home ran very differently than Tony's other home.

"I'm sorry," he said.

Rita cleared her throat and said without a hint of contempt, "Don't be sorry, Sandy. Not everyone learned to hug or to pray in their homes. We're a hugging and a praying family."

She smiled and said, "Carla, would you pray over this food?"

Carla did. Thankfully, for Sandy, the mother and daughter fell into a discussion of normal family life and local happenings; goings on at the church, Rita's health, and other mundane subjects filled the next twenty-five minutes.

As Carla and Rita finished their meal and continued talking, Sandy got up and cleared the table, hand washing the dishes in the sink. He did it

The Face in the Grave

automatically. This was his job in his version of Tony's home. It had always been therapeutic.

The sound of the running water combined with the simple contribution to kitchen operations gave him joy. He finished up and offered to refill the women's coffee cups before he noticed they were no longer talking but watching him.

He said with a grin, "We're a dishwashing family in my home."

Rita laughed. Carla gave a tight-lipped smile. It made him happy to see her mom laugh. He thought she probably hadn't laughed very much lately and a face that pretty needed more laugh lines than worry lines.

Carla said, "I'm going to show Sandy around the town today, Momma. Take him to the high school, maybe even up to Humpback Rock, if we get some energy. We've got to go back this evening."

Rita's smile faded. "Sure, honey. I wish you could stay and go to church with me tomorrow, but I understand."

"Mom," Carla said, with a note that said this was well traveled ground, "I can't stay here the rest of my life. And look, I just proved how easy it is to get here when we need each other, right?"

Rita nodded and gave a shrug that made her look like a sad little girl. Sandy felt a stab of melancholy and missed his own mother.

"We'll get back in plenty of time to hang out with you, Mrs. Dyson," he blurted out, looking to Carla to agree.

"And Carla told me y'all have the best pizza place of all time. Maybe we could pick up dinner and bring it here to eat together?"

Carla cut her eyes at him then said, "Of course we will, Mom."

Sandy made a note to ask about the look. Different families, different mothers, and mothers and daughters versus mothers and sons, he guessed. He had a lot to learn about all of it.

Carla said, "We're pretty tired from the all-nighter. Can Sandy crash on the couch while I get a nap? We'll get going around, what time, Sandy? Eleven suit you?"

Rita and Sandy both nodded and Rita showed Sandy to a cozy den with a well-worn and spacious brown leather couch. He was sound asleep before he took his second full breath, only pausing long enough to remind himself not to stick his hand in the waistband of his jeans.

Carla woke him up in what felt like a blink.

He was embarrassed to discover his right hand tucked comfortably in its usual sleeping position.

As he jerked the offending digits out of his pants, Carla smirked. "Like father, like son, I guess."

"Like… wha?" he said, trying to remind himself who and where he was.

Carla said in a conspiratorially low tone, "That's pure Tony, right there. I stood here a moment before I woke you up. It was a little freaky how much you looked like him!"

Her eyes were as big as her voice was small.

"He slept just like you do. I started to notice how much you look like him at breakfast. Especially the eyes, your eyes." She looked worried.

"What?" Sandy said.

"I told you. Rita's sharp! The longer we hang around here the more chance she sees something we don't need her to see yet. And if I notice, it's a no brainer she will. That's why I wanted to get us out of here quickly today."

Sandy suddenly understood the look Carla gave him.

"Sorry. She just looked so sad at you leaving so soon. It made me feel bad for her and I miss my mother too."

"What are you two whispering about in here?" Rita said, materializing at just the right moment as only mothers can do.

Both Sandy and Carla started and Rita laughed at their faces.

"Gosh guys! You act like you just saw a ghost. Don't we all get caught making out at least once in our lives?"

Carla went bright red. Sandy sat up fully from his resting position on the couch.

"Ah… naw… see… ah… Missus Dyson, we weren't making out," he said.

"No!" Carla managed to say.

Rita pursed her lips. Carla went a shade more red. For an instant it got very quiet between the three of them. Sandy felt it widening like a chasm. He went dizzy looking over the edge.

The Face in the Grave

It was there in Rita's eyes locked on his; she knew. He didn't stop to consider the impossibility of this feeling. She knew. She knew their secret and they were all about to fall into it and drown together.

Just at the moment he felt himself leaning forward to take the tumble, Carla said, "I know that look, Mom. And you're wrong this time. You are! We barely know each other. We're just friends."

Even Sandy heard the false note in her protest. He waited for Rita to shred this apart. Instead, sadness crept into her face again. She tried to push it back with a weak smile and said, "Not knowing each other well didn't stop me and your dad."

Carla snorted. "Mom!" Her eyes rolled up in exaggerated embarrassment, but Sandy felt the relief in her expression.

He ventured, "Mrs. Dyson, I am sorry I didn't say this earlier; I'm sorry for your loss."

He began to add that he'd just lost his father too but thought better of it. The chasm that had threatened to swallow them was just closing, no sense risking tearing it open again.

Rita sighed. "Thank you, Sandy. It's been hard around here without my Tony. He was a rock."

The word "my" grinded on Sandy's ear to the point it came close to evoking a physical response.

Carla said, "We should probably get going if we're gonna have time for Humpback before we pick up dinner."

Dinner. Sandy now saw what Carla already knew. This home and these interactions with Rita Dyson were honeycombed with the potential for trouble. It would have been better if they were leaving right now instead of subjecting themselves to an hour or two where any innocent comment might expose their secret.

"…my usual from Ciro's," Rita was saying. "It'll be so good to just do something normal together."

Too late. It would be dinner for three tonight.

Chapter 21 - The Phone

Carla didn't speak as they drove the half mile on the two-lane out of Brand's Flat to the highway.

When they passed under the railroad tracks and turned east on Route 250, she slipped a hand into the front pocket of her green Wilson Memorial High School hoodie and pulled out a black iPhone in a black case.

"Dead as a doornail," she said.

"I was going to grab it out of his office and charge it in my room while we napped."

She paused and looked into his eyes.

"I got weirded out at breakfast when I saw him in your eyes. It was like a flash of lightning. Your face and his. So clear. If my mom saw this,"— she nodded at the phone without taking her eyes off the road—"I was afraid she'd make connections we aren't ready to make yet."

The Face in the Grave

Sandy took the phone, turned it over in his hands, and pried it out of its case.

There was a tiny indentation on the backside bottom of the phone. He ran his finger over it, feeling it like he felt the scar on his forearm from a childhood run-in with a glass door.

It was there. It was real. All of this happened; was happening.

He remembered his father knocking the phone off the kitchen table as he got up to clear his plate. The innocuous thump it made when it hit the floor; his father cursing under his breath, his mother giving her husband an admonishing glance that said "not in front of our son" louder than words.

He remembered his father running his finger over the little imperfection in the perfectly new gadget. It had been less than a year ago.

Sandy felt further removed from that version of his life than he did from the six-year-old bleeding from the shattered glass door. There was no fixing this, no new pane of glass or new phone or stitches that would put things right again.

The only thing now was to try to understand why this had happened and who their father really was. Maybe he was holding the key here in his hand. He plugged the phone into the charger.

Nothing happened. Sandy grunted. "Yeah. Dead as a doornail."

Carla said, "That's another thing Tony used to say. 'Dead as a doornail.' What does it mean? Do you know?"

Sandy smiled.

"I do. Words are big deals with my mother. Any time I'd ask what a word meant she'd get this look on her face and I knew what was coming. 'Go get the Webster's,' she'd say, and make me look it up. I've got a lot of useless words and phrases jammed in here." He tapped his forehead.

"I remember this one because it wasn't easy to find. Not in the dictionary. Had to look it up online. The idea is that you hammer a nail through some wood and then beat the sharp end down into the backside. It's called clenching and once you do it to the nail, it can't be reused or pulled back out… it's dead, you see?"

He glanced over to see Carla giving him an amused look, her head halfcocked. He flushed.

She said, "Go on, Mr. Webster."

He felt heat in his face and started to fire off a retort, but Carla laughed and put a hand on his. "Relax, brother," she said.

The combination of her hand on his—which felt nice—and the word brother—which did not—made his head spin. "Brother?!"

Carla squeezed his hand.

"Sandy, we've got lots to learn about our lives. Take it easy. We're church people. We use that for everybody. My mom calls me sister. She used to call Dad 'brother.' It's just a way of saying we all belong to God the Father."

Sandy felt the tension drain out of him.

"I'm sorry," he said. The phone buzzed in his hand. Carla felt it in hers. They looked at each other.

"That doornail ain't dead," she said.

Several notifications popped up on the screen. Carla, wide-eyed, pulled the car over to the shoulder.

"I've never touched his phone," Carla said in a conspiratorial whisper.

Several cars whizzed by, so close their wakes rocked the car on its suspension. Together they looked into the screen as if it were a Magic 8 Ball ready to tell them the answer to the question burning in their minds: who is Tony Anderson - Dyson?

Sandy scrolled through the string of locked screen notifications slowly. There were only three, none of which were familiar to either of them.

They said PROXIMITY ALERT.

Carla said, "That was another thing Tony was nutso about—he used to say 'what's the sense of locking your phone when you let everyone see your business with these notifications?' He made us go in and turn all of them off."

"Same for us," Sandy said.

"But he didn't turn these off for some reason. I have no idea what app they're from. Nothing I've ever seen before. Proximity alert? What app sends you a proximity alert?"

"It doesn't look like anything I've seen... these are from months ago. Looks like they came in the week he died and before the phone..." She

The Face in the Grave

hesitated to use the same word to describe the phone as she had just used for her father.

"Whatever it was, it looks like it was getting closer. See?"

Sandy pointed to the earliest notification.

It read:

Proximity Alert
Tracker #1237 in Charlotte
Status: active
Condition: yellow
Min eta: 120 min

The next one read:
Proximity Alert
Tracker #1237 in Richmond
Status: active
Condition: red
Min eta: 90 min

And the final one said:
Proximity Alert
Tracker #1237 in Charlottesville
Status: active
Condition: critical
Min eta: 20 min

Sandy flicked the screen up and it refreshed. Two more Proximity Alert notifications popped up.

They were dated within the past week and a half. His eyes grew wide. They read:

Proximity Alert
Tracker #823 Atlanta
Status: active
Condition: yellow
Min eta: 90 min

Proximity Alert
Tracker #823 in Jacksonville
Status: active
Condition: critical
Min eta: 45 min

Sandy poked the screen, trying to get to the full message. The facial recognition failed and the passcode screen replaced the lock screen image.

He groaned.

Carla said, "What?"

He said, "Didn't you see where the alert is?! It's in Jacksonville!"

He looked closely at the screen. "The alert came today!"

Carla shrugged, not understanding why any of this would disturb him.

"Jacksonville is right on top of Amelia Island! Fernandina Beach!! We've got notifications for both homes. And the latest ones are for my house!

Carla still didn't stir.

"And why is that a big deal? Wouldn't you expect Dad would have things delivered to both places? It makes sense to me. He's tracking packages, right?"

Sandy grimaced and shook his head.

"That's a funny way of keeping tabs on a package, don't you think? Proximity alerts? Condition red? Condition critical? It makes me feel like a countdown to something bad."

Carla remained unperturbed. They stared at the passcode screen.

A tractor-trailer went past in a blur. The car rocked back and forth in its wake, slowly coming to a rest. As it did, the phone's screensaver timed out and the screen went black.

Carla turned the ignition over, checked her mirrors, and punched the accelerator just hard enough to spit out some stray gravel as she pulled the car back onto the blacktop.

A passing look of indecision gave way to determination, a look Sandy would come to know intimately.

She pushed the gas hard enough to make Sandy check his seatbelt.

"I want to show you something," she said.

Chapter 22 - Tony's Place

Carla drove in silence.

She turned several times on to what seemed to Sandy more and more remote country roads. Houses grew less frequent until there were none and only deep green hills surrounded them as far as he could see.

Finally as she rounded a curve he saw a tall wrought iron gateway arching over what he took momentarily for a driveway to a mansion. When he read the flaked gold sign at the top of the arch he understood this was not a home for the living but for the dead.

It read "Mt. Solon Cemetery."

Entering the property and following a serpentine ribbon of blacktop, they passed white and gray headstones of various shapes and sizes sprouting from the hillside like uneven teeth in a verdant jaw.

The Face in the Grave

He looked over at Carla questioningly but she didn't acknowledge him. The silence in the car grew deeper with the particular quiet of a graveyard.

She followed the drive slowly as it wound to the top of the hill and then halfway down the far side where there was a rectangular mausoleum of roughhewn gray rock.

A doorway split the structure in front of a four space parking area. An ominous weathered bronze door closed the entrance.

To Sandy the door screamed 'no admittance,' but Carla threw the car into park, and without a word, got out and went to the door, pushing it open effortlessly.

It took Sandy a second to realize he was alone, sitting frozen in his seat, paralyzed by the silence and surroundings.

Less than twenty-four hours ago he had been sitting in Webb Center at ODU waiting for a ride to the beach. How had so much happened in such a short period of time?

He got out of the car and followed through the open door to the house of the dead.

Carla stood at the far end of a central hallway. Metal plates affixed on polished granite squares of brown, gray, and black patchworked the walls on his left and right. They were the same bronze finish as the door.

Each displayed a name and dates. Some had sayings or Bible verses. The light grew brighter as he slowly walked toward Carla, then dimmed. He looked up to discover the reason.

The mausoleum had a vaulted ceiling with a skylight extending the entire length of the building. The interior lighting ebbed and flowed as clouds passed over the face of the sun.

The sound of his feet crunching on leaves fallen from vases of long-withered flower arrangements echoed too loudly in the emptiness. The sense of aloneness he had experienced when his mother went to the hospital crept into him like a finger of winter poking into his chest.

Carla did not look up when he reached her side. The determined look was still there but it was joined by streaks from silent tears.

The sunlight returned at the moment he reached her, illuminating a marker in the wall that stood out from its neighbors, new and untarnished. He read the marker.

Anthony Dyson
April 7th 1967
May 12th 2021
Faithful husband, loving father. Rest in peace.
Romans 8:1

"What's that mean?" he said, pointing to the Bible verse.

Carla responded in a monotone, talking to the wall in front of her instead of Sandy.

"*'There is therefore now no condemnation for those who are in Christ Jesus.'* It's from a sermon we heard a couple months before he died. He never really acted very interested in church things. Mom always worried about his salvation. Something about that verse caught his attention. He asked her to show him where it was in the Bible. Wrote it down on a yellow sticky note. When we buried him, I guess Mom used it to make herself feel better about him and God."

Carla trailed off.

Sandy thought she might be getting ready to cry again. He took half a step toward her and started to reach out to embrace her. Carla snapped away from his touch and turned on him.

Her eyes were fiery, her lips tight with barely contained rage. Sandy stepped back.

"A countdown to something bad????!!!!" she screeched, spitting the last word out at him like a dagger.

"Wha…?" Sandy started to say, completely lost in what was happening, his face drawn and blank.

"The alerts! The phone! A countdown to something bad? Here's something bad, Sandy! Here. What could be worse than this?"

She was choking on hot tears, but she continued, answering her own rhetorical question.

The Face in the Grave

"Oh, I know. Try this. How about watching your dad die at the dinner table? Just stop breathing in the middle of a sentence. Eyes go blank and yet still look at you?? How's that for worse! How's that for something bad about to happen!"

The last was more a shriek than a comprehensible sentence. Carla collapsed on the marble floor, breaking into wracking sobs.

Sandy approached her cautiously, but when he gently touched her shoulder she reached up and pulled him to herself, burying her face in his chest.

Sandy was scared and... what? Pleased? By this turn of events. Scared by the violence of Carla's sorrow flowing over her and over him like a river from a burst dam, wondering when it would stop, where it might find a resting place.

Pleased by the warmth of this girl next to him, needing him, grasping him, and pleased to find her strength had edges where he could feel useful.

After a long time, her heaving breaths slowed and evened out. He felt the cold of the stone floor rising into them. He thought she had fallen asleep when he heard her whisper in a pitiful childlike voice, "He rescued us. Mom always said that. He rescued us. And now what? Our rescuer is dead. Our rescuer is a fraud."

She let out a long breath and straightened her legs.

"Help me up," she said, raising her hands to him.

Sandy tried to help her but discovered one leg was pin prickly asleep and uncooperative. He flopped hard on the floor, grunted in pain, and rolled over, ending up on top of her. A man's voice startled them.

"Hellooo! What's going on here!"

The inquiry was tinged with anger. It came from a sparse old man dressed in well-worn bib overalls, rubber muck boots, and a straw hat who looked as if he just stepped down off a tractor.

He advanced toward them, red-faced, snorting. "Get out of here, you hooligans! Don't you have any respect for the dead?!"

Carla and Sandy tried to untangle themselves from each other and stand, but their legs couldn't keep up with their fear of the old man.

They plopped back on the floor and scooted back against the mausoleum wall. Looking up, they were in the direct line of the sunlight streaming in through the skylight. Both held a hand over their eyes to shade them.

The old man was upon them.

"That's right. Cover your faces. Shameful creatures. Defiling this place with your lust."

Carla found her voice.

"What are you talking about, mister?! We came here to see my dad." She pointed at the marker above her head.

The old man looked at it then at her. The anger drained out. It was replaced with recognition and embarrassment.

"Miss Dyson? Oh, Miss Dyson, I'm so sorry. I remember you and your mother. Here, let me help you up."

Sandy started to tell him to go to hell, but he was surprised when Carla offered the man her hand. He helped her to her feet. Sandy struggled onto his feet, still unsure of the support of one numb leg.

The old man ran a hand across his brow, knocking his straw hat back. He was shaking his head and clucking his tongue.

Carla said, "Do I know you? And what did you think was going on in here?"

"Oh, Miss Dyson, you wouldn't believe the things I find in here. I'm the caretaker of the graveyard. Keep it nice for the living and the dead. Dig the graves. You wouldn't have seen me at your father's funeral. I stay out of the way, but I watch. I know my people once they've left a loved one here with me. This place,"—he gestured—"is lately becoming a make-out spot for teenagers."

He rolled his eyes and shrugged.

"Can you believe it? Why? I don't know. But I chase some of 'em out pretty much every weekend. Had one just last week tried to pry open one of the vaults! Another one tried to steal the master key to the vaults. Broke into my shack at the top of the hill."

He paused to take a breath. "Can you imagine that? I've taken to sleeping in a cot up there a couple weekends a month trying to catch the delinquents."

Carla said, "I'm glad you're here to watch over the place. We were not here to make out although," she said, elbowing Sandy.

The Face in the Grave

"This is the second time today we've been accused of it. Maybe we need to go try it out someplace other than my mother's couch or my father's tomb."

The old man looked at Sandy to see how he should respond. Sandy looked back, interested in the making out part, clueless as to what to do with this mercurial woman.

Carla stifled a laugh. "Come on guys. Let's get out of here. Mr….?" She queried the old man with her eyes.

"Oh, ah, Lindstrom. Trey Lindstrom," he said.

"Thank you for keeping watch over my dad, Mr. Lindstrom," Carla said.

Chapter 23 - Shots Fired

Back in Carla's car, they followed the one-way loop of the cemetery drive from the mausoleum through the small grove of trees that concealed Trey Lindstrom's caretaker's shack and back to the wrought iron front gate.

She was silent again, but now the quiet wasn't stretched and taut, it was easy. Sandy timidly put his hand on top of hers on the armrest between them. As confusing as the past twenty-four hours had been, he felt close to this girl and was glad to be with her.

Carla turned her hand over and interlaced her fingers with his. He didn't ask where they were going next. He didn't care.

After a quick stop at Coffey's market, where Carla told him to wait in the car and came out with a brown paper sack, they headed east, passed through Waynesboro, and ascended Afton mountain.

The Face in the Grave

At the top they came to a sign telling them that from here the road north was the Skyline Drive and the road south was the Blue Ridge Parkway. Carla took them south.

A quarter of an hour's drive brought them to a pullover with a large, paved parking lot with a smattering of cars in it.

Getting out of the car, Carla rummaged in the back seat, pulled out a knapsack, and said, "There's a case of water in the trunk. Would you grab three or four of them?"

Sandy was grinning.

"What?" Carla said.

"Tony again. Always made us keep a case of water in the car. Is there a box of C-rations back there too?"

Carla smiled back and nodded.

"Yeah. He was always like, 'You never know when you might get stranded on the road.' Mom was like, 'Sure but do we need enough food to feed Cox's army?' She said it was like living with one of those doomsdayers… preppers." She sighed.

"But you could tell in his eyes when something was important to him, and it was, so we went along with it."

"Same at my house," Sandy said. "And who or what is Cox's army?"

"I dunno. My mom's full of sayings I don't have a clue about." She took the Coffey's paper sack from the back seat and motioned for Sandy to follow.

"Here's one; when someone made fun of us she'd say, 'Who said that to you? I wouldn't give a lukewarm cup of spit for anything that girl says,' and when we were little and something went missing and we kept asking where it was, she'd say it was 'up Mike's butt.'"

Sandy laughed. "Who is Mike?"

Carla laughed also. "That's the worst part! There is no one named Mike! No uncles or cousins or people at church. I don't think I knew of anyone named Mike till I was a sophomore at Wilson. And here I was this little kid and everything that went missing was up Mike's butt!"

Sandy was following Carla up a gravel pathway leading up a hill away from the parking lot.

"Where are we going?" he said.

"I showed you something awful; now I want to show you something wonderful," Carla said without stopping.

The gravel gave way to a well-worn dirt trail through a tunnel of trees just beginning to show tinges of the orange, red, and yellow of the coming fall.

Here at elevation it was cooler than the valley, but Sandy still broke a sweat after fifteen minutes on the gentle upslope. Carla had gone quiet again and he followed her, content with the soundtrack of the mountain.

When they'd hiked the better part of an hour they came to three successive cutbacks where the going got steeper and the trees gave way to a gray rock face bathed in dappled sunlight. His breathing became more labored.

Sandy wanted to slow down but Carla showed no sign of tiring, so he labored on. Finally they passed into a copse of trees overgrowing the trail. Carla stopped. She took a sip from her water bottle. He was amazed to see her breathing normally, no sign of exertion.

"This is it?" he said.

"No. I always pause here for a minute. I want to pretend I'm going out there for the first time." She pointed to where the trail disappeared between two boulders. "This is my special place. It's almost more church than church to me."

Sandy felt stupid, an outsider to either place she called a church. He said, "I've never been in one."

Carla arched an eyebrow at him and said, "If that's true, this is a good one to start. Come on." She took his hand. They walked between the boulders. The clouds cleared as they emerged onto a flat stone plateau broken at intervals by uneven mounds of rocky humps pointing skyward at varying angles, like the knuckles of giants outlined against deep azure beyond them.

Carla walked Sandy to the furthest outcropping at the edge of the cliff they'd skirted on the way up the trail. He was a flatlander. He had never seen anything like this.

A luxuriant green valley opened before his eyes in all directions. He saw purple-blue mountains at the furthest edge of the horizon. The panorama took him in like he'd fallen into a painting come to life.

The Face in the Grave

He could taste it, smell it, feel it in his chest. Maybe it was the swirl of emotions of the past twelve hours or the contrast of the Mount Solon mausoleum with the mountain top, or both; he felt wonderfully dizzy.

He felt in an instant he'd come to understand a reality that was at once both ancient and fresh.

He didn't know how long they stood there. He didn't want or need to talk. Carla squeezed his hand. She said, "Humpback Rocks."

He nodded. "If this is what 'church' is, I've been missing out. This must be what it's like to fly except you don't need a plane."

"Maybe," Carla said. "I've never been on a plane."

Their eyes met in what was becoming their look acknowledging common experiences—or lack of them.

"Tony never wanted us to fly. Matter of fact, he never wanted us to travel. And we didn't, much. He'd say—"

Sandy finished for her. "There's plenty to see right here where we are."

They laughed. A phone buzzed in the backpack. They looked at each other as Sandy took the knapsack off his back and began rummaging around in it.

"Probably my mom," Carla said, reaching for the sack.

Sandy found the phone that was buzzing. "Nope," he said, pointing to the screen, "it's mine."

He answered, and started to say, "Hi Mom, you can't believe the…"

"Shut your face." A gravelly male voice cut him off like a slap to the face.

Sandy held the phone away from his face, rechecking the caller ID. "Who—"

"Don't worry about who," the man said. "'Who' is none of your business. I'm gonna tell you your business and you're gonna listen."

Sandy started to interrupt. The man cut him off.

"No. No talking. Listening. That's you. That's now. Your mother will appreciate it if you listen. If you talk…"

There was a brief scuffling sound and Sandy heard his mother's voice, afraid, confused, verging on panic.

"Sandy! Sandy! Tell this man he's got the wrong house, the wrong person, the wro—"

Scuffling again. The gravelly voice again.

"So Sandy, you're going to listen until I tell you to talk and when I tell you to talk you're gonna tell me what I want to know. Your father is a dead man walking. No way around that. No protecting him. No hiding him. But it's up to you whether or not you're gonna be an orphan."

Carla was studying Sandy's face like a movie screen with no audio. She motioned for him to put the phone on speaker so she could hear. He did.

The man continued, "We know your father has three quarters of a billion dollars of the family's money. We know he's hiding out in Virginia and now," he paused, "thanks to your mother's cooperation, we know who you are and where you go to school."

The word "cooperation" clanged off Sandy's brain like a clacker in a brass bell. His vision narrowed. His head swam. Sweat poured into his eyes. The world went sideways and he dropped to one knee.

The phone clattered from his hand onto the rocks, cracking the screen. Carla picked it up.

The man was talking. "What was that? You listen, you stupid fuck. You don't want to break this connection, hear me? You hang up before I give you your instructions and Momma is gonna lose another finger. I'll put her in these cute little Tupperware containers, a piece at a time, till you learn how to follow instructions. Take the whole collection and send it to you when we're through."

Sandy spewed his breakfast on the gray-brown stone of Humpback Rocks, narrowly missing Carla. The sick-sweet smell of vomit made her gag, but she held down her gorge with an effort.

Sandy heaved a second time, emptying his stomach. Between retches he managed to gasp, "Okay. Okay. I'll do whatever you need me to do. Just don't hurt my mom. She's not well. Please…"

Carla pulled a bottled water from their knapsack and handed it to Sandy, who took it, washed the foulness out of his mouth, and poured the remainder of it over his head. Carla signed for him to follow and she led them out of the sunlight to a shaded area under a stony outcrop.

The Face in the Grave

He regained his senses enough to say, "I understand."

"Good. Good boy. Now here's what you're gonna do. In three minutes I'm gonna end this call. When I do you've got one hour to get your father to call this number back. That's sixty—"

"That's impossible!" Sandy blurted out. "He's d—" Carla grabbed his arm and ran a finger across her throat. Her eyes were wide, her mouth tight.

"You're opening that face of yours again. What did I tell you?" There was a scuffling sound. A woman in the background cried out in pain.

Sandy screamed into the phone. "Stoooooopppp!"

He gripped the phone so hard he felt it might crumple like a paper cup. Anger and fear raced through him, lighting everything inside him on fire.

The man was back. He was deadly calm.

"Don't tell me what you can't do. Time to grow up, Sandy. Time to be a man. Time to pay for the sins of your father. And there are a billion of 'em so the cost is steep. The family wants its money back. Your father took it."

Before Sandy could say or do anything, Carla grabbed the phone and said, "It's not enough time." She spoke steadily, firmly, no shred of doubt or fear in her voice.

The man on the other end of the line wavered for the first time, caught off guard. Not expecting to deal with anyone but Sandy.

"Who is this?"

"Don't worry about who I am," she said, mimicking his line. "I know Tony and I know how to get the money. Can't get him for you that fast, but I can get you the money. It's gonna take twenty-four hours. Tony… that would take a lot longer. That's the deal."

Sandy looked at Carla's face. It matched her tone. Serious. Flat serious. Confident. In control. Everything he was not.

Who was this girl? Was this an act? Had the threat to Sandy's mother made her flip a switch or lose a gear?

He wanted to take the phone from her and recant everything she just said. Beg for the unknown man to give him the opportunity to start over. He reached limply for the phone. Carla brushed him off firmly. She was still speaking.

"And if you harm that woman—if you breathe on her—there's no place in this world that will hide you from us. You and anyone you love will never be safe again down to your children's children's children."

Carla paused. Gravel-voice started to talk. She cut him off.

"Twenty-four hours. Keep the phone nearby because I'm gonna call and check on Mrs. Anderson whenever I get the notion. And she better be able to talk."

Without waiting to hear the response to this, she punched the 'end call' button and handed the phone to Sandy. He looked at the black screen in his hand numbly.

Carla walked back to the edge of the cliff and stood with her back to him. Fear, anger, and confusion boiled over. It vented through his mouth.

"Wha…what was that?!" he screamed. "You just killed my mom! That guy wasn't fooling around! And you!" He crescendoed. "Who are you? Where did all that mafia-sounding bullshit come from?! And 'your children's children's children'?"

He approached Carla and stood behind her. She didn't move or acknowledge him.

"In case you haven't noticed, we aren't Special Ops and we don't have any idea where Tony's money is, or what that guy's even talking about. Family? What's going to happen in twenty-four hours when we have nothing to give them?"

"Hook," she said without turning around.

"What?"

"That last line. It's from the movie Hook."

She turned around. She was holding Tony's phone. She held it up to him. A notification badge flashed on the screen.

"I picked this up when you took your phone out. This came out while you were… you know, puking. Look at it."

He did. It was from an app called Coinbase. It said:

BTC up 3%
ACCT BAL $713,000,000

The Face in the Grave

"I don't understand," Sandy said. "What's that got to do with anything? Hook? You? Me? That,"—he pointed at the phone—"turned you into Tony Montana?"

"No. I'm not Tony Montana… but our father might be. Must be. That notification is cryptocurrency. It's Bitcoin. I know that much. I heard him talking about it. He told Rita he was using it to pay for my first semester at ODU."

Sandy thought about it. "Yeah. I heard that too. He talked about crypto. But my college money came from a savings account. So?"

"So, didn't you see the balance?! That's almost three quarters of a billion dollars! That's what the man said. 'Tony has three quarters of a billion dollars of the family's money.' Who has money like that? We never lived like that. You never lived like that. Where'd that money come from?"

Her eyes were wide. The tough guy was gone.

"The only people who have money like that and talk like that are bad people. Criminals. The mob. I just… I don't know. Maybe I watched too much of The Sopranos. I just thought the only way to talk to them was the way they were talking to you. And if it's true, if Tony stole their money, they're never gonna stop till they get it back." A shiver went through her body.

"And Hook?" Sandy asked.

"It's what Captain Hook says to Peter Pan when he won't give him what he wants." She looked sheepish. "I don't know where that came from, but it sounded tough in my head."

"What does Captain Hook want with Peter Pan?" Sandy asked.

"A war," Carla said.

Chapter 24 - Gordon's Revenge

Stick Gordon looked at the cell phone's black screen, then at the pale white face of Shirley Anderson. She was tied hand and foot to a chair at her kitchen table.

The same place she'd checked out of the world just months ago, unable to fit her husband's disappearance into her head.

Now she was trying to fit something else in there. Something altogether unbelievable.

This man and his two flunkies had obviously come to the wrong house. They had the wrong Tony. The fat one, the one they called "Stick," threatened her.

The other two obviously feared him and jumped when he told them to do anything. They knew things though. They knew things about her husband—his appearance, his comings and goings, when he had been gone and how long—things that were hard to explain.

The Face in the Grave

Nevertheless, she repeated to herself they're in the wrong house, they're looking for someone else, they'll discover they're mistaken and leave.

"Who's the girl?" Gordon said, breaking in on her thoughts.

"I-I-I don't know," she stammered. "Sandy, my son, is in college. He must have met someone there."

Gordon snorted. "Yeah. Sounds just like a college girl to me. That's either a Fed or someone who knows the score."

He got up and approached Shirley.

"So far, we've been real nice with you, lady. But that can change. I told your boy we'd hurt you and…" Gordon's immense girth pressed against Shirley.

His breath stank of coffee and garlic. He put his fat face inches from hers. In a movement surprisingly agile for a man his size, he stepped behind her chair, lifted it half a foot off the floor, and dropped it.

The impact conducted through the chair legs and rattled every bone in her body. She cried out. Gordon took the back of her neck in a meaty paw and squeezed. Her vision went narrow.

"Who's the girl?" he said in her ear.

Shirley squinted. She flinched and tried to shrug away his hand.

"I told you, I don't know. You've got the wrong people. You're in the wrong house. My Tony never stole a thing in his life."

"No lady, it's you that's wrong. Your husband is a thief. He's the one that got the wrong people." He tightened his grip. Shirley cried out again and gasped.

"You know what?" he whispered in her ear. "I once held your husband over the edge of the Grand Canyon by his feet for sleeping with both my daughters in one night. I was this close,"—he pinched his fingers tightly on her neck for emphasis—"to dropping him when my boss told me I couldn't do it. He's been living with a horseshoe up his ass since then. Untouchable. Teacher's pet. But now…"

Gordon chuckled.

"Now there's no one or nothing gonna stop me from dropping him off a cliff. He's a dead man, your Tony. You and your kid? That depends on how cooperative you are in setting right the things he's done. You be a good girl and tell us what you know and maybe I don't make you watch me throw your boy over that cliff after your husband."

He loosened his grip on her neck. Shirley sobbed.

"Please. I don't know anything about anything. Look around… does it look like we're rich? You see my house. My car. If my husband stole all your money, where is it? I can tell you one thing, it isn't in our bank account. I'll show you. You can have everything in all our accounts if you let us alone. Sandy is a good boy—"

"Who's hanging around with a woman that talks like that?! Maybe you don't know your son so good."

"Well."

"Well what?"

"Maybe I don't know my son so well. 'So good' isn't the correct way to say it."

Gordon snorted. He sneered at his henchmen, turning to them.

"Got that, you two? Tony Diderrick's wife's giv'n us English lessons."

Without warning the fat Italian mobster unwound and backhanded Shirley Anderson full in the mouth, his gold ring cleanly slicing open her lower lip. Her head exploded in pain. She tasted blood.

She passed out.

Cold water splashed in her face and she sucked in a chest full of air contaminated with flecks of blood, mucus, and water spray.

Her white blouse was stained with blood dribbling from her gashed lip. She sputtered like a weed eater trying to start.

Gordon said, "How well was that, bitch? Any more suggestions on how I can improve myself?"

Chapter 25 - Striking Resemblance

The hike down to the car from Humpback Rocks was painful to Sandy. His calves and shins, unused to this kind of exercise, complained about the pressure placed on them by the downslope.

Carla led the way down as she'd led the way up, not looking to see if he were keeping pace and not speaking.

Once in the car, he asked, "What's the plan?"

Carla held out Tony's iPhone and said, "We've got to get this unlocked. It's the key to everything."

"You know how to do it?"

"No idea. Why don't you google it while I drive? I need to check on my mom. If they found your house it only makes sense they can find mine."

Sandy got out his phone and started searching for ways to unlock iPhones. It struck him.

The Face in the Grave

"How did they find my house? Tony managed to keep two families who never knew the other existed. Obviously, he knew what he was doing. Took precautions. How?"

"You heard that guy, didn't you? It wasn't just two families, it was three. But the third family, if it's what I think it is, is a family that's a lot harder to keep in the dark than us. He said Tony took 'the family's' money. Who talks like that? Only the mob. You never watched The Sopranos, did you?"

"No. Not really my thing."

"Well, it is now. It's our thing. We are the Sopranos… living in it. What did you find?"

"It's not looking good. I forgot about this story. Came up in the search."

"What?"

"There was this terrorist attack on the Navy base in Pensacola and they got the guy's iPhone. The cops couldn't get in it and Apple either couldn't or wouldn't help them. They said something about there not being any 'back door' or something like that."

"So there's no way to get in an iPhone that's locked? What if you just forgot your code?"

"It looks like you can get back in by doing a reset, but…"

"But what?"

"But you have to erase the phone and restore it from a backup."

They made eye contact.

"No way Tony left that loophole open," Carla said.

"If there is a backup somewhere, it's just as locked down as his phone."

Sandy nodded. "I never saw him connect it to a computer, and he always told us never to connect our phones to any Wi-Fi unless he cleared it. Crazy anal about it."

They fell silent. Carla's heart rate increased as they got closer to Brand's Flat.

Talk about the phone kept her mind occupied, but as they fell silent she felt dread flooding in, filling every space, taking away even the oxygen she tried to breathe. She rolled down the window, gulping in .

She pulled her car onto Jericho Road, barely able to keep panic from taking over. When she turned into the driveway and saw another car she cried out before she recognized it. Sandy tensed at her cry. She held out a hand.

"Sorry. Sorry. It's the preacher's car. I just... I wasn't expecting anyone to be here."

"Preacher? What's he doing here?" Sandy asked.

"I don't know. Probably just checking in on my mom. He's been good about that since Dad died."

She paused next to the car. Sandy went to her.

"What?"

"I've got to get my heartrate under control and get my face together before we go in there." She looked at him. "I'm not ready to unload this on my mom yet, okay?'

Sandy nodded his assent. The ride down the mountain and the silence of the car had the opposite effect on him.

Whether it was the wild swings of emotion he'd experienced in such a short period of time or reaching a sheer limit of what his mind could take in, he was feeling numb, almost detached from his body and from this insane, unbelievable moment.

He didn't seem to have a will of his own at the moment, so he borrowed Carla's.

They went into the house. Carla's mother was sitting at the kitchen table with an athletic-looking man with black hair showing a touch of premature gray at the temples. He rose when he saw Carla and Sandy enter. He hugged the girl paternally and turned to Sandy.

"Jack Franklin," he said, holding out a hand.

Sandy took it. It was a hard hand, not what he expected from a priest. His father had always had soft hands, reflecting what Sandy assumed was a soft occupation.

They made eye contact. It took him a second to realize he wasn't introducing himself.

"Sandy Anderson," he stammered.

"Nice to meet you, Sandy," Franklin said. "Sit down with us? I'm just here making my Saturday rounds." He turned to Carla.

The Face in the Grave

"Pleasant surprise to get the chance to see this girl."

Rita Dyson offered to pour them coffee. Carla refused but Sandy nodded yes.

"Never turn down a free cup o' joe," he said absently.

Sandy did not notice how Rita paused mid-pour and gave him an intense look before continuing to fill his cup.

Sandy said, "So you're a 'preacher'?" Emphasizing the last word, unsure of its proper usage.

Jack looked amused. "Yes. You seem surprised. Why?"

Sandy flushed. "It's nothing. I guess I've never met a priest before. You're not what I pictured."

He was more comfortable with priest than preacher but it still came out hard.

Carla said, "Not priest, Sandy. Jack's our pastor. The youth pastor of our church."

"Priest, preacher, pastor… aren't they all the same?"

Carla started to answer but Franklin cut in.

"You're right, Sandy. Basically they're all the same thing. And minister. And reverend. It's just different names churches use for their leaders. Some just sound more formal than others. Around here, with my church,"—he indicated Carla and Rita—"we're pretty informal. I go by 'preacher' or 'pastor' but I prefer 'Jack.'"

"Names are always better than titles. But you didn't answer my question. What about me doesn't fit your picture of a priest?"

Sandy thought a second. "You just look like a normal guy. I guess I had an image in my head of robes and black suits and…" He hesitated.

Franklin filled in, "Older?"

Sandy said, "Uh-hmm, and fatter."

Rita laughed. Jack joined in. Sandy hesitated and then began laughing too.

Rita said through giggles, "Well you would've been right in the ballpark if you'd of been here when pastor Mays was our pastor."

Jack gave her a mild, admonishing glance. "Be nice, Rita."

Carla said, "You can't say she's lying, Pastor Jack."

"And I didn't say he wasn't a good man!" Rita protested.

136

"But he was as round as he was high."

This led to another round of giggling between mother and daughter. Franklin got up.

"Okay, you two. It's good to hear you laugh. I better get on with my rounds. Don't get up. Sandy, nice meeting you. Love to see you at services in the morning."

Sandy started to say he and Carla would be leaving in the evening to return to school, but realized their plans of the morning had been overcome by events.

A shadow fell across his face as the situation pressed upon him.

Franklin took the hesitation as reluctance and nodded at Carla. "It's not as bad as you think, right Carla?"

"No. No, Pastor. I'd love to be there. It's just that we have to get back to school. We're only here for today." She cast a sideways glance at Sandy.

"Oh. Well that's too bad. Next time. Nice to meet you, Sandy." He fixed Sandy in a thoughtful stare and appeared to be about to make a comment he thought better of before continuing to the door.

"Let us know if you need anything, Rita." He looked at his watch. "Got to go and get an oil change at Freeman's. The old man is still kicking. Gonna invite him to church as well."

"Good luck with that," Rita said.

"You never know. I hear the daughter is home for a visit. Maybe she'll soften him up. What's her name?"

"Maggie," Rita said. "That's interesting. She never moved back from Norfolk after she joined the Navy. That's where these two go to school." Rita swept an arm toward Sandy and Carla.

"I graduated from Wilson with her. Tell her I asked after her, Pastor."

"I will," Franklin said. He left.

Rita Dyson returned to the table and sat down deliberately. She took her coffee cup between both hands and stared over it very intently at Sandy.

He was oblivious to her stare but Carla was not. She recognized in her mother's look the prelude to an interrogation. She didn't know what had triggered it but she felt it coming and needed to break it up.

"Nice of the preacher to come and check on us," she said.

Rita answered without breaking her gaze at Sandy.

The Face in the Grave

"Yep. He's a good one. Been real attentive." She put her cup down. Here it comes, Carla thought. She felt her heart rate hammer up again. I can't have this talk now. Not until we get some answers.

She pushed her chair back. It squealed loudly against the wooden floor as she stood up.

"Sorry, Mom. I know we were going to stay and have dinner but we have to head back right away. Right Sandy?"

Sandy looked startled. He picked up the look in Carla's eye. "Ah, yeah. We need to get back."

Rita Dyson said, "Carla, what's going on? Really? You've always been a terrible liar. And your new friend... he's worse."

She now fixed Carla in her gaze. Carla sat back down. No one spoke. The silence grew.

Carla sighed. Sandy thought the whole story was about to come out. He suddenly wanted to be anywhere but here. Silent tears streamed down Carla's face. They held him fast. He couldn't leave this girl to face this alone.

Finally Carla spoke. "Momma. I promise you I will tell you everything." She looked her mother in the eyes steadily.

"I will. But not now."

Rita started to cry too. "Where did he come from?" She pointed at Sandy.

"It's got to do with him, whatever it is."

There was sorrow rather than condemnation in her tone.

"He... he looks like your father. He uses your father's expressions... what kid his age calls coffee 'a cup o' joe?' They don't. And 'stay out of your own way'?"

She turned on Sandy.

"Who are you? Is this some kind of sick joke? Are you trying to get to this poor girl by acting like her father? Where did you pick up these things? How did you know? Are you some kind of internet stalker? You think she has daddy issues you can use to get to her?!!"

Rita's tone climbed as she added accusations. Sandy remained silent. His eyes were big, darting from Carla to her mother and back.

"Mom!" Carla said. "Stop it! Sandy's done nothing wrong. He's been nothing but a gentleman to me from the moment I met him."

Turning to Sandy she said, "Let's go." He got up.

Rita began crying harder. "I'm sorry. I'm so sorry. You... I... it's just things have been so hard since your dad died. My mind races through ways I might lose you too. And Carla, I think that'd be the end of me. If I lost you too."

Carla went to her mother and put her arms around her.

"Momma, you're not losing me. I promise. And I promise I'll tell you everything. Just not right now. Trust me. And Sandy? He's one of the good ones. Trust me on that too."

She pulled her mother's face, wet with tears, to look her straight in the eyes.

"You didn't raise a fool or a pushover."

Rita smiled and half-laughed through her tears. She nodded. Carla hugged her tight and let go.

She then followed them out the door and back to the car, standing and waving as they pulled away.

Chapter 26 - Pastor Jack

Federal Agent Jack Franklin sat in his black Ford Taurus in a blind cut-out on Jericho Road.

It was risky laying up here. Anyone coming into Brand's Flat from the highway would see him. That wouldn't be too much of a problem. Most of the folks back here were the 'keep yourself to yourself' kind unless you were trespassing.

The cut-out led up to the archery range, which was privately owned but generally shared with anyone who liked to shoot. If the girl or her mother came out, they'd have to be looking in the rearview to catch a glimpse of him. But he needed to call his boss and get some instruction before he got too far from here.

The Face in the Grave

Better to stay close until he knew what his orders were. The boy showing up here with Carla Dyson clearly changed the rules. He just had to know how much of a rule change.

When his higher-ups suggested this gig to him a year ago, he'd thought it was a joke. He also thought it would be impossible to pull off.

They weren't joking and they did pull it off. How, he really didn't know. Money and connections, he guessed. Always money and connections.

Miracles could be accomplished with enough money and connections.

Unbelievable as it was, he was "Pastor Jack," newest youth pastor of Fishersville United Methodist Church.

It wasn't as big a stretch as you'd think for a guy who grew up in Jersey in the home of a couple of lapsed Catholics.

His mother had sent him off to Vacation Bible School at the UMC on the block over from their house every summer since he could remember, trying, unsuccessfully, to keep him out of trouble.

He'd learned a little about the Bible from the frayed flannelgraphs the octogenarian women teachers used year after year, and a lot about the birds and the bees in the glossy magazines smuggled into class by the middle school boys.

His mother wondered at her son's continued attraction to the Methodists as he eventually said summer Bible school wasn't enough and began going to weekly services. It even stirred her to attempt a short-lived revival of the family's Catholicism, which Jack vetoed after attending a single Sunday Mass.

He gave the usual reasons: too much kneeling and standing, too much talking in a language he couldn't comprehend, too many men in robes.

He didn't think his mother ever knew it was really the disrobed women he could see at the Protestant church that made him reject the faith of his fathers.

Who knew it would lead to this?

A pretty good gig; keeping an eye on a prime target like Tony Diderrick was bound to be good for his career. He'd actually been sad when the crook keeled over. He assumed it would be the end of things here.

But here he was, six months later, doing what he'd been told to do: sit tight and keep tabs on Diderrick's wife and kid. He didn't ask why. They wouldn't have told him anyway.

You don't ask those kinds of questions if you want to move up.

The phone picked up.

"Go." The nasally voice of his boss.

"You said update you if there were any developments. The girl showed up here early this morning with a boy from school. Name is Sandy Anderson. The mother's real spooked by him. She told me it's not like her daughter to drive up here in the middle of the night with a boy she just met. She's worried he's got some kind of scam going. I don't know. Seems like a normal thing to me. It's college. They're hookin' up. No big deal."

He waited to hear what his boss would say. There was a long pause. He thought for a second the connection was lost and he'd have to call back and repeat the whole thing.

"Boss?"

"Stay on the girl and the new kid. I want hourly reports until I tell you different. Don't get made. Don't let anything happen to them. Be ready to bring them to me when I give you the word."

He didn't wait for Franklin's acknowledgement. The line went dead.

"Yes, sir," Jack said to the blank screen.

Chapter 27 - Surveillance and Surprises

Carla eased her car out of the neighborhood.

"What was that all about?" Sandy said. "I'm a stalker now? This morning your mom was encouraging us to make out! Or am I losing it?"

Carla shook her head.

"Since my dad died it's been like this. She swings back and forth. Sometimes I wonder if she's bipolar. The weeks before I left for school were hell. One day she's crying that I'm leaving her forever, the next she's crying because I'm going to college and she never did. It was enough to make me think I was the crazy one." She laughed grimly.

"I understand some of that. My mother went catatonic when Tony didn't come home. She went dark like someone threw a switch."

Carla turned onto a road leading to a school and a complex of one-story buildings.

"Where are we going? What is this place?" Sandy said.

The Face in the Grave

"This is where my high school is. Went to elementary school there."

She nodded toward the first brick building they passed on the access road.

"The rest of this is the Woodrow Wilson Rehabilitation Center. They built it for the veterans coming home from World War Two. Now it's for people from all over who've been injured and need help getting back on their feet, or in some cases learning how to live without them. My school, Wilson Memorial, is out here on the back side. We need a place to sit and talk a minute but I think we better stay out in the open. Just in case."

Sandy smiled. "You really think like a criminal or a cop, I can't figure out which. Where'd that come from?"

Carla didn't smile.

"I'm surprised you don't. Evidently it's in your genes."

Sandy didn't know what to say to this. They fell silent as she pulled into the middle of the empty high school parking lot and turned off the car.

The weather had turned beautiful. The sky was an electric blue accented against enormous full clouds towering up forever. A gentle breeze carried the slightest hint of fall.

"Top ten day," he said, grimly smiling, cracking his window casually and sighing deeply.

"Not a day for so much trouble."

When he looked over, Carla was looking at him intently.

"I'm an idiot," she said.

He squinted at her with one eye quizzically.

"Yeah. Right there. That's another Tony look. How did I miss all the similarities? It isn't just the sayings, Sandy. It's your looks. Your mannerisms. And she picked up on it. I guess it's because she knew him better when he was younger and I was just not that aware. But jeez…"

Sandy didn't want to think about this. Even with all that was happening in Florida with his mom he still held out hopes for something with this girl.

Looking and acting like her father even if he wasn't her biological father didn't seem kosher. He sat up and tried to look like someone else.

This got a smile out of Carla in spite of herself.

"You can't change your face, goofball. And it isn't just your face anyway. You know Tony wasn't a man who used a lot of words. That just makes the words he did use stick out even more. And you use a lot of his words whether you know it or not."

"Can we talk about this later?" Sandy said.

"I'm sorry we set your mother off, but at least she's safe for now. God knows what's happening to my mom…" He trailed off, ashamed that he'd not thought of this since they'd left Carla's house.

Carla said, "Hand me your phone and unlock it."

He did.

She punched in the number from the call on Humpback and put it on speaker as it began to ring. Gravel-voice picked up.

"What?" he said.

"Put her on the phone. Now." The schoolgirl was gone again, the criminal-cop was speaking.

"The fuc—"

"Now, asshole, or the deal's off. And we both know your boss will have your pinhead squashed in a vice if you blow this. Put her on or I'll cut a deal with someone less stupid."

There was a momentary silence followed by a brief scuffling sound.

"Hello?!" Shirley Anderson sounded tired and afraid.

"Mom!" Sandy said even as Carla motioned for him to stay silent.

"Mom! Are you okay?!"

"Sandy!!" The woman on the other end began sobbing. A string of unintelligible words followed by more scuffling. Gravel-voice was back.

"Enough," he said.

"Listen, little girl. I don't know who you think you are, but I promise you this. No one talks to Stick Gordon like this. You hear me? I don't care who you work for or what happens to the family's money. When this is over I'll cut out that tongue of yours and shove it up your—"

"Okay, big man. Big man who likes to talk big when he's shoving around old women. You keep that phone close." She hung up.

"God, Carla!!" Sandy said. "You're crazy!"

Neither of them noticed the black Ford Taurus that had taken a position across the road from the high school.

The Face in the Grave

Jack Franklin rolled up his heavily-tinted window and replaced the parabolic mic he'd been using on the seat beside him. He grimaced. Stick Gordon.

Did his boss know about this? It would be like him to keep things compartmentalized. Not let the right hand know what the left was up to. It came along with the territory. But this was too dangerous a game to play when you knew where the pieces were.

A guy like Stick Gordon? Never get caught out without knowing where that psychopath might be. And the woman and the money? And the girl? Carla Dyson talking like that?

He fingered his phone. He knew the boss expected updates and this was something he should report but he hesitated.

He'd kept himself alive playing his gut. Gordon was the kind of guy who tied up loose ends and enjoyed doing it. Franklin had no illusions that he himself could become one of those loose ends at any time, maybe he already was. He was used to that idea.

But it was the girl who threw him. He'd never seen anything like this out of Carla Dyson. Who was she?

Being undercover kept you out of the loop.

He put the phone down.

I'm gonna wait this out a little longer and see what else might show up on the board, he told himself.

He picked the parabolic mic back up and pointed it at the girl's car.

Chapter 28 - An Outrageous Plan

Sandy was thinking the same thing as Jack Franklin. Who was this girl he was sitting with in an empty high school parking lot?

For an instant he played with the idea she might be in on Tony's alter ego life, the one link between the two. Maybe even groomed to take the old man's place someday.

He shook his head as if to get the thoughts out. Stupid.

Was she acting this whole time? Keeping up the charade? The intense talk in the coffee shop across from ODU? The things they'd shared about their lives on the drive through the night? The tears at their father's grave?

He didn't think so.

He thought that was the real girl. But... but the way she flipped a switch and went full gangster was scary.

The Face in the Grave

And, he reminded himself, he'd lived his whole life with a man who was evidently a mobster, a man who'd thoroughly deceived him and his mother.

The thought of his mother penetrated him again like a cold blade in his belly. When he looked over at Carla she was studying him intensely.

She said, "What? Why are you shaking your head?"

Suddenly he felt very vulnerable. For the first time since he'd met Carla he hesitated to tell her his mind.

"It's nothing," he said.

"My head hurts. I guess I'm trying to fit too many new things in their places too fast and they just won't go."

He gave her what he hoped was a reassuring smile. He saw something pass through her countenance, something he couldn't put his finger on but he didn't like that he'd put it there.

It felt like he had betrayed her, that their relationship had taken a hit when he decided not to show her how he was feeling.

He immediately regretted it and wanted to fix it, but the moment and the words passed him by.

Carla was speaking. The camaraderie of last night was drained from her inflection. They were separated now, two people, not one pair trying to find a way through this crazy situation.

Her tone made the ice knife in his belly turn and stab deeper.

"I've got a way we can get this phone unlocked," she said to the steering wheel, and then turned to him. He didn't like the look in her eyes.

She'd gone blank to him a moment before, but that wasn't it. There was a gleam of outrageousness there.

He hesitated and then asked, "How?"

"These phones have facial recognition, right? It's what I use. It's what he used." She left the idea floating there between them.

Sandy nodded but had no clue how this could help. Carla's eyes burned into him, asking him to see what she saw. He tried.

"So we get a picture of his face?" he offered.

"Will that work? How sensitive is it?"

"Very," she said.

"I have these girls I went to school with who are identical twins and they showed me how their phones only worked for the right one. It made them happy, actually. They liked that it made them feel they were individuals and not just one or the other twin."

"So will it work with a picture? Do we even have a picture of Tony that's clear enough to use?" Sandy asked.

"No. I don't think it works with a photo. Even if it did, I doubt I have one clear enough to try it."

Sandy looked at her, unsure where this was going. "So…?"

"So we need his face to unlock this phone." She pointed to it.

"Okay, Carla. We need his face. We don't have his face. No one has his face. Tell me what you mean. I'm not seeing it."

She took a long breath.

"I need you to listen and not say anything until I'm done." She looked at him. He nodded.

She went on, "Your mother is in trouble and we are the only people who can help her. This"—she picked up Tony's cell phone and held it up to her face—"is the only way we can do that. We get this unlocked and not only do we have what the people holding her want, we have access to enough money to get anything we need."

Her eyes were bright, her voice was steady.

"All we have to do is get Tony's face in front of this screen and everything else falls into place."

In a flash, Sandy understood. He started to object. She held out a hand.

"You promised," she said.

He shut up.

"It's the only way. Thank God he's not in the ground. We don't have to dig him up, we only have to unlock that mausoleum vault and open his casket. I think we could do it in twenty minutes or less."

She paused and then went on rapidly as if she needed to get all of it out before she faltered in the craziness of her own idea.

"If these people really are mobsters, they'll come for us. They'll never let us alone. And if Tony stole the money from them like they say, the cops won't leave us alone either… everything we have comes from his work for

The Face in the Grave

them. Our families will be broke. They'll take our homes. They'll take our bank accounts. Our college money… all of it."

Sandy, who had his mouth open, ready to shut the whole scheme down as soon as Carla stopped talking, shut his mouth. He'd hadn't thought through the implications of having a mobster for a father.

His whole future was on fire. Not only his, but his mother's.

He flashed back to a vision of her, catatonic in the Jacksonville mental hospital. He would be damned if he would see that again or something worse.

He gave Carla a tight-lipped nod and said, "How are we going to do it?"

Chapter 29 - The Groundskeeper's Sleep

The drive to the graveyard was silent.

They'd stopped at a local hardware store for supplies. Carla insisted they do this in Harrisonburg twenty miles north to avoid the chance of running into anyone who might recognize her.

Sandy was again impressed with her forethought and glad if he was going down this tunnel he was doing it with her. She even thought through splitting up their purchases so as not to raise the slightest suspicion.

The trunk of Carla's car now contained the tools she thought they'd need: flashlights, crowbar, drill gun, mallet, two stepladders, and a last minute addition and reminder of the gruesome nature of the task they'd set out to accomplish: two industrial strength respirator masks.

The night sky was alternately black and bright with heavy clouds passing over the face of a full moon.

The Face in the Grave

As they drove up to the access road to the graveyard, Carla shut off the headlights and crept along the serpentine black drive. She slowed as they approached the mausoleum.

"I didn't think through one thing," she said.

Sandy looked at her, incredulous. Carla had thought of every angle.

"What if the groundskeeper is in his shack tonight? He said he'd had to run kids off at night lately and he was sleeping in the shed some weekends. What if tonight is one of those nights?"

Sandy shrugged.

"I didn't think the guy was serious. Who'd actually sleep in a graveyard if they didn't have to?"

Carla said, "I wouldn't, but we better go and check it out."

She paused and said, "And not only that, but remember what he said about having the keys that lock the vaults?! Stupid. I should've thought of that. Maybe we don't need all this stuff. It'd be a lot easier to break into the shack and get those than breaking into the vault."

Both sounded insane to Sandy but he'd already accepted the fact he was living in a waking nightmare.

"Let's go see," he said.

Rounding the turn into the grove of trees they'd driven through earlier in the day, they saw the shack in dappled moonlight. It was one a.m.

Carla stopped one hundred yards from the building and shut off the motor. The cicadas and crickets were in full voice.

They got out of the car, leaving the doors open.

Sandy came around to Carla, feeling his way as the moon again disappeared behind the clouds. As he did, they touched in the dark. He found her hand and took it.

They advanced together toward the groundskeeper's shack. Halfway there, Carla pressed his hand. There was a dim light showing in one of the shack's high rectangular windows in a garage door facing them.

They halted, unsure of what to do next. Retreating behind, a tree they huddled together.

"He's here!" Sandy whispered.

"Maybe. Maybe not," Carla answered. "It could just be a security light. We have to go see."

"And if he's in there?"

"We'll deal with that when it happens."

"How?! What if he sees us?!"

"I don't know."

"Why don't we just ask him to help us?"

In the dark Sandy felt Carla shrug and knew what was coming.

"And explain how our father is in the mob and stole all their money? How we're here to use his face to unlock his cell phone? He'll help us all right. Help us meet the sheriff."

Sandy exhaled.

Carla squeezed his hand. "It's us alone, Sandy. And we can do it. Trust me."

Sandy heard a tinge of hurt in her voice. The mistrust he'd expressed in the high school parking lot, the look he'd put in her eyes. He could take it back right now.

He found her face in the dark and kissed her as an answer. She kissed him back. Holding hands, they stepped out from their hiding place and moved to the shack.

The lighted window in the garage door was too high to see inside the structure. They circled around it, looking for another door or window. Rounding the left side they saw two things at once.

There was a door open, with dim yellowish light spilling out in an elongated rectangle, and at its very edge, a hammock slung between two elm trees. A bare leg hung over the side of the hammock, a frayed white tube sock on the foot.

They stopped and held their breath.

A pause in the ebb and flow of countryside noise brought their breath back. Gentle steady snoring came from the hammock.

They smiled at each other in spite of their fear.

Carla motioned them to the open door. Standing at the opening, she put her lips to Sandy's ear.

"Wait and watch. I'll go find the keys." He nodded.

She left him and slipped in the door to the shack.

The cicadas swelled again. The moon appeared directly overhead. Sandy felt like he was naked; as exposed by moonlight standing there as he

The Face in the Grave

would ever be on a beach at noonday. He started to sweat and looked for any place he could hide if the snoring figure in the hammock stirred.

Carla was taking a long time in the shed. Did she even know what she was looking for? He decided to go in and took a step toward the door just as Carla was exiting. They collided in the opening.

She dropped the metal object she was carrying. It fell half inside the doorway and half out, thudding in the dirt then bouncing on the concrete floor with a ching that sounded louder than a gunshot and stopped both their hearts.

They froze. The woods went silent. The snoring ceased and they heard the groundskeeper take a deep yawning breath.

His leg swung up into the hammock. Carla, her eyes the size of bar coasters, reached down, snatched up the dropped tool, and took off in the direction of the car. She didn't look back.

Sandy remained frozen in place for a half beat, then followed, passing along as quietly as he could.

When he reached the car, Carla was already backing away.

"Get in!" she hissed. "Did he wake up??!"

"I didn't see. Maybe. I don't know."

"Can't worry about it now," she said. "Open the glove box." He did.

"Hand me my gun."

"Gun?! No!"

"Just hand it to me, Sandy. I'm not going to shoot anyone. But if old Farmer Brown there comes looking for us, he's not coming empty handed. It'll keep us on even footing."

Sandy had never touched a gun. It was cold and heavy in his hand. It felt serious.

He handed it to Carla who put it in her lap as she guided the car back to the mausoleum.

Chapter 30 - Entering and Breaking

They gathered the hardware store purchases from the trunk of the car. Carla kept looking back toward the grove of trees and the groundskeeper's shack. When they got to the mausoleum, its imposing bronze door was closed. Sandy opened it and started to enter. Carla stopped him.

"Let me go and unlock the crypt and set up the ladders. If he's coming he'll drive his truck up here and you'll hear it coming. If he's coming it won't be long. Come get me. I'll call you when I've got it ready."

Even in the cool night air, Sandy's shirt was drenched. He didn't like the idea of Carla in the building alone or the groundskeeper catching them in the act. He hesitated.

Carla read him again. "I'll be okay. It will take both of us to do the really hard part." She tried to hand him the gun.

"I don't know anything about guns," he said. "You better keep it." He managed a forced smile. "Probably end up shooting myself."

The Face in the Grave

She shoved the weapon in the black bag with their graverobber implements and brandished the keys she'd purloined from the groundskeeper's shack. "Okay. It'll take me a minute to figure this out, then I'll come get you."

Sandy nodded and for the second time in ten minutes found himself standing an uneasy watch while Carla went to do the dirty work. It offended his image of his manhood, but only for a moment. Carla was redefining his image of womanhood and inevitably it forced him to rethink its counterpart. He stared off in the direction of the trees where any minute he expected to see the headlights of the groundskeeper's truck and hear it rumbling toward them.

Then what? Pull a gun on him? He shook his head, trying to fit yet another incredible thing into his brain. It was one a.m. on Sunday morning. He'd known Carla Dyson less than thirty-six hours. His missing father was a dead mobster, his mother was a hostage to the mob, he was falling in love with a sister from a second family his father kept secret, and he was standing outside a graveyard mausoleum in the middle of nowhere as a lookout while she broke into a grave. If a UFO landed here and now and little green men got out and offered him a ride, could it be any stranger than the last day and a half?

"Okay. I think I got it," Carla whispered, touching his arm and breaking his reverie. "See anything?"

"Nope. Not even little green men," he said.

She gave him the half-amused smirk he was beginning to covet. "Night's still young."

He followed her into the mausoleum. He saw she'd set up the two step ladders opposite of each other at the foot of Tony's crypt. She pointed at the marble faceplate.

"I got it loose using the key tool, but I don't know how heavy it is so I want to do it together. I hope we can get this done and leave without a trace we've been here." She mounted the far step ladder and motioned for Sandy to use the other one. Facing each other, they instinctively paused.

"Almost feels like we should say a prayer or something, doesn't it?" she said.

"Yeah, I guess. But are there any prayers for this?" Sandy said.

"I guess not." She hesitated one second more, then said without closing her eyes, "Jesus help us."

They loosened the crypt's faceplate, bracing themselves for its expected bulk. It turned out to be barely a quarter inch thick and lightweight. Another thing that wasn't what it appeared to be. Sandy took the plate easily in hand and placed it flat on the floor to one side. They were left staring at the glossy mahogany end of Tony's coffin in the square recess, a brass-edged wooden handle fitted in its middle.

"This works like a drawer," Carla said. "I saw how they slid it in before I left on the day of the funeral. Grab that handle and we should be able to pull it out."

They each grasped the handle and pulled. The coffin slid out effortlessly into the middle of the mausoleum with the sound of metal rollers. It was between them, chest high as they stood on the step ladders. The top was divided in half by a thin line.

"Which end...?" Sandy gestured.

"I don't know," Carla said. "It was closed at the church and they moved it around. Your guess is as good as mine. You ready? Where's the phone?"

Sandy looked chagrined. "In the car. I'll get it." He started to get down off the ladder, then said, "Don't open this without me."

Carla smirked. "I wouldn't. I won't. Hurry up."

Chapter 31 - Graverobbers Interrupted

If Sandy had been more familiar with the ways of country living he would have sensed the abnormal quiet that had fallen around the mausoleum, but he wasn't and the only experience he'd had of nighttime country sounds had been a quarter of an hour ago when he'd been solely focused on whether or not a leg dangling over the edge of a hammock was moving.

As it was, he felt the absence of sound as an internal thing—the fear over what he and Carla were about to do.

He retrieved the phone from the cup holder between the front seats of her car in the parking lot and walked back toward the bronze door. He was a step away from it when a figure stepped out of the shadow of one of the shrubs flanking the door.

The Face in the Grave

As he stifled a scream the figure materialized into the person of the groundskeeper. He held a shotgun loosely at his hip, pointed at Sandy's chest, its double barrels staring at him menacingly, holes in the night.

The old man's eyes said "hold your tongue" as clearly as any words could convey. He motioned for Sandy to go inside and moved around behind him.

In the dim interior of the mausoleum, the two marched to within a yard of Carla before she saw what was happening.

When she made a move to step off the ladder, the man broke his silence.

"Stay where you are, missy."

She did what she was told.

Sandy started to say, "I'm sor…"

The groundskeeper cut him off.

"You're both sorry. Damndest thing I ever saw in twenty-three years I've been here. 'Sorry.' Grave robbers? The hell—"

Several things happened at once. The groundskeeper went down like a felled tree, the sound of a dull thud punctuating his unfinished sentence.

The man who delivered the blow to the back of his head stood over the prostrate form. The shotgun spun away under the extended shelf holding Tony's coffin.

Sandy turned to see who else had invaded their insane casket opening and dimly recognized the priest or pastor or whatever they called him from this morning at Carla's house.

Carla was down off the step ladder scrambling to retrieve the gun. In an instant she had it in hand.

"Move, Sandy," she said. "Come over here away from him."

Jack Franklin put up his hands.

"It's just me, Carla. No need to point that at me." His tone was even, calm, smooth.

"Sandy! Move over here!"

Sandy did as she said. He was in a daze. The aliens had landed after all.

"What are you doing here, preacher?" Carla said, trying but failing to match his even tone.

Franklin took half a step closer to them. Carla leveled the gun at his chest. He stopped.

"I could ask you two the same thing," he said.

"That's true. But neither one of us just knocked a man cold from behind without a warning. Doesn't seem very Christian to me." She managed to get all her thinking into the one word: Christian.

Franklin put his hands down and let his shoulders sag.

"You're right. I just snapped, I guess. I saw a man holding a gun on you and reacted."

He gave an unconvincing grin and repeated himself. "No need to point that gun at me."

Carla said, "And how do you explain you being here to see that man holding a gun on us? You come up here to pray?" Again she put her suspicions into one word.

Sandy held out a hand and tried to push down the barrel of the shotgun. Carla shook him off.

"Don't be stupid, Sandy. The only way he's here is that he's been following us. I want to know why. Haven't you learned anything in the past twenty-four hours? Our own father isn't who he said he was. Maybe this guy isn't either."

Sandy withdrew his hand.

"Get my gun," Carla said. "It's in the bag."

Sandy retrieved it and stood next to Carla, holding it gingerly at his side.

"Well, preacher?" she said.

Wordlessly, Franklin gave the two an appraising up-and-down look. He exhaled, long and audibly, considering.

"Okay, Carla. Okay. But put the gun down first."

Something in the way the man spoke set off warning bells in Sandy's head. He was too calm, too sure of himself. Who sounded like this with a gun pointed at him?

He took a step away from Carla, and raised the revolver in Franklin's direction. She grunted her approval.

The Face in the Grave

"I don't think so," she said. "We've been through a lot in a short period of time. You're going to need to give us a good reason to trust you before we put these down."

The badass who'd been dealing with Stick Gordon was back. She matched Jack Franklin in deadly calm. He shifted on his feet. He shrugged.

"My name is Jack Franklin. I'm a special agent with the FBI. I'm undercover. Sent here to keep tabs on your father." He nodded toward the rolled-out casket.

"He's a high priority target. Involved with the Fratelli crime family."

Sandy lowered his gun at the mention of the FBI, but Carla didn't move.

"And if you know what's good for you," Franklin said, taking on an air of authority and fixing Sandy in his gaze, "you'll put down that weapon and start explaining what you two are doing here."

Sandy took a step toward Franklin and started to speak. "We—"

"Get back, Sandy," Carla said.

"Anybody can say they're FBI, Mr. Franklin. Prove it. You have identification? A badge?"

Franklin didn't blink. "I'm deep undercover. I told you. We don't carry anything that could compromise us, anything that would blow our front. Look," He quickly pulled out the lapels of his suit coat, causing Carla to raise the shotgun hastily. "I'm not even carrying a gun."

"Pretty convenient," Carla said.

"Fits your story. Where's your car, Jack? Got a gun in there?" Franklin's eyes said he did.

"Here's what's going to happen. I'm sure you understand, if you are who you say you are, how we can't trust anybody."

Sandy cut his eyes at the girl. She'd changed tones again. Now she sounded like a scared young girl, reasonably cautious after finding out her father was in the mob.

He wondered again which one of these people was the real Carla.

She said, "You want us to trust you? I'm going to ask you to trust us first. Sandy is going to get some paracord out of my hiking bag in the trunk of my car and he's going to tie up your hands and feet while we finish what we came here to do. If you let us do this I think we can trust you."

A full thirty seconds passed before Franklin nodded his assent.

Carla watched his eyes. She thought she could see them moving like an accountant's keypad, adding it all up, looking through to the end game.

Sandy tried to whisper his disagreement to Carla but she wasn't listening.

"Go get my hiking bag," she said.

Sandy wasn't good at tying knots, but under Carla's supervision he secured Jack Franklin's hands behind his back. She then directed him to walk to the far end of the mausoleum, where she kept the shotgun aimed at the man's chest.

She had Franklin sit with his back to a thick marble stand made for holding flower arrangements and showed Sandy how to lash him to it.

After he was secured Carla, put down the gun and said, "Okay, Mr. Franklin. One last thing. Where are your car keys and cell phone?"

"Down in my car outside the gate," he said.

"Don't carry anything that gives away your presence by making noise," he said, matter-of-factly.

Sandy said, "Carla, this is enough, right? Would a mobster let us tie him up? This is proof enough for me."

Carla said, "I'm going to check out his car and see. I'm not convinced yet."

A groan and a scuffling sound came from behind them. The groundskeeper was struggling to his feet.

"In for a penny, in for a pound," Carla said. "We can tie them together back here. After we're done with our job, we can decide who to trust."

In a few moments, the still dazed groundskeeper was sitting tied-up with his back to the same marble stand as Franklin. He managed a few disoriented words and offered no resistance. His head slumped to his chest.

"You pack a punch, Mr. Franklin," Carla said.

"Hope you didn't do any permanent damage to Mr. Lindstrom. How would the FBI feel about that? Knocking out an innocent old man?"

Once again she'd shifted tone. The sweet, scared girl was gone. The tough, suspicious girl taking her place.

Sandy took her by the arm and led her back to the side of the casket.

The Face in the Grave

"I think you proved your point!" he whispered forcefully. "Would a mobster let us tie him up?? Let's untie him and get him to help us! He can do something for my mom!"

Carla took a deep breath and looked into his eyes.

She whispered back, "Sandy, it proves nothing. Would a real FBI agent let someone tie him up? We can't trust anyone right now. And we've got no leverage—nothing to negotiate with until we get this done."

She pointed at the casket. "Once we have the phone unlocked, we call the shots. Either way. You think the cops don't want control of the money as bad as the mob? Remember—we're talking about our homes, our families, our future. You don't know what it's like having nothing; I do. I remember living out of a car and heating up our dinner on a camping stove. I'm not going to let that happen again if I can help it."

Sandy nodded. Pointing to the casket, he said, "How do we get this open?"

Chapter 32 - The Face in the Grave

Sandy ran his fingers along the edge of the coffin lid, looking for a recess or latch, like he was feeling under the hood of a car. He found nothing. Upward pressure on the lid yielded zero movement. He made eye contact with Carla.

"When they closed this did they put nails in it? Or screws? I don't see how they sealed it. Do you?"

Carla said, "They asked us to leave before they closed it. But the coffin was sitting in front of the church. There's no way there was any hammering going on or anything like it. Here." She handed him a flashlight.

"Let's look over the whole thing. There's got to be something we're missing. A hidden latch or panel."

Their search revealed a small black hole just below the lid. It was half the diameter of a dime and metal-rimmed.

"That's it," Carla said. "It's another hidden key like the one I used to take the front panel off the crypt. Maybe the same tool works the lock." She climbed down from the ladder and was back quickly.

"Hold the light on that hole."

The Face in the Grave

Sandy did. She slid the hexagonal end of the tool into the hole. There was a satisfying clunk of metal on metal as it seated perfectly. She twisted the handle and there was a muffled click of a latch being withdrawn.

The sound of disturbing someone's eternal rest turned out to be surprisingly mundane.

"That's it," Sandy said. He felt his heart rate rise. They looked at each other. Are we really going to do this? was in both their eyes. They exhaled together.

Just as they reached together and began pulling up the lid, a loud groan came from the dark at the far end of the mausoleum. They dropped the lid with a thunk. Carla stifled a scream and came close to falling off her stepladder. Sandy grabbed her flailing arm and steadied her.

"It's just the old man," he whispered, momentarily proud of himself for keeping his wits for once when Carla hadn't.

She took a deep breath and let it out. "I forgot about them," she said.

"I guess our plan to do this and leave no trace is blown." She smiled weakly.

"That's a good reminder. We need to do this so they don't know what we're up to. No reason to let anyone know we have access to a billion dollars with this." She pulled out Tony's phone and held it close to her chest where only he could see it.

"For all they know we're here to get something out of his casket. Best to let them think that."

"You think the old man's hurt bad?" Sandy said. "We can't leave him here if he is."

"One thing at a time, Sandy. Let's get this open and the phone unlocked. Then we'll figure out what to do with them."

Sandy nodded and said, "Ready?"

Carla nodded in response and they lifted the lid of the coffin again. It opened easily. It was disturbingly light, Sandy thought.

He'd had movie visions of the top of a mummy's sarcophagus taking two and three men to lift and toss to the side. The way the top flipped up seemed too inconsequential for the act they were committing.

The coffin top opened toward Sandy and the two men they'd tied up at the other end of the mausoleum. He jumped down off his step ladder and quickly dragged it to Carla's side.

When he mounted it and stood, looking into the opened casket, Sandy was met with another sight he'd not anticipated.

The dead man's face did not greet him. He thought he had steeled himself for that.

Instead, a white quilted cloth covered the body. If he'd been anywhere else at this moment, almost anything could have lain under it. The fact that his own father, and the first dead person he would ever see, was there, rushed at him like an unseen car passing as he was about to step off a curb. His vision went blurry. He wavered. Carla touched his arm.

"Okay?" she said.

"Yes," he said, swallowing hard. "You've already seen this. My first time."

She patted him. "It'll be alright," she said. But the tough girl wasn't in her voice.

She reached into the casket and pulled back the quilted cloth. For an instant Sandy thought they'd opened the wrong crypt. The man lying there in the dimness bore little resemblance to his father.

It took him a moment to register what he was seeing and what was putting him off; it was the stillness, the utter lack of animation.

So a dead man was really dead. Not moving. No longer in motion. No longer capable of it. An object. He swallowed again.

Meeting death for the first time pried itself forcefully into his imagination and he knew he'd never be able to see any living thing the same way again. He gripped the side of the coffin as if he might fall in with his dead father.

Carla peered down at the corpse, her head tilted to one side. She'd seen other dead people.

She said, "I've been to lots of viewings. They always say the same thing: 'He looks so good,' or 'Doesn't she look natural?' I guess that's what people say to be nice. I never saw anyone who looked either." She pursed her lips thoughtfully.

Their eyes met as the same telepathic thought penetrated: will it work?

The Face in the Grave

Carla took the phone from her pocket and hit the power button. Before she could position it in front of the dead man's face, the keypad with a miniature lock symbol came on.

Sandy pried one hand loose from the side of the casket and reached for the phone. "I've got a better angle," he said.

Carla handed it to him.

As Sandy positioned the phone over Tony's face, the back of his hand touched clammy, slack flesh, and he got his second lesson on the nature of death. He dropped the phone.

It made a sickening hollow thud as it bounced on the corpse's chest before disappearing down the dark crack between the body and the far edge of the casket. He pulled his hand back and rubbed it against his pants leg, as if he'd touched a hot stove, and as if attempting to wipe away the memory of what he'd just felt.

He looked at Carla sheepishly. "Sorry. I wasn't expecting that."

"It's okay. That's another thing."

"What?"

"Some people at viewings want to touch the dead person. I've even seen them kissing them." Her shoulders shuddered involuntarily.

"I only ever touched one the first time because my mom told me I should. It was this old lady from the church who used to teach my Sunday School. I touched her hand. I wished I'd never done it. The feeling doesn't go away for a long time." She reached out and took Sandy's death-burned hand in both of her hands.

"It'll be alright."

Sandy nodded. He felt childish but the warmth in Carla's hands and eyes made it safe to be whatever he was right now.

"I'll get it."

He put a knee on the narrow ledge of the crypt drawer and pushed himself up far enough to lean over the body and reach into the crack where the phone had fallen.

Feeling for it, he encountered another object. He pulled it out.

It was a leatherbound Bible. He showed it to Carla and questioned her with his eyes.

"Mom wanted him to be buried with it. It was in his hands. Must've slipped off when they moved the casket." She took it from him and placed it on the top of her stepladder.

Sandy went back to his search for the phone and soon had it.

He positioned it in front of Tony's face and hit the power button, cocking his head so that he could see if the facial recognition was working. The lock icon remained as before.

He tried it a second time. No change.

"It's not working!" he said, desperation creeping into his voice.

"Let me try," Carla said. "Switch places with me."

As she got off her stepladder she knocked the Bible off. It hit the ground and skittered off toward the edge of their lamps. Sandy got down and started to retrieve it.

"Leave it. We'll get it when we're done," Carla said.

"Hold your light here." She pointed.

Carla took the phone and repeated the process Sandy had just tried. After her own two attempts failed she stopped, thinking.

"You have your iPhone?" she asked. Sandy nodded and took it from his back pocket. "Give it to me," she said. He did.

She said, "Close your eyes."

"Wha--?"

"I want to see something."

He closed his eyes, holding tightly to the edge of the coffin, feeling a bit of vertigo.

"Now open them," Carla said.

He did what she asked.

"That's the problem," Carla said grimly.

"What?" Sandy said.

"Face recognition doesn't work if your eyes are closed."

She let the sentence settle, the two of them hanging over the words as they were hanging over the coffin.

"Shit," Sandy said.

"Yeah," Carla said. "Shit."

"What are we going to do? That's it! We're dead. My mom's dead. We gotta get Franklin. We gotta trust him."

The Face in the Grave

Carla set her jaw in the familiar way. "No."

"No?!"

"No. We don't have to do that yet. We can try something else." She was looking down into the casket soberly. Sandy followed her gaze. Without another word she handed the phone back to him and reached into the coffin. When Sandy saw what she intended to do he grabbed her arm.

"Don't!" he choked out.

She brushed him off. "I'm not leaving here without at least trying. You don't have to look if you don't want to."

Sandy swallowed hard. "Give me his phone," he said. "It'll be easier."

She handed the phone over and reached back down to the body. Sandy positioned the phone over the dead man's face, leaning further over the casket than he had before, feeling more as if he might fall in.

Carla took in a long breath, and with her palm on her father's forehead reached two fingers over his eyelids.

"Ready?" she said.

Sandy tried to say "yes" but nothing came out. Carla gingerly attempted to slide open the cold flesh off Tony's eyelids. They did not move. She pulled back with more pressure. There was slight movement.

The skin started to give way. Sandy saw a sliver of milky white before the eyelid snapped back closed.

"What's wrong?" Sandy said.

"It feels like there's something holding it closed," Carla said. "I think something is in there under his eyelids. Something hard." She grunted, shifting her weight, bending further down over the body.

She realized till now she'd been at her task as if trying not to wake a sleeping person, not to mention the natural repulsion at feeling the clammy skin. This person was dead. No hurting them; no waking them.

She fought the urge to wipe the feeling off her hands. She doubted it would ever go away.

Taking a deep breath, she used both hands on Tony's right eye, peeling back the upper and lower lid at one time. There was an audible sickening pop as she did.

"What…what is that?" Sandy said.

A flesh-colored oval of plastic sat on top of the eye. It was covered with raised dimples like the reverse image of a golf ball.

"It must be how they keep a dead person's eyes closed," Carla breathed.

"I never thought of that. You're gonna have to take it out, Sandy. I'm using both hands here."

Sandy swallowed hard and looked at Carla again. Each step of this was taking him further into a macabre world he had no desire to explore.

"Do it. Don't think about it," Carla said.

He fumbled with his flashlight in one hand and put the phone back in his pocket. Do it. Don't think about it.

Using two fingers he tried to pluck the object off the exposed eyeball. It wouldn't come. Reflexively he took his hand back and wiped it on his jeans. Then he reached back in and pulled the grotesque dead man's contact lens off his dead father's eyeball.

He never forgot the sickening feeling as it peeled away like a piece of masking tape from the milky orb. They gasped at the sight.

Tony's eye was no longer Tony's eye any more than the rest of his body.

It was dispossessed not only from life, but from this world. It was an alien thing; a milky white ball with a bottomless pit of black in its center surrounded by the slightest hint of brown iris that had dilated to eternity.

Completing the image, the ball was dissected side to side by a blood-brown streak. Carla released her hold on the eyelids and stood up straight on the step ladder.

It was her turn to wipe her hands on her jeans.

The two fixed each other in a grim look that said louder than words "what the hell is this and what are we doing?" This time Sandy regained his senses first.

He said, "Let's do the other one. Just do it, don't think. We've come this far. We have to see if it'll work."

Carla nodded but said, "I don't see how it will work."

They repeated the process on the dead man's left eye, then paused as if on cue.

The Face in the Grave

"Whatever happens," Sandy said, "I'm not putting those things back in his eyes." He pointed to the plastic eyelid holders he'd placed on Tony's chest.

"No. No need for that," Carla said, the barest hint of humor creeping back into her voice and face. "I'm ready. Got the phone?"

Sandy retrieved it from his pocket and nodded, positioning it over the body again.

Carla repeated her earlier attempt at opening Tony's eyelids, resting her hand on his forehead and pulling up. Sandy powered on the phone.

They both held their breath as it flickered on. The tiny lock icon remained the same: locked.

Carla started to release her grip. Sandy said, "Wait a sec." He flipped the phone down on Tony's chest then back up, mimicking the motion of someone picking up their phone.

The lock icon sprung open.

"Oh God! It worked!" Carla said. "Here, give it to me. Don't let it turn off!"

Sandy did.

"Reset the passcode," he said.

"You two have a plan for getting out of this?" A sardonic voice from the far end of the mausoleum intoned.

Chapter 33 - Closed Coffin

Jack Franklin freed himself of Sandy's pitiful paracord knots a few minutes after Carla and Sandy tied up the groundskeeper behind him and left them in the dark.

He stayed put, knowing they'd have to return to him eventually and he'd have plenty of time to deal with the two. He wanted to see what they were up to, and the best way to do that was to stay where he was, watch, and listen.

He'd seen some truly strange things in life, but tonight was without a doubt the top of the list. He'd thought at first the two were after some item left in the casket. A watch? A ring? Something sentimental the girl's family had second thoughts about leaving there?

He could understand that, even if a midnight trip to a crypt on their own seemed like the hard way of getting it back.

He was used to people taking matters into their own hands and doing it under the cover of darkness. But these people? Two teenagers? When the two lingered so long over the open casket, it felt like something more.

The Face in the Grave

It wouldn't take this long to search the belongings of ten dead men—another thing he knew firsthand. He had come close to getting up and surprising them, but the groundskeeper's inopportune and sporadic groans kept him from it.

A poorly timed grunt from the old man might be enough to cause them to look his way at the wrong moment. So he waited.

When he finally heard the girl say, "It worked!" he decided to speak up.

He heard shuffling around and more of the hushed whispering they'd been exchanging for the past quarter hour from behind the top of the open coffin.

Carla Dyson emerged from the gloom holding the groundskeeper's shotgun. Behind her the coffin lid shut and the lights it had obscured flooded into Franklin's eyes.

Reflexively, he threw a hand over his dilated eyes. The girl pumped a shell into the 12-gauge's chamber with the universally understood sound of 'don't try it.'

"You're full of surprises, Mr. Franklin," she said. "I had planned on leaving you here tied up and letting the groundskeeper come back and untie you after we left him in his hammock. But it looks like you've gone and changed that plan."

Franklin, still shielding his eyes, tried to give her a disarming look.

"You really ought to take care with pointing guns at people. Didn't your dad ever tell you not to point one at anyone unless you intend to shoot them?"

He made a move to get up.

"My dad never touched a gun. Hated the things," she said.

"My mom? She's carried a gun since the day my natural dad beat her half to death." She paused.

"She bought me a pistol the day I turned eight and taught me to use it. And she told me never give a man the chance to get his hands on you if you think he's got hate in his heart and means you harm. Mr. Franklin, the only reason I haven't shot you already is that you haven't tried to put your hands on me. But if you get up right now, I swear I'll shoot you and stuff you in that coffin right beside my dad."

Her voice was steady, her eyes deadly earnest. Franklin eased back into a sitting position.

Teenager or not, the girl had steel inside he hadn't expected. Much more like the Jersey street kids he grew up with than the sweet country girl he'd seen in the church youth group.

He believed she would shoot him just as readily as the boys from East Orange.

"Okay, Carla, okay. No reason we can't all get out of here in one piece. Tell me the new plan."

Carla said, "Since you're so good at untying knots, you can untie Mr. Lindstrom and carry him back to his shed. It's in that grove of trees at the top of the hill. Put him in his hammock and make sure he's not hurt bad. It's your handiwork so it's your mess to clean up. You're gonna do that while we finish up here. Once you do that you can do whatever you want."

Franklin raised an eyebrow at this.

"What choice do you have? You're asking us to trust you but you're the one who just admitted you're playing a role. Me? I haven't been acting like I'm a preacher when I'm not. I'd say you've got more reason to trust me than I have to trust you."

Franklin tried the disarming grin again. It looked all the worse for the circumstances, like lipstick on a pig. He held up one hand and used the other to slowly help himself to his feet.

He started to say something, thought better of it, and knelt beside the groaning groundskeeper. He made short work of the knotted paracord binding the older man's hands and legs.

Grunting, he got him to his feet. Lindstrom slung an arm over Franklin's shoulders. His head slumped against Franklin.

There was a trickle of blood coming from one ear. He swayed slightly.

"C'mon, old timer. Let's walk," Franklin said.

The two made their way to the door of the mausoleum and out. Carla stood back, letting them pass, then followed them out the door at a safe distance.

"Sandy?!" she called from just outside.

"Yeah?"

The Face in the Grave

"Keep closing things up. I'm going to make sure Mr. Franklin keeps going. You think you can figure out how to put everything back by yourself?"

"Yep. Almost got it already."

Carla went to her car and continued watching the painfully slow progress of Franklin and Lindstrom. As the two got further away it was hard to distinguish them from each other. It was like watching a slow motion three-legged race that came in and out of focus in the scattered moonlight.

When they were far enough away that she felt safe returning to the mausoleum entrance, she backed up to it, keeping her eyes on the fading forms.

"Done in there?" she called over her shoulder.

"All but the name plate," Sandy called back. "I can't see how it fits."

Carla strained to see Franklin and Lindstrom one more time. They'd been right at the edge of the hilltop grove of trees when the moon was obscured again.

She said, "Grab everything you can carry and come put it in the trunk of the car. Then you can hold the shotgun while I put the plate back on."

A moment later Sandy emerged, lugging all their supplies and one of the two step ladders.

He threw all of it in the trunk and returned to Carla's side, breathing hard. She handed him the groundskeeper's shotgun. He looked at it doubtfully.

"I'll be done before he could possibly make it back," she told him.

"But if he shows his face, all you have to do is point this in his general vicinity and squeeze the trigger."

Before Sandy could protest, she'd shoved the gun in his hands and disappeared inside.

She replaced the surprisingly lightweight faceplate of her father's grave quickly and paused only briefly when she was done. None of this had gone to plan.

She'd wanted to leave no evidence of their macabre mission. Even now she thought it might remain a secret. Franklin, whoever he was, didn't seem like he would be interested in telling this story, and Lindstrom might have been knocked on the head so hard he wouldn't remember any of it.

She swept the surroundings of the crypt with her flashlight, looking for anything that might give their presence here away, and saw it laying in shadow under the step ladder. Tony's Bible.

She grimaced. Put it back? Impossible.

The alarm clock in her head warning her that Jack Franklin could arrive at any second was screaming. She had no illusions that Sandy would threaten the man, much less fire the gun.

Much more likely Franklin would take the gun away and have them at his mercy. She snatched up the book and tucked it under an arm while she folded up the step ladder. Figure out what to do with it later.

Right now they had to move.

Chapter 34 – Getaway

Carla had a bad moment when she got in her car and turned the key over. Nothing.

Sandy said, "Why won't it start?"

"Don't know," she replied.

Carla had a horrible movie image of the villain sneaking up on the unsuspecting victims in their car. She checked all the mirrors then remembered why the car wouldn't start.

She'd drifted to a halt here, not wanting to risk any extraneous noise. She shoved the transmission lever to Park and released the emergency brake. The car started immediately. Carla breathed. Her heart was hammering.

They drove to the cemetery entrance in silence. Sandy looked at the dashboard digital clock glowing its ghostly blue green. "Is that right?!" he said, pointing at it.

"Yeah." Carla said.

The Face in the Grave

    They both thought how much had happened in less than thirty minutes. They were in a time continuum of their own, like the long seconds a driver experiences when he realizes he's about to be in a collision, every detail incredibly compressed into crystalline clarity.

    The question now was how badly they'd be injured. Would they survive impact?

    As Carla turned right, out of the cemetery onto the paved two-lane country road, Sandy said, "Look! That must be Franklin's car!"

    The black Ford Taurus's red taillights flashed in Carla's high beams. It was parked in the unmowed high grass of a tractor entrance to a farmer's field a hundred yards from the cemetery entrance. Carla slowed.

    "Wonder if he was telling the truth about leaving his keys here," she said.

    "Maybe we should check. If they're here it'd give us a bigger head start. No doubt he's coming after us."

    Sandy didn't like the idea of stopping now that they'd gotten this far away from Franklin and the graveyard, but he liked the idea of the man chasing them down even less.

    "I'll check," he said.

    He got out of the car and went to the Taurus. The door was unlocked. He found Franklin's cell phone and keys laying in a side compartment in the door and pocketed them.

    He looked under the seat and discovered a square box. Pulling it out and opening it he saw the parabolic mic Franklin had used to listen in on them earlier that day.

    He didn't know what it was but decided to take it with them. The glove box was empty with the exception of the car's registration and a pack of gum. He was closing it when a shrill honk from Carla's car horn made his heart skip a beat.

    He looked back and saw her frantically waving him back. He ran to the car. Before his door shut she was accelerating away.

    "Wha—?"

    "Headlights on the cemetery road!" she exclaimed.

    "Stupid. I should've thought of that. The caretaker's truck! Franklin must've taken it to come after us!"

Sandy craned his neck, looking back. He saw flashes of yellow-white swinging back and forth on the cemetery road. He turned around. Carla flicked off her headlights. The windshield and the world beyond it went black.

"Carla!" he said

"Don't worry. I've done this plenty of times on these roads," she said.

"Franklin may be lots of things but one thing he's not is a country boy! He'll probably stop to get his car and by the time he does we'll be gone. With any luck he didn't see us yet. Won't know which way we went."

Sandy grabbed the handle over his seat and held on, disbelieving that anyone could stay on the road with no light to show the way.

But Carla guided the car surely. After a few moments he relaxed his grip.

"Which way are we going?!" he said. "What's next?"

Chapter 35 - Pursuer

Jack Franklin drove the groundskeeper's beat up pick-up truck unsteadily down the hill.

He'd deposited the old man, still moaning, in his hammock before discovering Lindstrom's ancient F-150 parked on the far side of the shed.

The keys were in it, and although it started easily, the manual transmission and the vehicle's insistence on her own master's well-worn handling frustrated his progress.

By the time he got to the bottom of the hill and exited the graveyard he had no idea which direction the girl and boy went and he was more than ready to ditch the fidgety truck for his car.

Although a little embarrassed by letting the girl get the jump on him not once but twice, he wasn't too worried.

He'd let the two grave robbers complete their task out of curiosity and instinct, not out of fear or their flimsy attempt at tying him up. It paid off, too, for although they'd kept their voices down mostly, he heard enough to discover their bizarre raid on Tony Diderrick's crypt had something to do with a cell phone.

If they were only there to retrieve a phone someone left in the casket it should have taken them much less time than they lingered over it.

That left only one option he could see; as crazy as it sounded they must be using the dead man's body to unlock a phone. A fingerprint? Facial recognition?

That meant they had Tony Diderrick's cell phone.

Had it been in there since the man died? Had they brought it with them? What was it that was worth going to all this trouble for?

He didn't know those answers yet, but he would.

Pulling up to the spot where he'd left his car he saw where a car recently had rolled over the knee-high grass on the roadside.

So they'd come this way. Cutting off the truck, he got out and discovered his keys and cell phone were gone.

The keys weren't a problem. He still had plenty of Jersey street kid in him and he had it hot wired and moving in less than five minutes. The phone could be replaced. It was an inconvenience and not even a setback really.

He wasn't going to call for backup yet anyway; not until he was sure what was going on. Not until he was sure he'd get proper credit that was coming to him.

Besides, he liked these kids, especially the girl. She might be from a nowhere splotch on the map, but she had something about her he admired.

She was tough and smart and anyone who grew up the way Franklin grew up respected those two things more than any other characteristics. She reminded Franklin of himself. He smiled.

Got to give them both credit. Whatever they were up to they had moxie.

He drove and thought about what might be on Tony Diderrick's phone and what Carla and Sandy would do next. He was confident he'd figure it out before they did.

He had many more years of thinking like a criminal on the run than they did.

Part 3

Chapter 36 - DNA of Connection

Jack Franklin quickly cleared out his sparsely furnished apartment. He threw his clothes in a secondhand army jump bag and boxed up the remainder of his possessions in three medium-sized plastic containers that fit in the back seat of the Taurus.

He'd lost the girl and her companion after they fled the graveyard and they'd been cagey enough to stay away from the obvious place to regroup: the Dyson's home in Brand's Flat.

He didn't need anyone to tell him his next move.

One way or the other it was time to move. His cover was blown.

It didn't matter whether or not they believed he was FBI—they knew who he wasn't and that meant a quick exit before the situation got more complicated.

Once packed he drove to the 7-Eleven on Route 250 just outside of Brand's Flat and bought a burner phone to replace the one Carla and Sandy took from the car. No chance they'd get anything out of that phone, he thought. It was locked down tight as a drum.

The Face in the Grave

He took a deep breath. The sun was almost up, and he knew what was coming for him. He decided to get a jump on it and head toward Richmond.

He was not looking forward to spelling out the events of the past few hours to his boss. He waited until he was on the interstate and punched in the boss's number.

He was amazed again that the man never sounded surprised or sleepy at any hour of day or night when he'd called.

He got the same gritty, no nonsense greeting he always got. "Go."

He went. He described everything that had transpired since he'd called the day before. The urge to edit out the embarrassing parts was strong, but he resisted it. Franklin had learned long ago that the boss never relied on a single source on a job. He always had back up; always had more eyes on a target, more sources reporting events.

A job this big? There'd be backups watching the backups. You never lied to the boss. It was always a bad idea. On this job it would be an exceedingly bad idea. He finished his tale and waited.

"The janitor?" the boss said.

It took Jack a second to put it together. "Ah, the groundskeeper? What about him?"

"Dead?"

"No."

"He make you?"

"No."

"You sure?"

"Pretty sure. I knocked him cold from behind. When I took him back to his shed he still wasn't seeing straight."

"Mmhmm. But he did see the Dyson girl and the boy with her."

"Yes."

"Local law enforcement involved?"

"Don't know. Don't think so."

"Why'd you clear out your apartment?"

"I assumed you'd want me out of here. The girl knows I'm not who I say I am."

There was a long sigh.

"Here's what you're going to do. Obviously Diderrick's kids don't want the law involved in whatever they're up to so we can't squeeze them with that…"

"Kids?" Jack said.

"How's that? The boy is Diderrick's too? They looked more like boyfriend and girlfriend than brother and sister."

"Complicated. They're not blood. We've been tracking this since the start of the year. It seems they didn't know about each other. We didn't either until our contacts at 23andMe tipped us off that we had close matches for Tony Diderrick's DNA in Florida and Virginia.

"The tests just happened to come in within a week of each other. God bless these teachers and their family tree assignments. Our guy regularly scans 23andMe's database checking for matches of DNA profiles for the Bureau's most wanted.

"So it comes up Diderrick has a kid in Florida. His name is Sandy Anderson—the kid you just lost. The real jackpot was the spot-on match of Diderrick himself that came up in Virginia. It's how we knew where to send you. We didn't bother with him since we already had our man. But them showing up together…"

"So they are brother and sister," Jack asked.

"No. Carla Dyson is Rita's daughter from another relationship. When we sent you to Virginia we already knew Diderrick was there. We sent the Richmond office out there to put eyes on. It's why you're there.

"But, for all we knew, Tony wasn't aware he had a son in Florida. You find out all kinds of interesting and useful shit when you start tracing DNA… stuff some people really want to know and stuff other people really want to forget. Stuff that can be very useful as leverage… even over a guy like Tony Diderrick."

Jack Franklin pondered that for a second. He'd always thought of the FBI as the "good guys." Not necessarily the ones wearing pure white hats—life on the street had taught him there were always blurred lines between good and bad—but at least he'd never thought they wore black hats.

This total disregard for privacy and due process, this wanton willingness to abuse power, unsettled him. It blurred the lines even more.

The Face in the Grave

He saw it vividly: a love child you never knew about, Mr. Senator? A criminal your family denies is your flesh and blood, Madame Speaker of the House?

He wondered how they'd gotten access to the genealogy company's records. It didn't take much thought.

The federal government was the biggest bully on the block. If they couldn't get something with a sugar cube they could get it with a stick.

All he could say was, "Yeah, I'd imagine so."

He added, "So what do you think now?"

"Like I said, them showing up together changes things. It doesn't seem likely they just hooked up coincidentally. First law of criminal investigations—"

"There are no coincidences," Franklin finished for his boss.

"What do you want me to do next? Debrief in Richmond?"

"No. Not yet. I want you to keep an eye on Rita Dyson. We're sending a team to the Anderson place in Florida first thing this morning. We need to keep our bases covered until we can sort out what the two kids are doing.

"I want eyes on Rita. Make sure she's there and hold your position until I get back with you."

Chapter 37 - Depth in the Dark

Sandy and Carla sat in her car at the first overlook off I-64 at the top of Afton Mountain and watched the sun burning off the low fog hugging the ground in little pockets in the valley below.

They had taken turns keeping watch and getting a few hours of sleep through the night before making the phone call to Stick Gordon.

The idea for a way out of their situation had come to Carla as she slept fitfully. It was the money. Of course it was the money.

She'd awakened with the question clearly before her mind: why would Tony take the mob's money?

Her stepfather was not a good man. He'd worked for a notorious crime family, how long she didn't know, but long enough to rise to a position where the Fratellis trusted him with their books and access to all their funds.

Obviously he'd been a party to countless criminal acts and facilitated the perpetuation and growth of the organization. Bad man. He'd married women in two different states and deceived them about his identity. Bad

The Face in the Grave

man. He'd established two families with children who did not know who he was. Bad man.

Tony Anderson or Tony Dyson was undeniably a bad man.

So why did a bad man steal three quarters of a billion dollars and take it to his grave? Was this the pinnacle of his badness?

Tony didn't do anything with the massive wealth he'd stolen. The accounts he'd set up for his families were pittances. There was no trust fund. No nest egg.

It appeared the only provision Tony made for his dual families were modest college funds for his children and paid-off mortgages for the houses in Brand's Flat and Fernandina Beach—neither of which were extravagant by any means.

Extravagant? Tony must have had access to large sums of money for many years, yet nothing about him hinted at wealth. Not a whiff. Not a fancy car or a piece of jewelry. Ciro's pizza was their version of fine dining.

From what she knew of Sandy's home life, the duplicitous man she called dad was consistent—no trappings of wealth there either.

From every appearance, this bad man had stolen the money for no reason at all. It existed only in ethereal Bitcoin and the only access to it was this phone resting in the dirty cup holder of her used Camry.

She picked the phone up and punched in her unlock code, reminding herself that they needed to come up with a way for each of them to easily access the phone.

Sandy's face and her code would work.

She randomly opened several apps before tapping on the notes app native to the iPhone. The list of her dead father's notes popped up. They were in chronological order.

The most recently accessed note caught her attention. It read simply: *church*.

Tony was taking notes in church? She clicked on the note. There were dated entries for the Sundays Tony had been in town.

They began about a year before his death. Sermon titles and Bible references followed each date along with a line or two of his thoughts and questions.

Scrolling back to the earliest entry, she found one that was longer than any of the others. The sermon was The Rich Young Ruler. The text for the talk was taken from the book of Luke, but Tony had taken time to find the same story in the books of Mark and Matthew.

He'd written down the other Bible verses the pastor referenced during his sermon. They were old hat to Carla, things she'd heard harped on from the pulpit of her church since she could remember.

The love of money being the root of evil, your treasure revealing where your heart is, and the parable about investing your money and not burying it like the unwise servant; all things she knew from well-rehearsed sermons and Sunday School lessons.

But to Tony, they'd been novel. The sermon obviously affected him.

Carla remembered the Bible she and Sandy took from Tony's coffin. She retrieved it from the back seat. Fanning through it, she saw a flash of yellow highlighter and thumbed to the page.

As far as she could tell it was the only marking in the book, which was stiff with disuse despite her mother having given it to Tony with his name embossed on the red-brown leather cover many years ago.

Her mother's copy of the Bible looked more like the much-used family recipe book, full of tabs, underlinings, and multi-colored highlighted passages. To pick it up was to risk either an actual page or some scrap of paper falling out and fluttering to the floor.

The highlighted passage in Tony's Bible was from Paul's first letter to Timothy, the famous admonition about money:

Those who want to be rich, however, fall into temptation and become ensnared by many foolish and harmful desires that plunge them into ruin and destruction. For the love of money is a root of all kinds of evil, for which some have strayed from the faith in their greediness, and pierced themselves through with many sorrows.

Tony had highlighted the two verses with yellow highlighter and underlined "ruin," "destruction," "pierced," and "sorrows."

There was a church bulletin tucked in the back few pages of the Bible. It was for the Sunday the sermon was preached. Curious.

The Face in the Grave

What would make a bad man read the Bible? What had gotten Tony's attention?

Carla picked up the phone again and opened the web browser. She typed in "Fratelli Crime family" and fixed the date range to search around the date in the bulletin.

The top result caught her eye.

Richie Fratelli, known to be one of three brothers atop the Fratelli crime family, had been brought in for questioning over the gangland style slaying of his older brother, Frank, and the car-bombing murder of the third Fratelli brother, AJ.

What did all this mean? What did it have to do with Tony?

It made sense to her that death and violence went along with being part of a crime family, but violence and death perpetrated upon other people, not members of the family.

From her made-for-television and cinematic understanding of monsters and the mob, the one thing you could not do was hurt or kill someone who was… what was the word? "Made."

Yeah. Goodfellas. The Sopranos. You don't kill family members. Unless… unless you wanted to start a war.

She had taken all this in after she and Sandy ditched Jack Franklin in the graveyard and made a quick stop at the Sheetz for gas and food.

They pointed the car east after the briefest of debates on whether or not they should check on Rita. They ditched that plan; most likely place for Franklin to find them.

When they got to the top of Afton Mountain, she told him to pull into the first overlook on the eastern side of the mountain.

Dawn was still hours away and they were exhausted from the night's activities.

Sandy said, "We need some sleep before we do anything else. You rest first and I'll keep watch, then we can swap out, okay?"

Carla put the phone down, nodded and yawned. The adrenaline vacuum caught up with her all at once and she suddenly felt an overwhelming weariness like she'd never felt before.

She managed to recline her seat and mumble, "…sure you'll be able to keep awa…" before falling into a deep sleep.

Sandy wasn't sure he could stay awake. He had been on the nods before pulling into the overlook. He took the first watch because he thought it was the manly thing to do and because it seemed to him Carla was doing all the heavy lifting as this crazy story unfolded.

He stared at the blue-green numbers on the car's dashboard digital clock. Three minutes passed. Getting through the next three hours, if they passed as slowly as those minutes, would be like wading through quicksand or running against a strong wind.

His chin fell on his chest and he snapped awake. He checked the clock, fearful he'd slept through his whole watch. Only two more minutes had passed. He shook himself, and leaving the car running, eased out into the brisk mountain air.

He contemplated the strange nature of time. Two days had passed like a flash of light, yet here he was, crawling through minutes. How did time accordion like that?

He was aware of time, its weight, its relentlessness, its insistence, but he was also aware for the first time in his life of its foolishness, its construct.

He flashed back to the body in the crypt, utterly still, and thought how it represented time. Tony had no time. Time, whatever it might be, was over for him. No need for a wristwatch on a corpse.

He wondered if people were ever buried with their watches—how strange that would be to put your ear to a coffin and hear the tick tick tick of time running in the timeless grave.

A car zinged by on the highway with a whoosh of air. The night cold crept into his feet and up his legs. He stomped his feet and did a handful of jumping jacks. He could see his breath.

Cold. Breath. Every thought bent inevitably back to the crypt.

Cold skin. Breathless body. In the dark on the side of Afton Mountain the skies had clouded over, burying the moon, and Sandy Anderson felt the weight of his own mortality settle upon him for the first time in his young life.

He stifled a groan of grief and fear and wished for the sun to rise and this night to pass. Life would be different now.

The Face in the Grave

No way back to life without death, but perhaps daylight could burn away enough of the funereal tar in his soul so he could see some way forward.

He was surprised by the intensity and rapidity of this attack on his undefended mortality and wondered how he'd never considered a need to defend it until now, but there it was and here he was: defenseless.

He made laps around the car in this wounded condition until Carla relieved him just past four a.m. They exchanged nods.

Sandy got into the car and Carla took up his track. The sleep Sandy had tried to avoid now avoided him. After fifteen minutes of tossing and turning in the passenger seat, he rejoined her. She raised an eyebrow.

"Can't sleep," he said.

"I didn't really sleep myself," she said.

"Too much…" She let the phrase fade away with her visible breath.

They made laps together in silence for a few more minutes before Carla stopped and retrieved the phone.

"The money," she said absently.

"Huh?" Sandy said.

"It's the money that's got us into this."

Sandy gave her a look that said, duh, and so what and tell me something I didn't know all at one time.

Carla ignored it. She was a verbal processor—needed to take ideas out of her head and spread them out in front of someone like dumping out a box of puzzle pieces on a tabletop.

She didn't need the tabletop to do anything other than be there to catch her thoughts while she rummaged around looking for the edges and began framing up the picture. Sandy sensed her mood and shut up.

"Tony steals a billion dollars and takes it to his grave. We get squat. But he never lived like he had a lot of money. He had to have had plenty of it. He suspected all along that money was trouble. Maybe he found it out long before he met our mothers. Who knows? We don't even know what we know about our father." She tapped the screen of the iPhone.

"But these notes he made in church and the timing of the mob boss's death, that clicked. He must have really cared about those people. He saw what the money did to them. That they'd kill their own brother to get it. He decided to take away all their motivation for killing each other."

Sandy interrupted. "Yeah, and give all of them the motive to kill him!"

"Yeah. He did. But he loved us too."

She rolled her eyes even as she said this. "He kept the money away from us because he knew what it would do to us. And when he decided to take away their money, you can bet he had a plan to keep us safe. He knew how to keep his location secret, didn't he? He knew how to keep two families in the dark about where he was half the time. He planned to disappear from his third family—the mob. Or maybe they're first…"

"So let me get this straight. You think our bigamist mobster father got religion and that's why he stole a billion dollars? I'd of thought getting religious might mean not stealing. And maybe telling his two families what a piece of shit he's been to lie to them… and to use what money he has to take care of his children…"

Sandy stopped and pulled Carla around to face him. His face was flush and there was heat behind his eyes.

"Or am I missing something? If this is what they're peddling at your church, I think I'll pass."

Carla wasn't listening to Sandy. She'd found the edges to the puzzle she'd been pondering in the dark. She got in the car and began thumbing through files on Tony Diderrick's phone.

Sandy said "Hey!" in protest of being ignored, but got in beside her.

"What are you doing?" he said, not able to hide the hurt tone he hated in his own voice.

"The money. It's the thing that got us into this and it's the thing that we can use to get out of it."

"What about all that religious bullshit you just laid on me? Root of all evil?" he said.

"It isn't the money that's the root, it's the love of the money. And evil people love it. You love your mom and they're using that against you. They love money. We can use that against them." She held up the phone.

"Tony didn't just have the mob's money here, he had their hearts." She had been swiping through files while they talked. She paused.

Her eyes lit up. She added, "And their secrets."

Chapter 38 - Rat Trap

Stick Gordon's phone rang.

It was 8:48 a.m. according to the digital clock on the console of Shirley Anderson's oven.

He and his boys sat around the kitchen table in various stages of repose. Gordon rarely slept, had not slept a full night in thirty years owing to a bad case of insomnia and an equally bad sinus condition three separate surgeries and a CPAP machine couldn't touch.

He slept—when he slept—in fits and starts sitting up in chairs. He'd come to see it as an asset and believed it kept him alive when most of the guys he'd grown up with in and around the family were not.

Much harder to whack a guy when you couldn't catch him sleeping.

Shirley Laughton slept. Her head was slumped forward, her chin rested on her chest, and her breathing was steady and sonorous but not quite a snore. The ringing phone did not produce any reaction from her; fear had given way to fatigue and it held her fast.

The Face in the Grave

It was the kid's phone. The woman's son, but it was the girl again, the trash-talking cunt, whose voice came over the speaker when he tapped the green receive icon on the phone.

He was adding up her insults like an accountant in green eyeshades, relishing the thought of what he'd do to her once he'd gotten the boss's money back.

"Put Shirley on the phone," she said.

"Good morning to you too," Gordon sneered.

"You didn't ask nice. You didn't say please. I'm gonna enjoy teaching you some manners."

"When I speak with a dog I speak their language, Stick Gordon, you fat ass."

Gordon swallowed a retort. The girl knew his name? She picked up on his hesitation.

"That's right. I know who you are. I'll tell you who else knows you. The FBI. They'd love to talk with you. They'd probably give you a good deal. Send your fat ass someplace nice—"

Stick Gordon suppressed the thick wad of anger rising in his chest.

"You've got the wrong one, little girl. You've had it wrong from the first time we talked. You see, I'm not a negotiator. I'm death. There's no way around me and no stopping me. I don't talk. Not to the feds, not to you. And I told you to keep the cops out of this or—"

"Who said I did?" Carla cut him off.

"And I am a negotiator. I've got things of value that people are interested in. You're just one of 'em. I've got a deal for you I think you'll like."

"You're not good at listening. I don't make deals, especially not with some little girl who thinks she's a badass. You don't know who you're talking to. The people, my people, aren't actors, sweetheart. We don't play."

"Yeah, but you already did, didn't you? You made a deal with me. Gave me forty-eight hours to produce the family money. Or Tony. You already played. I think you should check your bank account. Make sure you check the right one. It's Denby right? Claude Denby. The banks open in less than five minutes, Mr. Denby."

She clicked off.

Gordon looked at the blank screen. Bank account? Like all the foot soldiers in the family, he lived on cash money. It was the family way. Banks were not trustworthy. Banks could be robbed. He robbed banks.

Having a bank account was frowned upon for that very reason. The only trustworthy place to keep your money was with the family on their books or in cash in your own pocket.

A mobster who kept his money separate from the organization was like a husband who kept a credit card his wife didn't know about; a breach of trust that could only mean one thing: unfaithfulness.

A hint of infidelity might drive a wife crazy but drove the Fratellis to murder, a fact with which Stick Gordon was intimately familiar.

A second fact pressing itself into his consciousness at the moment was the existence of his own very private, very secret savings account he'd opened seventeen years ago under an assumed name.

The start had been innocent enough. He'd gone to a local bank in Newark to case it for a robbery. In order to get a good look at the layout and security he sat with a cute young account specialist who patiently explained the advantages and disadvantages to the bank's various savings plans as Gordon scanned the best way to remove all their money while also giving careful thought to the best way to remove all her clothes.

He used one of his fake IDs—Claude Denby—and tossed in a couple G's—pocket change for him even back then—thinking while he signed the deposit slip that he'd soon be back to withdraw it with a lot more than three percent interest.

When the bank job got canceled he forgot about it, till three months later when he got a statement from the bank in the mail and realized he'd absentmindedly used his actual mailing address while filling out the bank forms.

Not good. Sloppy. But there was something about seeing that money there in black and white:

Balance - $5014.03

It looked solid. Not like the pocket full of cash that regularly swelled and disappeared as the days and weeks passed.

The Face in the Grave

And so he'd begun quietly adding to his accidentally-laid nest egg, changing to the new paperless option so there wouldn't be any more statements showing up in his mailbox.

He got the same satisfaction he'd gotten from that first bank statement when he checked his account balance every week or two. Claude Denby had amassed the tidy sum of $737,000 since then.

He'd also obtained a social security number and a passport. Claude paid taxes and lived in Delaware. He was a perfect empty suit Stick Gordon thought about wearing some day when he took off the one he had worn since he was a teenager working the streets.

That one was stained with blood, and when he'd still been able to sleep in a bed at night, it made him sweat through the sheets and wake up shoving his own fist in his mouth to stifle his screams.

He fingered his phone and watched the clock on the stove. At 9:01 he logged into his account at Garden State FCU. The screen refreshed. He flicked a finger to scroll to the bottom of the page.

His grip tightened on the hard rubber encasing the phone. There was an entry for an electronic funds transfer at 0900 for one million dollars.

He stared at the new balance:

$1,737,666.07

As he stared, the screen switched to an incoming call from an unknown number. He answered.

"What kind of game are you playing?" he said.

"No game," Carla said.

"You just got one million dollars for the deal you cut with me to find Tony."

"What deal? There wasn't a deal."

"Sure there was. You gave me one day to find him and I agreed to give you one million. Your portion of the family's money Tony stole. Great deal for you, Gordon. Or is it Denby? Which name should I use? You should think about which one you should use. Which one has a future."

Carla's tone turned icy hard.

"Because when I disappear with the rest of the money you're gonna need a name no one's ever heard of if you don't want to end up in a jail cell or a hole in the ground."

There was a long silence on the line as Stick Gordon checked and rechecked the angles. He played his only card, knowing the girl held the nuts, knowing he had to play this out anyway.

"I've still got the woman…"

"And I've still got a billion dollars of the Fratellis money."

"There won't be enough money in the world to put her back together after I'm finished with her."

"And there's not enough money in the world to buy you a new name after I tip off the feds and the Fratellis. Listen, Gordon, we don't need anything much and you should think over the possibilities. We don't want this money. We just want the woman back. But you… you see how easy it was to make you one million dollars richer since this morning? It could just as easily been two hundred million or… let me see."

There was a momentary scuffling sound. The girl's voice got distant. She came back on, louder.

"It could be $724,124,548.23." She paused to let the number and the offer she was making sink in, then said,

"It could all be yours."

Stick Gordon glanced up as Carla said, "it could all be yours," realizing he'd never taken the phone off speaker.

His two guys—the muscle heads he referred to mentally as Lenny and Squiggy—sat across the kitchen table from him.

Their faces were set to boardroom passive, but their eyes had gone wide. Too bad, Gordon thought. That was life in the family… and death. Hear something you shouldn't hear and wind up in a barrel at the bottom of the Passaic River.

In an instant he flashed back over forty years of this life-and-death lifestyle. People he'd put in barrels and times he'd been sure he was going to be next in a barrel with no one to tell his wife and daughters the truth of where he'd gone or what happened to him. Just like these two would soon be gone without a trace, it could have been him.

He studied their faces. They'd never see it coming.

The Face in the Grave

"What makes you think I'm a rat?" he said into the phone, casually clicking it off speaker and holding it to his ear.

"We both know you're a rat, Gordon. Everyone in the Fratelli family is a rat. What I'm asking is this: do you want to be the king rat? Or do you want to keep running around in the maze taking orders from a rat that's fatter than you?"

She cut the connection.

As if the phone call had over-pressurized the car to a bursting point, Carla and Sandy simultaneously opened their doors and got out.

"What happens next?" Sandy finally said.

"We stick to the plan. Give him time to consider the offer." She paused.

"And we make a few more phone calls."

They returned to the car and emerged a quarter of an hour later, wide-eyed, hearts hammering. They lapped the car together, letting their heart rates level out and their stomachs settle.

It was full light on the mountain; a clear, beautiful day. They stopped at the front of the car and gazed out over the vista opening to the east from the side of the mountain.

Pockets of low fog checkered the ground between hills rolling away at their feet. Depth and distance lost meaning momentarily and with them the gravity of all they'd experienced in the night. They both felt lighter; almost light enough to step off into the sky and leave this present darkness.

Carla started to speak. A man's voice from behind them broke their reverie before she could utter a word.

"You two got the jump on me the first time we met. And you've sure made a lot of trouble for me. So do yourselves a favor and don't make any sudden moves."

They turned to see Jack Franklin, his gun drawn.

Chapter 39 - Unlucky

The serenity of the moment popped like a soap bubble, everything flooding back in with Franklin's voice. The mob. The dead father. The stolen money. The hostage mother. And the feds.

All of it. It threatened to swallow them.

The panic that flashed across their faces registered with Franklin. He lowered his gun. Kids. Scared kids. He put a hand out toward them. Calm. Let's pull this back.

"No need for this to go south," he said.

"Huh?" the blond kid said, his face twisted up between fear and confusion. Diderrick's daughter cut her eyes at him.

"He means he doesn't want this to go badly," she said. "You never heard that saying before?"

The boy shook his head, but said, "Yes." Obviously too much going through his circuits to process even this simple thought.

The girl got up off the hood of the car and faced him. The boy followed.

The Face in the Grave

"How'd you find us?" she said.

Franklin's turn to look sheepish. The truth was he'd been headed to Richmond, ready to own how he'd been owned by these two kids and to explain how they gave him the slip.

It was not going to be a pleasant meeting. Probably a career ender when the whole story was told. He'd never be able to live it down. It was pure chance that he'd been coming down Afton Mountain when his boss told him to stay and keep an eye on Rita Dyson.

He'd taken the next overlook, searching for the quickest way to turn around, and there were his perps. He half believed it was a hallucination—wishful thinking—before swinging his car into a parking spot and approaching them. The girl was staring at him, reading his thoughts.

She said, "Got lucky, huh?"

He started to deny it, then grinned in spite of himself. He liked the girl. She was sharp. Very sharp. Would've made a good agent herself. He nodded. "Yeah. Lucky." He added, "Guess that'd make you…"

"Unlucky," she monotoned.

"So what now?"

"It depends," he said.

"You've caused me a lot of trouble. A lot of trouble." He looked for a second as if he were on the edge of a precipice. Deciding. He sucked in a deep breath and let it out slowly.

He fixed his eyes on Sandy, then Carla.

"I liked being your pastor. It sounds crazy. I was doing it as a cover but it wasn't fake to me. That's hard to believe. You've endured a lot of fake lately. When I took this assignment I didn't know it would go this way. Didn't think through it.

"They needed someone who could pull off being a convincing youth pastor, and well, that didn't leave many guys who were good options. This case… it's the biggest thing to come along in years. If I did a good job, it was high visibility.

"A guarantee to make a name for myself, move up. It must seem like it's a lie but I'm not a bad man. I believe all the things I said to you and the others. I'm a Christian, I mean—"

Sandy erupted.

"You? A youth pastor? Cover? No no no, man. No. That's messed up. If anything was ever messed up that's it. You and your religion are just as messed up as Tony and his money."

He was talking to the agent but looking in Carla's eyes. She winced. He went on, turning to face Franklin.

"You, you're an undercover cop pretending to be a pastor? How does that work on any level?!"

Jack had been watching Carla's reaction. He snapped from her face to Sandy's suddenly.

"Who're you? What do you know about anything? I came here hunting down a man in the middle of terrible things. I didn't end up here because I followed a girl home from college like some lovesick puppy. The real world makes us make tough choices, boy."

It was Sandy's turn to wince. He searched for something, anything to say to move the attention off of him, but found nothing.

His face burned in the cool morning air.

Carla spoke. It came out like a melancholy sigh.

"It seems nobody is who you think they are. Not in this story. Our story."

Sandy and Jack felt the deep sorrow emanating from the girl. It punctured the moment like a needle in a hot water bottle. The tension drained out of both men. Sandy tried to take Carla's hand. She didn't respond.

Carla stood rigid, staring with vacant eyes into the side of Afton mountain, seeing her former life fading with the Blue Ridge morning mist. She took in a deep breath. Her eyes regained focus on the agent.

"What now?" she said again, more command than question.

Something in the way the girl looked at him decided it for Jack Franklin. He jumped.

"Maybe we can help each other," he said.

"Taking you in does nothing for my career. No one's interested in putting you away. I'm not. Don't know there's anything to pin on you anyway... besides maybe taking a federal officer hostage." He grinned lopsidedly at this.

"And I'm not particularly interested in telling that story."

The Face in the Grave

Sandy thought the agent's face might be burning like his own only moments ago.

"I want to put the bad guys away. I know some of the worst of them are involved." He hesitated half a beat. He wanted to see their reaction to the name.

"Stick Gordon."

The girl's face remained slack. The boy's face did not.

"Yeah," he continued, "one of the worst. Not your average muscle. Not the kind of guy they send to just erase somebody—make 'em disappear. No. When the family sends Gordon to do a job, they know he gets off on inflicting as much pain as he can before he kills. Crazy bastard saw a show called Shōgun. Ever hear of it?"

Franklin didn't pause to see if the two had or not. He wasn't looking at them at all. He was recalling a scene his mind rejected. He went monotone.

"Shōgun. This warlord boils a man alive. Does it slow so it takes hours and hours for him to die. Gordon decides to copy the warlord. Decides he can do it better. Took a snitch out in the desert. Big ass stainless steel vat. Propane tank. Took three days for the guy to die. When they finally pulled his body out it fell apart like an overcooked chicken."

Franklin paused and swallowed hard.

"Want to know how I know this?" Again he didn't wait for either of his audience of two to acknowledge the question. They were both swallowing hard themselves.

"Because Stick Gordon videoed the whole thing. Sent it to the Bureau. He also sent it to half a dozen witnesses to a mob hit in Cleveland who were scheduled to testify. Case never went to trial. Not one of 'em would say another word to us after that video. Everyone got amnesia."

Franklin let out a long slow breath.

"That's the guy you're dealing with here. Don't know what your next move is, but unless it involves putting that fat son of a bitch away or in the ground…"

Sandy was looking sick to his stomach. This was the man standing over his mother?

He bent over, hands on his knees, fighting back the fear, anger, and hopelessness that were trying to strangle him.

Carla patted him on the back in that universally impotent manner of the overmatched. She resented this man intruding in their lives telling his boogeyman story. She wanted to disbelieve him. She wanted to take control of her out-of-control life—find a foothold from which she could push off from all the lies and terrible truths and start a new life in a new direction.

But she knew instinctively that Franklin told the truth about Stick Gordon and her abundant self-confidence was running low.

"You got a plan, Mr. Agent Man?" she said.

Chapter 40 - Lion's Den

Stick Gordon, a congenitally impatient man, was growing impatient.

He felt it crawling up the center of his chest like lava rising in the underground ducts of a volcano. He'd run out of patience for Tony Diderrick years ago.

Sitting on his hands taking orders from some bitch of a girl on a phone was making him itch. He decided he'd take one more phone call from the girl, give her one more taste of the fear in his captive's voice, then he'd kill the woman with his bare hands and text the video of the act to the girl.

He'd be careful to keep any identifying marks out of the frame of course. He'd learned that trick on the job like everything else in his gruesome profession.

Trial and error.

There was a missing Utah prosecutor stuffed in a suitcase at the bottom of a landfill bearing mute witness to him learning that trick. It had made a relatively simple hit on a small-time player in a pawn shop in Ogden into a three-month long ordeal.

The Face in the Grave

Mr. Pawn Shop tried to get a cut of family money laundered in his establishment from a semi-legal prostitution operation out of Vegas.

Since the family used many such establishments across the country to wash its soiled dollars, the Fratellis sent Gordon to Ogden to dispose of the would-be thief and to make an example of him that would discourage anyone else from emulating him.

Gordon came up with the idea of videotaping the man's demise—he'd always been an innovator when it came to killing and terror and it was the era when camcorders and VHS tapes emerged.

How effective would that be? Cut off a few fingers, stuff them down the guy's throat, tape his mouth shut till he suffocates on his own flesh and blood and catch it all on camera.

Let that get around to these other bums and there'd be a big downtick in bucking the system. Only problem was the idiot running the camcorder missed a little detail. Gordon wanted Mr. Pawn Shop's glasses on him while he worked on him—thought it was a nice touch—let 'em see it all as clearly as possible.

Except the footage didn't just capture the horror in the victim's eyes. It also captured a fully recognizable image of Stick Gordon reflected in the man's eyeglasses.

A year later, when the case of Mr. Pawn Shop's murder was colder than the mutilated body in his coffin, one of the two existing copies of Gordon's tape found its way into the hands of the Ogden DA.

That mess had taken a lot of skill and time to scrub away and landed the DA in the landfill, his pieces mingled with those of the idiot who'd videoed the murder in a battered old Samsonite.

It had been easy enough to lure the cocksure attorney to a meeting with an imaginary video expert who promised to deliver an admissible image of Stick Gordon with his advanced video tape enhancing techniques.

Making his original videographer into the point of contact for the Ogden DA had been a stroke of artistic genius as far as Gordon was concerned. And another way to send a message.

Fuck with me or fuck up when you work with me? That's a bad day. He only regretted he hadn't taken the time to capture the new masterpiece of murder on tape.

Gordon rapped the table with stubby fingers in a staccato piano riff and contemplated the semi-comatose woman across the kitchen table. An easy kill. Law of the jungle, baby. The way he'd lived his entire life. Evolution. Stronger, faster, smarter, wins.

He fully expected one of these flunkies he dragged around with him to figure it out sooner or later; put a bullet in the back of his head more than likely. Probably the ginger. That one always had a little something behind the eyes that was either a little crazy or a little shrewd—he could never decide which, probably both.

There was a touch of Gordon himself in that one.

But what that stupid fuck didn't know was Stick Gordon had no plan to be—what's that thing they called in basketball? Posterized.

No. Gordon had no plan for his demise to be a message to anyone. No suitcase in a landfill or bloated body in a river. No video. He had an escape plan.

He had stayed alive by getting more shrewd as his body became more frail—not that it was frail now, just not what he used to be. He had the problem of all apex predators.

When do you become vulnerable to the next generation? When do you pull the plug? A lion didn't have options. It was defeat and then death alone when their strength failed.

But Gordon was going to disappear like... well like the man he was hunting down right now. He paused on that one. How had that old fuck gotten away with it? How long had the accountant laid the groundwork for leaving the family behind? Money, he mused.

It was money. Had to be. With enough money, you could be invisible or bulletproof or both. Diderrick had done both.

His hands in the family money was the only reason he wasn't fish food in the Colorado River all those years ago. That made him bulletproof. And then somehow, he'd disappeared.

Gordon thumbed his phone and tapped the icon for his bank account again for the hundredth time since the girl's last call. How the fuck had she done that? How had Diderrick done that? A dark thought crossed his mind.

If she could make money appear in his account, what's to stop her from making it go away? And did she or Diderrick know about his two other

The Face in the Grave

accounts? The two that were going to line his retirement nest, not down south, no, in Canada.

Who'd ever think to look for a retired mobster up there?

South America? The islands? Sure. Not Gordon. He'd be in a cabin in Manitoba. The thought of anyone fucking up his escape plan went through him like a shot of grain alcohol. He felt the heat rise. He saw Diderrick's face, heard the smart ass girl's voice.

He pushed back from the table. Time to go. Right now. Kill this bitch and these flunkies. Ginger first then the other two, who'd be too stupid or scared to do anything.

This lion was going to give his last roar and head north. Instinct had always served him and it told him it was time to move now.

The woman stirred as Gordon got up. She opened her eyes and stared at him, sensing the change in temperature in the room as if an emotional furnace had clicked on. She knew. She started to scream.

Gordon put the phone on the table, intent on shutting her up. Damn the Fratellis and damn the girl. It was his time now.

He walked over and stood behind the woman. The pitch of her screams increased with each step he took.

He rested his meaty hands on her shoulders momentarily and observed her head like a squirrel assessing the best way to crack a nut.

He put one hand to either ear, palm flat, elbows out, and began squeezing.

His phone rang.

Chapter 41 - The Right Bait

There was a confused moment as Gordon connected the call and punched the speakerphone button.

He was breathing hard from the effort he'd just been expending upon Shirley Anderson. Shirley Anderson was wailing in a combination of fear and pain.

One of Gordon's two flunkies had knocked over a glass of diet soda as he'd attempted to answer Gordon's phone, and was swearing profusely as the brown liquid waterfalled over the edge of the kitchen table.

Carla tried several times to speak and clarify she had Gordon before she knew she did. She was glad she'd kept her own end off speaker. Sandy was already on edge.

Hearing his mother like this would surely have put him over it. As it was his eyes were the size of saucers while he listened to her shout into the phone, finally hearing and being heard.

"Gordon!"

The Face in the Grave

"Yeah, girl. I don't have time for you. I'm gonna shut this bitch up and finish cutting off the frayed edges around here."

He paused to scream at Flunky Number Two, "Leave the fucking soda! Stuff a rag in this bitch's mouth!"

Back to Carla, "Pray I don't decide to come find you next."

Carla was cool. She went to that place she'd discovered in the past two days—a part of her she'd never known was there. Her voice was not ragged at all.

"And where would you look for me, you fat tub of lard?"

She waited half a beat, long enough to hear Gordon suck in a breath and begin his retort, when she added, saccharin sweet, "Canada?"

The stream of vileness caught in Gordon's throat. He choked on it.

"S'matter, Gordon? Haven't you figured out you're not in charge here? Check your offshore accounts lately? Your nest eggs? You may want to sit down before you do. Someone may or may not have gotten the authorities to lock them down while they investigate the source of all that money. It's not all bad. You've still got your job. But I doubt Richie Fratelli will be too forgiving if you kill the only person who can reconnect him with the family's money. Especially when I let him know it was you and not Tony that took it."

Gordon found his voice. "That's a lie!"

"Oh? I'm sure you'll have an easy time convincing Richie. Seems like a reasonable guy. Not someone who would, say, kill his own brothers because he thought they might have more money than him…"

Carla let that hang in the air.

Stick Gordon had gone from rage-drunk lion to cold-sober mouse like a dropped hammer. His world clanged off the ground, reverberating with the sound coming through the phone.

The girl was still talking.

"Your two boys there with you are gonna help us sort this out, Gordon."

Ginger stopped dabbing at the spilled soda. He and the other flunky were looking at Gordon quizzically.

"How's that?" Gordon found his voice.

"The three of you are going to make a trip together. There's a private plane waiting for you at Fernandina Municipal. It leaves in two hours. You and Hunter and French are going to pay me a visit and we'll finish our business."

How did this girl know the names of his muscle? How did she know they were there?

He instinctively swept the room with his eyes, looking for cameras, wondering if the place was bugged. He motioned for his two men to keep quiet.

"Why would I do that?" Gordon said, trying to put authority back into his voice. "I'm holding all the cards, girl, and Mrs. Anderson is my ace."

"Not all of them," Carla said.

"I've got one I'm pretty sure you'll want to see before you scurry off down whatever rat hole people like you end up in."

"Yeah? What card would that be?"

"Really? You really are stupid aren't you? Or is your memory that bad? I've got Tony."

There was a long enough pause that Carla thought her ace might be a joker. That Gordon wouldn't take the bait.

She'd taken away all the man's options, cut off all his escape routes. It was a dangerous game with a man like Stick Gordon and depended upon two characteristics she sensed in the man: self-preservation and pride.

She was giving him the one way out that played on both.

Finally, he spoke. "Who do we need to talk to at the airport?"

"Go to the general aviation desk and tell them Fatso and his crew are there. The pilot is already briefed on the destination and he's been told you don't ask any questions. If you ask him where you're going he'll divert to another location. If you try to force him to talk he'll divert. You get on board and sit like a good boy. If you don't, this will be the last time we talk."

Another long pause. Carla could hear the fat man's labored breathing.

Finally he said, "And Mrs. Anderson?"

Carla breathed. She realized she'd been holding her breath and tried not to let it show.

"She goes to the airport with you. She has her own traveling arrangements. She leaves fifteen minutes before you do. If there's a hiccup

The Face in the Grave

in her itinerary, if she misses her connection, or if she's not alone when she leaves the airport, all bets are off. You understand? You follow the plan and you'll get Tony Diderrick. You don't? Those two with you are gonna get identical texts from Richie Fratelli telling them the first one who brings him evidence that you're dead is getting an early Christmas bonus."

Gordon looked at the two dull-eyed men still watching him. They'd do him. No questions. They'd be too stupid to ask if a text was really Richie.

They'd do him and probably split the money… or more likely do him and kill each other trying to prove it was one and not the other that did it.

This girl. This fucking girl. How did she know what she knew?

"Tell you what, sweetheart. I'll be on that plane. I'll send Mrs. Anderson on her way. But after I'm done with Tony… after I settle business with him? I'm gonna put off retirement. You'll be my last job. I'm gonna make you famous. When I get done with you, it'll be your name people use when they talk about suffering."

He hung up before Carla could say anything.

Chapter 42 - Antarctic Survival

Preparations for Stick Gordon's arrival went at breakneck speed.

Carla, Sandy, and Jack Franklin were discovering what the better part of a billion dollars could accomplish. How "impossible" and "we can't accommodate you" vanished under the weight of hard cash.

And how time was compressed. They were learning a new definition of the phrase "time is money," by purchasing chunks of it from people willing to hand it over for the right price.

Franklin knew he was a party to thirty different types of illegal activities getting Stick Gordon to Virginia with mob money. He was operating under another kind of authority, one from a saying he'd learned as a kid: better to ask for forgiveness than permission.

He was well aware their shoestring plan had gaping holes in it—dangerous holes—thousand-foot deep glacial crags which could swallow the three of them whole.

The Face in the Grave

He'd read all the accounts of Antarctic explorer Sir Ernest Shackleton after a middle school English teacher assigned him a book report on Endurance in eighth grade.

He learned a great deal because of that chance assignment and one of the great lessons was movement.

Movement.

When it was time to move, you moved; fast and without looking back. The bridge to safety may only last a moment and the bridge to success was its close relative. Go.

Don't give the ice time to shift under your weight.

Since his chance encounter with Carla and Sandy on the Afton Mountain overlook, he'd seen a way to both success and safety.

The Fratellis were more dangerous than the Antarctic ice fields that crushed Ernest Shackleton's ship like a matchstick, and if he didn't find a way to stop him, Richie Fratelli would crush them too.

The more he heard their story, the more determined Jack was to prevent that from happening. These kids and their mothers deserved better.

Add in a dose of guilt and shame that he'd been just another deceiver in their young lives, and it went beyond his desire to put bad guys away and look good doing it. But there was still a possibility he could do both.

And there was enough of a glory hound in him to mull over that possibility.

Still, he thought the odds were probably against him keeping his job even if they pulled off the outrageous plan they'd come up with. There'd be time to deal with that later.

If he could put away Fratelli and his main enforcer Stick Gordon, well, what more could a lawman want in a career?

He glanced over at Carla next to him in his car. Her expression was calm. This girl… where did she come from? How could something that looked so soft and kind be so tough?

He could see why Sandy was smitten by her. She was a wonderful enigma. His mind drifted to the dead man in the mausoleum. What did he have to do with this girl becoming the young woman sitting here?

Another thing that made no sense.

To Franklin, the Fratellis were monolithic. Evil. What was wrong with the world. The reason he became a lawman.

Dismantle them bit by bit like taking apart a machine. Each piece to be buried. Tony Diderrick was no exception. How could someone so evil produce Carla Dyson?

He'd met the girl's mother. Didn't think he could account for the girl through only her. Maybe he needed to reassess his idea of how people were either good or evil…

Carla broke up his reverie.

"Sandy? You're sure your mom will be okay?"

"No. But we don't really have options right now. Sending her back down to the hospital in Jax is the best I can come up with for the moment." He sighed deeply.

"You don't have to stay here, you know."

He locked her in a glare.

"You think I'm gonna leave in the middle of this? She's safe for now. What happens to her mind after all this settles is impossible to say. But I'm gonna be here to see it through. See that son of a bitch Gordon get what's coming to him." He paused.

"Besides, I could tell when I talked with her she's not all the way back to where she was before. She's tougher than I thought." He spit the last phrase at no one in particular, looking out the car window.

Carla caught Jack Franklin's eye.

"You think we can pull this off?"

He nodded, but said, "If we play it right. It's risky. But there aren't any easy ways out of this. You guys have been living in the dark right next to a den of poisonous snakes all these years. Could've been bitten plenty of times. Tony put some pretty extreme measures in place to keep you and your brother safe."

Sandy winced at the use of the word "brother."

"She's not my sister," he said, a touch too harshly. He heard the inflection and flushed bright red in the back seat.

"No offense," Jack said, not able to keep a smile out of his voice. He'd used the term purposely to draw a reaction.

Carla ignored both the provocation and the reaction.

The Face in the Grave

She said, "How did he get these trackers on these thugs?" She thumbed on Tony's phone again and tapped the app showing the location of Stick Gordon, the two men with him, and approximately sixty others.

"'On' isn't the right word," Jack said.

"These kind of men would never consent to any kind of tracking device." He let out a long breath, thinking.

"There was a rumor a few years back. Actually more than a rumor. This is classified. Shouldn't be telling you this legally, but…"

He shrugged.

"That horse is way out of the barn at this point. We got a briefing about what they call a 'black program.' Super-secret. It was only a concept at the time. The military was considering a type of tracking system for its special operators—Navy Seals, Rangers, Marine Recon.

"It was a form of nano-bot and the contractors who developed it tried to sell it to them. The nano-bot was designed to be swallowed. Once a person swallowed it, it would allow them to be followed with a new technology. It transmitted continually and lasted several years.

"The Spec Ops people rejected it. They hated it. The operators revolted. You can see why. The thing worked all the time—not just when they were on an op. Privacy issue."

Franklin watched his two students to see if they understood or believed this. Both were tracking.

"The Bureau heard about the program and tried to come up with a legal way to use it against the bad guys. It ran aground in Congress. Violated the Constitution in too many ways to count.

"When we were briefed it was just to make agents aware of the technology and warn us that it could be used against us if the bad guys ever got hold of it. We'd never even know it. The nano-bot was undetectable. The only way to disable it was a cocktail of chemicals that you'd drink to cause the thing to die. Then your body would flush it out. All scary stuff. Weird.

"Once all of this came out, the Justice Department demanded the company that developed it give over all their prototypes and destroy their research. They wanted it to go away. But, as we've seen, money changes things. Evidently it wasn't destroyed. It's the only explanation for what's on this phone."

"Once Pandora's box is open it never closes. The question is—does the Fratelli family know it's been bugged or did Tony do this on his own? Given that they never found him, or you, Tony must've done it alone." He shook his head. "How he managed to do it is beyond me."

Carla held up the phone and pointed to the red markers on the tracking app. "He did it the same way we did. You have enough money and you can make things happen."

Franklin nodded. "It was a dangerous game he was playing, though. And it had to take a lot of planning. If any of these thugs had the slightest idea what Tony was up to…"

Carla said, "He went to a lot of trouble to keep us safe."

Sandy scoffed. "He was lucky… and he's a bastard. He's wrecked our lives."

The car fell silent momentarily, each of them lost in their own thoughts, each tasting their own version of fear and anticipation. What would happen next?

For Sandy and Carla, who'd had their lives picked up and shaken like a snow globe in the past two days, there was the kind of awareness that usually dawns slowly on sheltered people in their late teens and twenties but had been shoved violently into their consciousness: there are no rails.

Anything can happen. Anything is possible.

And much of it will not be to your liking.

Like the sheltered individuals learn in bite-sized lessons, they were learning quickly that taking what comes to you and making choices without all the information or advice you'd like to have is inevitable.

You have to jump. You can't live any semblance of an actual life without the jump. It was a long way down from here and they weren't the only ones who'd hit the ground hard if the choices they were making went badly.

Another lesson: there is no such thing as a disconnected life. What you do, whatever you do, others are going to feel it. The old man who kept the cemetery and Shirley Anderson already did. More were going to shortly. Inevitable.

The Face in the Grave

Hopefully, their hastily constructed plan would put the hurt and the healing where they belonged, but lesson three in the crash course of becoming humans: there are no guarantees.

Carla prayed. Franklin ran scenarios. Sandy simmered.

In the next twelve hours they'd each take a turn at all three.

Chapter 43 - Jumping Without a Chute

Stick Gordon, for all his hardness, was not a good flier.

He ascribed to the John Madden philosophy of travel whenever he could and only flew when he was not in charge of his own schedule which, at this stage of life, wasn't very often.

The last time he'd flown was the family gathering in Italy, and he'd only consented to fly when Richie made it plain that his presence wasn't optional. Even Stick had things he feared more than airplanes and getting on the wrong side of Richie... well, the man would kill his own brother.

And the man had other men as ruthless as Stick to enforce the enforcers if needed. It was with this thought that Stick thumbed through the contacts on his phone.

He needed help. Another feeling he had not experienced in years. Put me on a fucking airplane? Make me ask for help? He didn't know where this ended but he knew the girl and anyone helping her he could get his hands on would suffer.

The Face in the Grave

It was this thought more than the thought of salvaging his life that drove him now. It made a dangerous man even more dangerous and a cruel man consider how much more cruel he might be.

He found the name he was looking for and punched the call button.

"Billy? Yeah. Stick. I know. Long time. I've got a problem I think you can help. Why should you help me? Because the price is right. No, no, not family business. Personal. Would I ask for that?

"I know you've got your own people to keep happy and you know that when the Fratellis are happy it's good for the Kuznetsov family too. Yeah. It's one of those deals. What's bad for business is bad for all our business. None of us need the attention, am I right? Good.

"This is very hot and if you're gonna help it's got to be right now. What assets you got available in north Florida and how fast can you move them in a pinch? Uh-huh. Look I'm not askin' yah to give up family secrets, I'm askin' for help with a problem.

"If you want to bust my balls, fine, but I'm tellin' you my problem is gonna be your problem if I don't nip it in the bud. Right. What's your cost?"

Gordon sighed at the number. It was old habit, nothing more. Money had no value right now.

The man could've asked for three times the amount and he wouldn't have blinked.

He said, "How you want it? I'll send you half as a goodwill gesture right now. I can count on you? Okay. Okay. I'll be in touch."

He cut the connection. From the plane's small porthole window he looked out over the Atlantic. The flight plan had been chosen to keep him in the dark as long as possible. No landmarks, only ocean.

But there was the sun and the time on his wristwatch. They were headed North and they were in a twin engine puddle jumper. Couldn't be going too far like this.

He sipped at the ginger ale he'd found in a small chill box in the rear of the aircraft. His stomach danced with the little craft's unsteady up and down; not exactly turbulence but not smooth either. Uneven. Unpredictable. No rhythm he could settle into and get the churning to stop.

Involving the Kuznetsovs in the Fratellis business wasn't unprecedented but it was unusual.

Doing it without Richie knowing about it first… that was way out of line. So far out of line it would likely amount to an irreparable breach of trust even if Gordon recovered the family's money.

He looked out the window again. The plane was descending. The surface of the ocean was now distinct with the white tops of rolling waves.

No. With that phone call he had jumped just as surely as if he'd have opened the cabin door and stepped out over the blue expanse below.

He'd jumped like a stuntman in a Mission Impossible movie.

No parachute.

He hoped he found one on the way down. But he was committed one way or another.

Chapter 44 - Parting of Ways and Means

The groundskeeper's shack was not an ideal staging place for their meeting with Stick Gordon and his men.

Although it sat on the crest of a hill overlooking the cemetery, the foliage around it precluded a view of the property in all but one direction and that was the backside of the place. All that was out there was a field with a cow pond so scummed over it looked like a green ice rink. The few head of cattle roaming the field dotted the landscape, making a lazy black, white, and brown kaleidoscope.

Franklin ascertained through Bureau contacts with local law enforcement that the groundskeeper was in Augusta Regional with a concussion, but otherwise unharmed.

Carla, Sandy, and the agent shared the land with the cows and the dead. It was a day that promised rain; shadowless, ominous.

The Face in the Grave

For the hundredth—thousandth?—time, Jack questioned himself. Backup? Was he so set on glory he would risk the lives of these two civilians?

He did want to bring down these people, and he couldn't say there wasn't a healthy dose of glory hound in the decision. He was an old soul when it came to "serving justice," but there were more ways than one to see justice served. More ways than letters of the law.

And if the Bureau got their teeth into a billion dollars of Tony's dirty money, he had been around long enough to know how muddy things would get.

Carla and Sandy and their families would not be an afterthought, they'd be no thought at all. The bureaucrats would Hoover up every last cent, every last asset, and they'd use any obscure statute they could find to do it. The kids would be destitute, homeless, futureless. That wasn't justice.

He added the Bureau's abuse of the DNA database and the existence of the covert tracking system Tony had procured to the mix and the situation tipped in this direction; as crazy as it sounded, Jack Franklin and these two kids were more likely to settle this justly than the Fratellis and the FBI.

He felt the weight of being the "adult" in the room. If this plan of theirs went wrong, losing money would be the least of their worries.

In a way, their plan encompassed the only exit point from the mob; death. The same thing Stick Gordon had in mind would be their goal too. He wanted them dead, they wanted to be dead too. Dead to the Fratelli family, at least.

Carla walked into the shed with her phone pressed to her ear. "Yes. Yes, sir. I know my father cared a great deal about you. Thank you. How long?" She held the phone out to check the time.

"Yes. That will work. Thank you again."

She met the eyes of the two men as she hung up.

"It's set. No turning back now."

Sandy and Jack showed the tension of the moment in their faces and in their wide eyes. Carla thought she must look the same way. There was no way back. But, she reminded herself, there had been no way back before either she or Sandy had even known who their father was.

They'd only been reacting to the facts as they'd been revealed. Playing the hand they'd been dealt. Now the cards were on the table and all the chips were in... well, not quite all of the cards.

The burner phone they'd purchased at the Sheetz in Fishersville buzzed in Franklin's hand.

"They're on the ground," he said.

"How long?" Sandy said.

"Twenty-five, thirty minutes," Carla said.

"Show me the tracker," Franklin said.

Carla thumbed on the phone and opened the tracker. Three red triangular icons appeared, superimposed on a map of the area.

"That's the Eagle's Nest airport." She hesitated.

"It's actually not much of an airport, really just a landing strip, an office and a few hangers."

Sandy looked over her shoulder. "They're not moving?" he said.

"Give it a minute," Carla said.

"The car's there. No bags. No people. They should be moving like we told the driver to tell them." Sandy said.

Franklin grunted. "Keep your shirt on, son. They'll be moving soon enough... and here sooner than you'll like."

Sandy bristled at the tone and the use of the word "son." He didn't like the way Franklin looked at Carla.

And he wasn't so much older than either of them.

"I hope you do better against Stick Gordon and his guys than you did against me and Carla, Preacher," he said, immediately regretting the emphasis he put on the last word, knowing he'd done it to remind Carla who she couldn't trust... and who she could.

Franklin gave him a sideways glance and pursed his lips in amusement.

"We'll see," he said. "A lot's changed since then."

Carla ignored them both, still focusing on the screen. "Still not moving. Text the driver and find out what's the hold up."

Franklin did. The response came quickly. They read it together:

Bathroom break.

"Bathroom break?" Sandy said.

The Face in the Grave

"When you gotta go…" Franklin said.

"You told the driver to keep them moving," Carla said. "Everything depends on keeping this moving, you said."

Franklin shrugged.

"What are you gonna do? What do you expect? Nature calls. And it isn't like we had a wide choice in getting a driver to do this, no questions asked. Give the guy a break. I feel bad enough putting anyone in a car with Stick Gordon even when we paid him enough to keep him and his redneck buddies in PBR for the next five years.

"Just hope he gets them here without getting a bullet in his head for his trouble."

Carla frowned. "I don't want anyone else to get hurt, but I don't like this. Now that he knows where we are, what's to stop him from bringing more thugs?"

"Nothing," Jack said. "But if he does, we'll know it, won't we?" He nodded at the unmoving red blips on the map. "Besides that, we don't have muscle as our protection now, do we? If we're wrong about Fratelli…"

Sandy said, "Text the driver again. Tell him they need to move now." The stress of the situation bled into his voice.

Franklin started to speak. Carla cut him off, and catching Sandy's eyes, said, "That's not gonna help, Sandy."

As if on cue, Tony's phone rang in her hand. She answered, putting it on speaker

"You ready to meet?" Gordon snarled.

"I'm ready for you to do what you're told," Carla said.

There was an ominous pause, then, "I think you're mistaking me for a pet. A dog. I'll tell you what's gonna happen now, you little bitch. You're gonna get that cheating fuck of an accountant and bring him to me right here right now."

"Why would I do that?" Carla said.

"Because…" Another pause.

"If you don't, I'm gonna give the word to one of my associates in Jacksonville who's sitting across the street from the hospital and he's gonna pay a visit to Mrs. Anderson and take her for a ride."

Sandy's eyes went big. Carla scrolled back to the tracker and zoomed in on Jacksonville. Nothing.

Gordon was still talking.

"You think I'd give up my cards that easy? You have no idea. All of you are living on borrowed time. All of you are gonna die today. Only question is how. Quick and painless or slow and painful. Starting with Mrs. Anderson."

Carla held a hand up to keep Sandy silent.

"You're bluffing again. You've got nothing and no one in Jacksonville. Get in the car with the driver and you might have a chance of saving your fat ass. He'll bring you to the meeting we agreed upon or you'll never see Tony or the money."

"Your driver? That's gonna be a problem. I don't think the hayseed's gonna drive anyone anywhere ever again. Dead men make bad chauffeurs."

The three looked at each other. Before Carla could stop him, Sandy shouted, "You touch my mother again—"

Gordon cut him off.

"All of you die today. Hayseed got the quick and easy way out. Give me Tony and you and your mother get the same. The girl… that's not an option. She's gonna pay off all her big words. I'll give you an hour to get here before Mrs. Anderson follows the hayseed."

The line went dead.

The momentary silence between Carla, Sandy, and Jack was as loud as a thunderclap. Sandy bent over double. Carla gripped the phone so hard it cut off the circulation in her fingers.

Jack discovered he was holding his breath. He exhaled, breaking the silence.

"Let me see the tracker app again, Carla," he said.

She flicked the phone back on and opened the app. It was still zoomed in on the Jacksonville area. Still nothing there.

The agent looked at the girl. There were tears in her eyes. It took him half a beat to catch up with their source.

"That poor man," she said.

"He didn't deserve that. And it's our fault. It's my fault."

The Face in the Grave

Jack reflected for a moment upon this response. He realized the girl was being human. This was the proper human response to the situation. And he realized somewhere along the line, at least in his capacity as an agent of "the law," he'd become something other than human.

The driver was collateral damage. The problem wasn't that he was dead, the problem was the need to apprehend the bad guys some way other than the way they'd planned it.

And that was a problem. His problem.

He was too used to dealing with truly inhumane people. And it was making him like them.

Sandy said, "My mom… she can't take another shock."

"He's bluffing," Jack said. "He doesn't know we have them all located."

Carla said, "But what if we don't? What if Tony left one of them out? Or they got a new thug on their team?"

Jack grimaced. "Not likely. Tony had a thorough plan. And he was a thorough man."

Sandy broke in, "It's not your mother's life that's at stake here if we're wrong, man."

Jack nodded.

"If we're wrong about anything, it's all our lives. Gordon's a liar and a thug, but you can believe him when he says he intends on seeing us all dead."

"The plan doesn't work if we don't get him here," Sandy said, looking at Carla. "Right?"

She held out a hand to him. "Let me think." She checked the time again.

"We've still got time. Jack, is there anyone in Jacksonville you trust? Anyone who can get eyes on Sandy's mom? Keep her safe in case Gordon's really got a man there?"

Jack thought this over.

"There is a field office there and an agent I trust more than the rest. I could call down and see they'd go check it out. If we do that, we're exposed on all sides. The family will know about us and the Bureau will too."

He rubbed his forehead. "At this point I don't trust one more than the other."

Carla looked at Sandy's worried face.

"We don't have a choice. See what you can do."

Jack scrolled through his contacts and punched in a number. He walked outside and made laps around the shack while he spoke.

Carla took out Tony's phone.

"I'm going to play our last card. We agree upon how much of this money should come to us? Sandy?"

He nodded. The number had been harder to agree upon than they'd thought. All of it was blood money, obtained by people like Stick Gordon for people like Richie Fratelli. They were more aware than ever that Tony had it right when he saw what money could do to a family, even a crime family, and decided to keep it away from them.

If it could do it to the Fratellis, it could do it to the Andersons and the Dysons. It was obvious Tony thought having enough money for a home and for college was enough. That was how he'd set it up and how they'd keep it.

With a few clicks, Carla transferred the Bitcoin to two accounts: hers and Sandy's.

"Okay. One more phone call. This better work. We're betting on greed more than lust for revenge."

"What are you going to do?" Sandy said.

"I'm going to give them everything and let them eat themselves. If Tony left them alone they might have torn themselves to shreds. Now I'm going to give it a little push and see what happens. If Stick Gordon thinks he can have this money and Richie Fratelli thinks it belongs to him…"

Jack returned to the shack.

"It's set. My contact there alerted Jax PD and will go check out the hospital herself. I trust her. She'll let us know the score as soon as she knows it. And it shouldn't take long. The office is less than ten minutes on foot from Jax Psych.

Carla nodded. "Here we go." She punched in Stick Gordon's number.

"Times burning, little girl," he said, coming on the line smoothly, menacingly.

The Face in the Grave

"Yes," Carla said. "And you know what they say about time being money. It's true." She had her composure back.

"I'm going to send you a location now—"

Gordon started to cut her off. She plowed ahead.

"Tony's dead. You'll see the proof when you get to the location. It'll be worth your trouble to go there. You'll also find his phone and access to all the money he took if you're smart enough to figure out how to open it.

"That's a billion dollars, give or take a million or two. But I'd hurry if I were you. You're not the only one looking for him or the money. Don't bother with your threats about Shirley Anderson. She's already been moved to a place you can't reach her.

"You've got a choice now, you fat ass. Money or blood. And it won't last long. Other interested parties are already on their way."

She hung up before the thug could say another word.

"Let's go," she said.

Not waiting for the men to follow, she turned and left the groundskeeper's shed.

Chapter 45 - Flight

The three made their way down the hill to the mausoleum together in silence.

Once again, they stood in front of Tony's crypt. Carla checked their faces one more time looking for agreement or objections. Neither man blinked.

She opened the maps app in the iPhone, clicked on the "share location" icon, and copied the link.

She then sent two text messages with the location in them and laid the phone down on the marble floor at the foot of the vault.

Jack said, "We won't be able to see where any of them are after we leave this." He pointed to the phone.

"Can't be helped," Carla said.

They started to leave, but halfway to the exit she turned and went back to the phone.

"What are you doing, Carla?" Sandy said.

The Face in the Grave

"I want to keep Tony's notes. His diary, I guess. I don't know why but it seems important. More important than the money or the tracking. He's the only father I've ever known for better or worse. I know the worst. Maybe it'll help me see the better."

Sandy thought about this, then nodded in agreement.

"You're right, I guess. I'm not sure I'm ready to think that way yet."

He paused half a beat and added, "Delete it when you're done. Don't leave it for them. Come to think of it, delete the tracker while you're at it. Why should they know how he fooled them?"

Jack interjected.

"Wait. You're not thinking through this all the way. We left the Bureau out of this till now, but they'll be involved soon enough. That phone—especially that tracker—could really help in putting away some very bad people.

"Every one of those red dots represents a murderer. I know I've been hard on them about the money. But when it comes to that, I do trust them. It's not the field guys, it's the bureaucrats we can't rely on to do the right thing."

"Okay, Jack," Carla said. "If Sandy agrees, I do."

Sandy nodded. "I guess so. Whatever we're doing, let's do it."

Carla copied Tony's notes and deleted them from his phone, doubling back several times to insure there would be no trace of them left that could be recovered. Finally, she removed the login code.

The only way back into Tony's phone was again the face in the grave; his face.

She laid it on the ground at the foot of Tony's crypt. The phone had been heavy in her hand. She felt the weight of all it represented lifting off her shoulders. Let someone else pick it up. Let someone else bear that burden.

They walked out of the mausoleum into dappled sunlight. In the parking lot they stopped.

"This is where we part ways," Jack said. "What's your plan now?"

Sandy said, "I've got to get to Jacksonville. Take care of my mother."

"I'm going with you," Carla said.

She met his eyes, daring him to disagree.

She found only gratitude in his face.

Franklin's phone buzzed. He stepped away and pressed it to his face.

Sandy went on. "All right. But we aren't leaving your mother behind. Agreed?"

Carla nodded slowly.

"No way to do that without spilling the whole story."

"I know," Sandy said. "It was going to have to happen one way or another. We may as well tell them both at once. Let them mourn together and figure this out together," he paused.

"There's a lot we'll need to sort out... as a family."

Family; he pondered that strange word. What did it mean now?

Jack hung up his phone and rejoined them.

Carla said, "How will we know what happens here? Will you tell us? We need to know so we know what to do next. Whether we can ever come back here or do we have to become ghosts."

Jack said, "That was my contact. Once you're in the air, call the number I'm going to text you and give the person who answers your ETA in Jax. When you get on the ground in Florida, call the same number. Someone will be there to pick you up and take you to Sandy's mom.

"Make sure they tell you "Grady sent me." Make them say it both times you call. That's the safety phrase. Don't speak to anyone or go anywhere with anyone who doesn't say this. Understand?"

Carla and Sandy both nodded. There was an awkward silence. Sandy said, "Thanks Jack."

Jack said, "Get out of here. I'll be in touch if anything changes you need to know about. Go take care of your moms."

On the way to her home, Carla contacted the pilot she'd contracted to fly Stick Gordon and his men from Florida earlier in the day. He was standing by, ready to take anyone anywhere she asked him to go.

She put him on notice to expect three passengers within the hour.

Rita Dyson was surprisingly pliable. Carla and Sandy debated about the level of detail to share with her and decided to keep it to a minimum based upon how willing Rita was to go along with them.

She turned out to be more ready than either believed she would be.

The Face in the Grave

Carla marked it up to her mother's depressed state. This was not the woman who raised her, only a shell; dead in the eyes and open to being told what she needed to do next.

To Sandy, the look was all too familiar. He'd seen it often enough on his own mothers face. It weighed his heart down and filled him with sorrow, realizing that this woman's sorrows were about to compound.

Better to process this together, he told himself, not for the first time.

Hard is not as hard when you have others to share it.

Chapter 46 - The Money Talks

Jack Franklin didn't trust the FBI with Tony's money.

He wondered how Carla and Sandy didn't connect him to that mistrust. Youth. Naivety. Whatever it was. He smiled grimly as he watched the two drive away.

He checked his watch and retrieved the phone from the foot of Tony's crypt. A billion dollars. He couldn't put his finger on the exact moment he decided to take the mob's money. He'd been sincere enough when he told Carla and Sandy he would not trust the Federal Bureau of Investigation with it. He'd meant every word.

Even in his young career he'd seen enough dirty cops to populate any number of Netflix true crime documentaries and some so dirty you'd never be able to write a believable fictional movie about. He had never been one of them. He'd played it straight. He'd been as pure as the driven snow.

And it got him nowhere.

He didn't think it was bitterness that had led him to this brink. It was… well shit, a billion dollars!!

The Face in the Grave

In the last six hours he'd seen what could be done with stupid amounts of money. Charter a private jet. Buy a chauffeur for a day. Make a bloodthirsty hit man abandon his bloodthirst. It fascinated him.

It was as if the whole world turned into a Monopoly board and he owned all the properties and pieces. Well, not him. Carla and Sandy. But he'd watched it. Now they were gone and the phone was just sitting there.

Shit! It wasn't like the twenty-dollar bill he'd found on the sidewalk in front of Toys-R-Us as a kid.

He stood in the doorway of the mausoleum, half in and half out, and mused about how this assignment led up to this moment.

They had wanted a man on the ground to keep an eye on Tony Diderrick. They had wanted him to get close and be trusted. He'd come up with the idea to pretend to be a pastor after he read over the case file. No one would have ever thought of it but him.

When the dust settled would he get any credit for that? Or would the smell of letting a college girl get the drop on him linger around his career like cheap perfume? He knew which it would be. No doubt.

He wavered there, letting the film of his future career run itself out in his mind.

His interactions with Sandy and Carla had been real. He wanted to help them when he saw up close the human impact of what was normally "working the case."

They had not deserved to be treated as collateral damage. Carla's family deserved better than a fake youth pastor to go along with their fake father. Jack saw it clearly when he looked in her eyes. No. He'd done what he'd done honestly enough. He knew himself well enough to know that was true.

But they were gone now. The phone called his name. It had whispered at first, but it got louder as he'd stood there. Now it was a shout. A BILLION dollars!

He ran up the hill to the groundskeeper's shed and retrieved several items: a crowbar, a sledgehammer, and a knife.

He had an unpleasant task and not a lot of time to accomplish it.

He had no time for subtlety and no compunction about leaving the evidence of robbing Tony's grave or leaving the man "in peace," whatever that meant.

Unlike the thieves who broke into the tombs of the ancient pharaohs and stole the goods that ensured safe passage to the afterlife, he had no superstitions. He had a good idea where Tony was. No amount of gold was going to pay his way across the River Styx into paradise.

And those thieves had little interest in the mummies of the dead kings. Jack did. He needed Tony's face.

That face was going to make Jack Franklin into one of the richest men on earth.

Chapter 47 - Money Keeps Talking

Stick Gordon had changed his mind, too.

Well, he'd changed it enough to reorder his plans. Calling in a marker from another Family's hit man all but punched his ticket with the Fratellis. He had little doubt of that. But a billion dollars?

That could buy a lot of safety... and revenge. He'd learned both of those things over a lifetime with the mob.

After all, just exactly why was Richie Fratelli untouchable? It wasn't just the name. It was the power that came from money.

He'd watched police and politicians fold like cheap suits under its weight. And although he enjoyed killing now, it hadn't begun that way. It had started out as a way to make a shit ton of money. Money he'd never have had a chance to make coloring between the lines like all the shmoes working their nine-to-five jobs.

He had to admit Richie had a touch; a way of greasing the skids with the right people at the right time with the right amount of greenback grease.

The Face in the Grave

But if one man could do it so could another. And he could learn.

He decided to make a start on his lessons before leaving the airport when he offered Vic Hunter ten grand to take Bobby French into the airport bathroom and leave him there with the dead hayseed.

Hunter complied without a minute's hesitation. The man never even questioned when he'd see the cash. That was good because Gordon planned on giving him a similar send off as soon as he got to Tony's phone.

The two got into the hayseed's car and set off for the dropped pin the girl left them, which showed up in a cemetery twenty-five minutes away, according to the maps app.

He smiled to himself. Yeah, a billion dollars would buy a lot of revenge, although he had no intention of contracting out his revenge on the girl. No. He was gonna take his time on that one.

What was the line from that movie? Yeah. Pulp Fiction. He was going to go medieval on her ass. This might even be better. Let her sweat. Let her look over her shoulder. Take up residence in her brain, maybe even let her believe she was safe.

Then show up in her rearview at just the right time to maximize her terror. He tried to imagine what it would look like but drew a blank. No face. He didn't have an image to fill the terrified girl's spot.

Oh, well. Money would fill in that blank too. Then he'd erase it. A particularly enjoyable thought came to mind. After he'd done a number on that mouthy bitch, the perfect ending.

He'd take her back to the spot—the exact spot—he'd hung her father over the edge of the Grand Canyon. He'd tell her the story. Watch her eyes. He'd get this on camera. And then… then he'd let go and watch her fall. A perfect ending.

He suppressed a laugh. Hunter glanced sideways at him.

"Keep your eyes on the road, fuckstick," he growled.

"Drive off the road around here it'll take a week to get out."

The man snapped back to his driving. Gordon smiled again. He liked snappy responses to his commands. Respect.

Maybe he wouldn't bury a bullet in that red hair.

Chapter 48 - Above the Clouds

Above the clouds it was a glorious day.

Sandy mused at the difference fifteen minutes and a few thousand feet made in perspective.

On the ground the gloomy cloud cover felt like a blanket you couldn't escape. Up here the sun shone against a deep blue expanse that felt infinite and free.

While Carla conversed with her surprisingly calm mother, he punched in the number of the agent Jack Franklin had given them.

He was surprised when a woman came on the line.

"This is Bradley."

"Ah, is this Agent Bradley?"

"It is." All business.

"This is a friend of Agent Franklin. He said you'd be expecting me to contact you…" Sandy waited what seemed like a long time to hear the phrase Jack had told them to expect from his contact in Jacksonville.

"Yes. I am. Are you on the ground already?" Bradley said.

The Face in the Grave

No recognition phrase.

Sandy started to disconnect the call. As he pulled the phone away from his face he caught the sound of the woman clearing her throat and saying, "Grady sent me."

He raised the phone back to his ear and breathed a sigh of relief.

"We aren't there yet. Last I heard we still have forty-five minutes till we arrive. You set to pick us up and take me to my mom? Shirley Anderson?"

"Yes," Bradley said.

"I've already made arrangements with the hospital. I'm going to get her myself. Our other friend is already under arrest. Had him picked up with an anonymous tip to the Jax PD. They were glad to get in on some action. I'll have your mother at the Fernandina airport when you get there."

Sandy felt himself tearing up. His mom was safe. She had a lot of recovering to do, and a lot of hard revelations to hear, but they'd deal with that together.

"Thank you for everything, Agent Bradley."

"You bet. See you soon." The line went dead.

Sandy thought wistfully for an instant that it would be nice to have another chunk of that money. Take these two shell-shocked women away somewhere nice and warm and dreamy so they could unpack the nightmare they'd been unknowingly living and begin to untangle the emotions and separate the false identities from the true. Make a fresh start in a fresh place.

When he looked up, Carla was watching him, reading him in that way of hers, better than anyone he knew.

Her eyes cut from his face to the form of her mother, asleep in the seat next to her. When she returned to his gaze, he saw understanding, agreement, and something else.

"Let me show you something I found in Tony's notes," she said.

Chapter 49 - Opening King Tony's Tomb

The crypt came open easily enough.

Two well-placed blows from the sledgehammer did the trick. Jack cleared away the remnants of the marble slab. Dust hung in the mausoleum's still air. The ringing in his ears from the hammer blows ebbed away.

The clock in his head was getting louder, pounding away now. As he slid the crowbar into the edge of the casket lid, the ticking in his head and the beating in his chest melded into one thing. It felt like his body was an alarm clock going off with no snooze button.

The crowbar could not find an entry point to force open the casket.

He climbed down off his stepladder and retrieved the sledge. A few taps on the end of the crowbar yielded splinters and a leverage point. He strained against the bar with no movement. He was perspiring profusely. His hands were slick with sweat.

He tried to tap the end of the crowbar again and connected with his hand instead with a mind numbing thwack, dropping the bar.

The Face in the Grave

    Cursing, he stepped down to retrieve it. He came back to his task fueled by anger as well as fear. Getting caught here with no way out would mean more than death for him if Stick Gordon and his thugs arrived.

    He abandoned the stepladder and any pretense of gentleness with the polished wooden box holding Tony's remains. He went at it from the floor with full swings of the sledgehammer, unhinging the lid which hung askew as the casket top yielded under the blows.

    He dropped the hammer and scrambled back up the ladder to see the body. Tony lay there, his billion-dollar face hidden under the grave quilt Sandy had hastily replaced the night before.

    Jack smiled grimly at that thought.

    He pulled the dead man's cell phone from his pants pocket, turned it on, and held it to Tony's face.

    Nothing happened. He did it again. And a third time. Still it didn't unlock. Panic rose in his chest. This has to work. That girl had done it. What was he missing?

    Then he noticed an oval of plastic resting on the corpse's chest and it hit him. That's what had taken Carla and Sandy so long. The eyes had to be open to unlock the phone.

    He swallowed hard. Shit. Nasty shit.

    He took the phone in one hand and used two fingers of his other hand to peel back the lids of Tony's eyes. He froze when he saw them. A sight that he knew he'd never forget seeing with his own living eyes.

    The sick wet sound and the feel of cold flesh folding under his fingers made his gorge come up. He involuntarily pressed down on the phone's on switch, almost dropping it in the process.

    He pulled back, ready to scream or puke or combine the two, and noticed he was in.

    The phone was unlocked.

    He jumped down off the ladder and looked at the home screen, the phone's light shining on his face as if he were Howard Carter seeing the glint of gold in the darkness of King Tut's tomb. His mind raced.

    Got to get out of here now. He started for the exit. A thought hit him. It was a fatal thought.

Better test this before I go. What if I need his face to open the Bitcoin wallet?

He opened the Coinbase app. It came up instantly. He thumbed through it, looking for the transfer button. How much to move to his own wallet as a test?

No need to be greedy. Fifty thousand was a nice round number.

Chapter 50 - Seed Phrase

"What did you find, Carla?" Sandy said.

"I think I found the key," she said.

"Key? To what?"

"To the crypto. The seed phrase. If you have it, you control all that's in a crypto wallet. It's a safety feature in case you lose access to your account. It lets you restore it. If you lose the seed phrase, and you lose access, you can never get it back. The crypto is gone forever."

Sandy's eyes got big.

Carla said, "I was thinking, we might have been a little hasty back there giving all this money away. Seeing her"—she nodded at her sleeping mother—"and thinking about what your mother and my mother are going to have to go through…"

"I agree," Sandy said.

"They're innocent in this. Isn't there such a thing as a court rewarding money for pain and suffering?"

The Face in the Grave

"There is. And they're in for a lot of it."

"You got a number in mind?" Sandy said.

"I don't know. Maybe. Do you?"

"It's hard. It's still blood money and that makes me feel funny."

"Me too. And who can put a real number on what we've been through?"

They fell into silence over the thought.

Finally, Sandy said, "There's no right answer to it. As bad as this money is, I want to do something good with it. Not for me, but for them." He hesitated.

"In fact, I think I want to give back the college money. It would always be there, you know? Every time I look at my degree I'll have to think 'I got this with dirty money.'"

Carla looked at him strangely.

"What?" he said defensively. He didn't recognize admiration.

"That's the truth. I'm glad you said that. Later, after it's done, if I'd have thought it, I'd have been stuck. Like what would I do? Try to give back my diploma? Thanks Sandy."

"So what can we do about it?" Sandy said, smiling inside. This girl's approval meant more to him than a college education. It was worth more than that. Way more.

"Let me show you what I found. If I'm wrong, all of this is a moot point… but I'm pretty sure I've got it right."

He was surprised when she pulled out Tony's Bible.

"You gonna give me a Sunday School lesson?" he said. "Where'd that come from?"

"Nope. I grabbed this out of the car when we were leaving. I don't know why. Maybe it was seeing Tony's notes. Something was happening to him there at the last. Maybe the same thing we just found out. He was making notes about things he'd heard in sermons. Especially about what greed does. He knew a lot about that firsthand. But there was this weird thing. Look."

She opened her copy of their father's notes on her phone.

"See how he kept them?"

Sandy looked. He didn't notice anything special. Each entry had a number, a date and a heading, just a few words followed by a paragraph or two. Very orderly.

An accountant's eye for records.

"I don't see—" he started.

"The numbered entries only go to twelve," Carla said, scrolling down through the first several entries to show him.

"One through twelve, even though there are about thirty entries."

Sandy shrugged. "What do you think it means?"

Carla's eyes were intense.

"There's something else odd about each numbered entry. Each one has a Bible verse in it. Some of the others don't. But all the numbered ones do. I looked up the first one. It didn't seem to have anything to do with his note so I looked up a couple more. Some match up but others are way out in left field."

Sandy shrugged again.

"The man wasn't exactly the kind you'd expect to know the Bible, is he?"

"No. But he did know numbers."

She pointed to the first entry. "Psalm 130."

She thumbed through Tony's Bible and found the psalm. "The first word is 'out,' she said, "and the verse is underlined."

Sandy started to protest, but the girl went on.

"I went through all twelve verses. All twelve are underlined. Nothing else in the rest of the book is marked. Just these verses. I took the entry number and found the corresponding word in each verse. It gave me this:"

She showed a scrap of paper to Sandy.

out gold free salt ready purple
fence bred great fist dog enter

"Am I supposed to make sense of that?" Sandy said.

"It's nonsense," Carla said, smiling broadly.

The Face in the Grave

"It's supposed to be something no one could make sense of—no way anyone would ever put those words together in that order. No one would ever be able to guess them and order them correctly."

She hesitated half a beat and said, "It's the seed phrase for the entire crypto account!"

It took a second for Sandy to have this sink in.

"We can move any or all of that money. Or… we could make it disappear forever." Carla said.

Beginning to grasp her meaning, Sandy said, "How can you be sure it's right?"

"We can test it right now! All we need to do is install it on a wallet and we'll be able to see everything in the account."

"If you're right," Sandy added.

Carla ignored him. She was already downloading and installing a new Coinbase account on her phone.

"I'm right," she said. "Watch."

The install completed. She went to the "recover account" feature and plugged in her code-breaking effort in the seed phrase it asked for.

And there it was.

A billion dollars in Bitcoin, give or take a couple hundred million here or there. They looked at each other, stunned.

"You gotta give it to him," Sandy said, "the man always had a way to make the numbers add up and he always had a plan."

Carla nodded, then looked down and gasped.

"What?" Sandy said.

Carla pointed at the screen.

"Fifty thousand dollars just went somewhere!"

"Huh?!"

Carla scrolled to transactions and showed it to him.

"Someone just moved a chunk of that money!"

"Who?" Sandy said.

Carla checked her watch. "Couldn't be Gordon. Not enough time to get to the cemetery."

They looked at each other as the truth dawned on them simultaneously.

"Franklin!" they said together.

"Why would he do that?" Carla sounded genuinely surprised… and hurt.

"Is he just making sure the money's there before Gordon arrives?"

Sandy shook his head.

"No. Can't be. How'd he even get into the phone, Carla? He had to open the crypt again… use Tony's face again. He said he didn't trust the Bureau with all that money. He is the Bureau!

"We left a billion dollars lying on the ground in that mausoleum on that phone. That's a lot of money to leave lying around. A lot of temptation."

Carla's lips went into a hard ribbon. She began pecking away at the screen of her phone.

"What are you doing? Sandy said.

"What I should have done in the first place. Tony was wrong about so many things, but he was right about one; money that will make you kill your own brother is worse than blood money. It's a replacement for blood. It gets in the veins and flows through your heart. It's a drug. It's addictive. It killed the Fratellis and it'll kill Jack Franklin too." She pressed a button.

"There," she said. "Done. The money is gone."

"Gone?"

"Gone. The only way anyone can ever recover that Bitcoin is with this seed phrase." She pointed to her scrawled note.

"What happens now?" Sandy said.

"I guess it depends on how crooked Jack Franklin really is. How much he bet on getting that money and if he was telling us the truth about calling for backup.

"And if he saw what just happened to the money. That it's not there anymore. There's about to be quite a collision in Mount Solon cemetery."

Chapter 51 - Unhappy Endings

Jack Franklin did not see the balance in Tony's account go to zero.

And he would never get the chance to spend the fifty thousand he'd moved as a test.

He hurriedly went into the iPhone's settings and changed both the passcode and the facial recognition to himself. He turned the phone off and pocketed it. Time to go.

He stepped toward the bronze door to exit the mausoleum and heard a deep voice that sent shivers through his spine.

"That's far enough, Agent Man."

It came from the shadowy end of the space. The space where less than twelve hours before, he and the old caretaker had been tied up together.

For a brief moment Jack thought he had awakened a ghost in this home for the dead. A pale white face emerged from the gloom. The man smiled grimly.

He was holding a .38 special at waist height, not pointing it at him, but gesturing with it casually.

The Face in the Grave

He didn't need to point it; his dark eyes were more menacing than the barrel of a gun.

Richie Fratelli.

He stepped into the diffused sunlight of the mausoleum's skylights. Franklin backed away instinctively. His own gun, holstered under his left arm, felt far away; too far.

"Stay put," Richie said in his raspy old man voice.

"You and me got business to attend."

He paused. Franklin couldn't tell if it was to catch his breath or to make a point. He'd never met Richie Fratelli, only seen him on surveillance videos. In the flesh he was every bit the caricature of a New Jersey guido.

Old. Fat. Slicked back black hair streaked with gray.

Jack's mind raced. How had Richie Fratelli found this place? Was he alone? What did he know? Fratelli was studying him, reading his face.

"Tony's kid," he said.

"Smart. Like her old man. Always a plan and a plan for the plan."

He nodded at the destroyed coffin.

"Got to hand it to them, the smart guys. Runs out though. The smarts. Sooner or later somethin' comes along they left out of the plan. Like dying. Funny, ain't it? Death is as sure as taxes but no one plans on it."

He waved the .38 in Jack's direction.

"How about you, lawman? You a smart guy? You plan on dying?"

Franklin went to speak but found his mouth had gone dry. He swallowed several times before speaking.

"No. I'm not a smart guy. And"—he gave the gun a hard look—"I'm not planning on dying."

He paused half a beat and added, pointing at his pants pocket, containing the phone, "The money is all on this phone. Only way to get it. If you kill me, you'll never get into it. The money will be lost."

"Will it?" Richie wheezed.

"No. You're not a smart guy. I just watched you unlock the phone with a dead man's face. I'm not a smart guy either, but I'm smart enough to know one dead man's face is as good as another. And I'm not going to need a crowbar to get at yours."

He leveled the gun at Franklin's chest.

As he did, a car door clunked shut outside. Footsteps approached the mausoleum. Shadows fell across the doorway between Jack Franklin and Richie Fratelli.

The snout of a revolver entered the room, wavering back and forth like a hunting dog, then a hand and an arm. Jack was thinking that whoever was attached to that arm would swing the balance of power in the room and determine who lived and who died in the next five seconds.

He held his breath, and keeping his eyes fixed on Richie Fratellis eyes, slowly drew his right arm up toward his shoulder holster.

Several things happened at once. The gunman stepped across the doorway and turned left toward the mob boss instead of right toward the law man. Choices. 50-50-90.

He was a big man. Huge actually, and he temporarily blocked Richie's view of Franklin, who reached for his gun just as the ear splitting sound of a gunshot deafened him in the confined space.

Franklin cried out in pain and fear, still attempting to pull his gun as the big man crumpled. The holster was snapped. He flailed at it as a second gunshot erupted and a bullet went through his gun hand and into the left side of his chest, a lucky-unlucky shot with him on the wrong end of the luck.

He went down like a dropped sack. Blood pooled around him. So much of it. His brain fired between two words as it shut down: blood, money, blood, money, blood, mo…

Richie Fratelli stepped closer to the writhing body closest to him, blood also pooling around it.

This body still breathed.

"Well, Stick," Richie said, "too bad I ain't the murder artist you are or I'd set up a camera and record this. But I'm just an old-fashioned wise guy. Never killed anyone for fun like you, you fat fuck. Dead's enough for me. Like pulling out a splinter. Just get the thing done."

Gordon tried to speak. All that came out of his mouth was a groan and a little blood.

"Gut shot," Fratelli said. "They say it's the worst way to die. Makes you real thirsty."

The Face in the Grave

Another shadow darkened the doorway. A scared voice called out, "Boss?!"

"It's all right, Vic," Fratelli said.

"Come in here and help me clean up."

The man came in. His eyes were huge.

"Okay, Richie," Vic said, failing to keep the fear out of his voice.

"You did good, kid," Richie said, "you did good."

Turning to the still-writhing Stick Gordon, he said, "Loyalty. Loyalty. See, Stick? You can't buy it. You can't put a price on it. You go outside the family? That's it. Everyone knows this. Vic here knows. That's why he called me up and told me about Jacksonville. About the Kuznetsov man you got involved in our business."

Gordon's thrashing was slowing; the death throes he'd observed and recorded in his many victims paying him out now. Richie Fratelli leaned down close to his hit man's face. His eyes narrowed to slits and his voice lowered to a deadly whisper.

"And he told me you were coming here to find Tony and take my money. Loyalty, Stick. You of all people should've known I never bought it with money. I bought it with blood."

The fat man ceased struggling. One long gurgling breath escaped his great mass. He was still.

Richie stood upright and surveyed the scene. He motioned to Vic.

"Watch where you walk now. This'll work out perfectly. Check the lawman. Don't step in any of this blood. If he's not dead yet, he will be. Pretty sure I plugged him in the heart."

Vic checked the downed agent. "Dead," he said flatly.

"Get the phone out of his pocket," Fratelli said.

"And get his gun. Wipe it down and put it in his hand. Dumb sonofabitch'll probably get a citation for killin' Gordon. Bury 'em with honors."

The henchman accomplished both tasks while Fratelli wiped off his own gun and placed it in Stick Gordon's still warm hand.

Vic handed over the phone.

"Ever seen a dead man make money?" Richie smiled at Vic.

The man shook his head.

"Watch."

Richie turned on the phone and held it up to Jack Franklin's face. "Look at this! He made it easy. Died with his eyes open," Richie snorted.

The phone scanned the dead man's face and unlocked. Richie saw the time flash on the home screen.

"Is it really that late? Shit. We gotta get a move on. I'm sure the stiff has got friends who'll come lookin' for 'im."

He swiped to the phone's settings and pecked in a new access code. "Get me to Charlottesville, Vic. You did what I told you about our problem in Jacksonville?"

"Yeah, boss. The Kuznetsov guy down there had a very bad day… as bad as these guys."

Richie smiled and wheezed, "Good, good. Let's go. I'm thinking you deserve a good meal for a good day's work… and a little somethin' extra for helpin' an old man take out the trash."

Chapter 52 - A Strange Family Reunion

The Gulf Stream touched down in the Fernandina airport and taxied to the private general aviation terminal.

Carla helped her mother down the stairs. Sandy followed. A woman in navy slacks and white blouse approached them from the terminal entrance.

She was a slightly-built Hispanic woman with a severe face and black hair tightly pulled back in a no-nonsense ponytail. She strode up to the trio and offered her hand to Rita Dyson before acknowledging Carla and Sandy.

Sandy started to ask for the safety phrase.

She cut him off.

"Agent Bradley. Jacksonville field office. Grady sent me. Let's get you to a secure location and we can talk."

The Face in the Grave

The group hustled off the tarmac, through the terminal, and into Bradley's black SUV without stopping. Once inside, Bradley said, "It's been quite a day down here. I've got to drop you off and run."

She looked in the rearview mirror and caught Carla's eye. "Joseph Mikailov was gunned down in broad daylight in front of Jax Psych."

When Carla failed to show any recognition, the agent went on.

"Joey Mikailov is—was—the Kuznetsov family's main leg breaker. That's Chicago. The guy we got in custody—we only got him because the stupid bastard decided to cap Joey and then stop for a Snickers bar at a convenience store not two hundred yards from his dead body; the clerk gave us his description, plates, everything—the shooter is out of Jersey. Minor player, but associated with the Fratellis."

The agent paused again and scanned back and forth in the rearview between Sandy and Carla.

"And just today I get tagged by Jack Franklin calling in a favor I owe him from all the way back in our academy days. He says to take care of you and not ask questions. But I've got to tell you… if we're seeing the start of a turf war between the Fratellis and the Kuznetsovs here in Jax, I'm going to need some answers.

"I got a boss breathing down my neck as it is. It took calling in a few favors of my own to get Mrs. Anderson out of the hospital and into a safe house. So… you two going to help me out here? Want to tell me what's going on?"

Carla spoke first.

"We'd like to help you, Agent Bradley, but we have no idea about crime families and turf wars. All we know is that Sandy's mother was in some kind of trouble and you would help us. Pastor Jack…"

"Who?" Bradley interrupted.

"Pastor Jack. Jack Franklin. He was—is—my church youth pastor up in Virginia. When we told him we needed help he seemed really anxious to take care of us."

Bradley was continuing to scan the two as this story unfolded. The girl was smooth, she had to admit. The boy was looking at her intensely; his eyes had dilated.

Sure sign his girlfriend's story was distressing him. But she went on without a hitch.

"My boyfriend didn't have anyone he could call in the city so Jack said he'd take care of it. Said he knew someone… you."

"Jack Franklin is your youth pastor? In Virginia?" Bradley said slowly, digesting this like an oversized pill.

Then something dawned on her and her eyes narrowed.

"Why did Mrs. Anderson need to be moved from the hospital?"

Sandy, warmed by Carla identifying him as her boyfriend, found his voice and jumped into the rhythm of her story.

"I don't know anything other than I got a call from her doctor telling me my mom had been admitted, but he thought she needed family more than she needed to be in the hospital again. Carla's pastor overheard us talking and said he knew someone who could help us out. Guess he meant you. And I don't know who Grady is, but he must be helping us too."

Bradley checked his eyes closely. This one wasn't as smooth as the girl. He wasn't a good liar.

She knew she could unwind him with a few deft strokes of interrogation, but her boss really was breathing down her neck and there really had been a mob hit in downtown Jacksonville and she didn't have time to babysit these two and the girl's mother, who looked like she was out of it.

"I'm going to drop all of you off at the house where Mrs. Anderson is staying and you can stay there till I can get back to you. There's everything you need there."

They drove on in silence, not to the west as Sandy assumed they'd go—not out of the city into the country, but to the south and east.

Soon he realized the agent was taking them in the direction of the south side of Amelia Island. He suppressed a smile. How funny would it be that the FBI had had a safe house no more than ten minutes from a man they badly wanted to find, the accountant for the Fratellis crime family, Tony Diderrick, his father. Pretty funny.

When the SUV pulled up at a condo just off the 1A1, he got out and stretched. The smell of the ocean greeted him. Home.

The Face in the Grave

Almost every other piece of his life had moved in the last week, but the ocean was still the ocean and its smell was still the smell of a familiar friend's cologne.

He had the sudden urge to plunge into it, paddle out and catch a wave, but another thought pushed the urge away. Mom.

He followed Bradley into the condo, afraid of what he would see of his mother.

Afraid of that blank stare he saw in her when she had realized Tony was gone.

"Mom?!" he said when he'd entered the condo. "Mom!"

He heard a chair scraping the floor and then saw his mother. She was smiling. Her eyes were bright.

"Sandy! Sandy!" She threw her arms around him and laughed.

"You're all right, Mom?" he said.

She said, "Uhm-hmm," muffled by his shoulder.

Pulling away, Shirley Anderson realized Carla and her mother were standing behind her son.

"Who are these folks?" she asked and moved to greet them.

Carla caught Sandy's eye.

Bradley said, "I need to be going. You know how to contact me if you need me. I'll be back here as soon as I can." The agent departed.

Carla took her mother by the arm and led her to the couch in the living room. Sandy did the same with his mother.

The two women looked at each other and then to the faces of their children.

"It's a long story, Ma. A really long story."

Chapter 53 - Off the Mountaintop

Vic Hunter drove Richie Fratelli along Route 250 over Afton Mountain and began the descent toward Crozet.

It was a foggy night on the top of the mountain; a bad night for high beams, city drivers, and impatience.

He was pleased with himself for betting on the right horse and ridding himself of following Stick Gordon around. He was also unused to fog and mountains, and he was nervous to please Richie and consolidate his gains and his new status near the kingpin.

With Gordon gone, why shouldn't he be the new main enforcer? He juggled these thoughts while he flicked the rented Cadillac's dimmer switch back and forth, trying to keep the car off the white line he assumed was on the edge of the mountainside.

The white wall of fog in front of him stole his depth perception. He was on and off the brakes as shadows flashed across the windshield.

"Da fuuuuck,," Richie said from the backseat.

The Face in the Grave

"Let it roll, Vic. We got places to be and you're making me sick with this jerkin' around."

"Sorry Richie," Vic said.

He started to explain why he was driving erratically, thought better of it, and drove on, trying his hardest to keep his foot off the brake and subtly guide the big sedan through what felt like a cloud bank.

He could hear Richie wheezing away in the backseat and he wondered how healthy the old man was. How old was he? Vic didn't know.

It was unhealthy to inquire about the health of any made man, but it was especially unhealthy to ask about the health of the boss.

Still… the old guy didn't sound so good.

In the backseat, Richie fumbled with Tony's phone. He prided himself on keeping up with the times, staying in the game, using new technology himself, and not just getting his minions to learn it for him.

He'd always been an early adopter. First guy to have a laser disc and camcorder, a CD player and then a smartphone. It was this hunger to stay relevant and up-to-date that had gotten him into this mess.

Well, it was that and a fair dose of pride.

When the dead accountant explained cryptocurrency to him, he had grasped the basics, it was true, but Tony talked fast and he talked with authority. Richie had a soft spot for the guy. He trusted him. But he also didn't like to look a fool.

And Tony made crypto sound so simple, as if anyone should be able to follow blockchains and mining and halving and virtual accounting.

What Richie did understand well enough and early on was that it would be very hard to intercept or to track payments using crypto and that meant a better chance to keep his money away from the law. This was good.

He also understood that crypto offered a new way to make money that no bank could offer. The value of money in a bank depended upon a supply that was a crooked game; the government could and did just keep printing money.

And they could do it any time based upon the whims of a politician.

And of course banks meant deposits and records and reporting of interest. Crypto changed all that.

There was a fixed amount of it that could never change.

The "mining" of new Bitcoin would eventually come to an end and the currency would stabilize at whatever rate the market held it to be. It was perfect for family business and Tony had been way out ahead of it.

The Fratellis had been in on Bitcoin, laundering and moving huge sums of money when the crypto was trading at a few dollars per coin.

The family was not poor by any means, but day-to-day operations could run close to the bone. Bribes and beatdowns might mean Richie and his brothers moving men and money around under the pressure of the clock.

And crime—at least the kind of crime Richie Fratelli committed—was finesse. Much more ballroom than break dance. Moving too fast meant mistakes and mistakes meant people took notice. Bad for business.

But then Bitcoin went to a thousand per coin, then ten thousand and twenty thousand each. Overnight the family had become the wealthiest east coast operation. Overnight.

And without lifting a finger, pulling in a marker, or breaking a leg. Billions. With a "B."

There was more money than anyone knew what to do with. There was so much money it made the family business seem… what? Useless? Why extort and bribe and muscle? What was the point if not to make money?

The brothers met up in Aversa to discuss this problem. The problem of too much money.

It was during this meeting Richie had heard his own two brothers suggest they give it all up. Take the money and run. Payoff the troops. Live life. They had close to a billion dollars each if they split the windfall three ways.

Richie had watched their eyes. He had seen the… what? Greed? Yes, but it was something more, something even deeper.

He had rode the train down to Naples and took a walk along the waterfront while he chewed on it. He stopped at a street vendor's cart and bought a cappuccino.

The two men, the mob boss and the street vendor, stood face to face and looked into each other's eyes. Richie saw no fear in the man. No respect.

The Face in the Grave

He pocketed the couple euros and went back to his newspaper to await the next customer. Richie wasn't used to being treated like a customer; a consumer, a dollar sign.

His father and his father's father built the family into a force to be reckoned with on the streets of East Orange.

He never remembered his father talking about money. Money wasn't shit. It was respect. It was your name. He'd say fear and respect are the same thing; interchangeable.

Here he was, the top of the organization they'd built, the name they'd built. And his brothers wanted money more than they wanted respect. They wanted money more than they wanted their name. He decided then. He'd take away their money and their name.

He was the only one who could handle it. He'd watched it for years. Suggesting it was time to get out of the game had been the last straw. Tony had shown him how to get the money. Richie knew how to take away his brother's names.

He'd been doing that to other men for a long time.

Back in the Caddy, He looked out the window. Vic was still struggling with the fog. Idiot looked like he might run them off the road at any moment.

Richie wheezed and mused. Now he was the last Fratelli brother. He alone had the name. He could give it to anyone he wanted. He had time. He'd comb through the nephews and cousins and find one worthy... or not. He could let the name die with himself.

And he would if none of them proved themselves. Yes. He had the name. And he had the money. Slick fucker, that accountant. Had to give him that. Using Richie's own plan to get all the money in one place. The money he'd made for them. Now he had it all back. All.

The name and the money.

He smiled to himself and opened the Coinbase app on the dead accountant's phone. There it was. Three quarters of a billion in Bitcoin. Another hundred and fifty million in Ethereum.

While he scrolled through the other cats and dogs of startup crypto currencies he'd dropped money into—a hundred thousand in Dogecoin, another hundred thousand in something called SafeMoon, he saw a red notification pop up. He tapped it and looked at a string of notifications. The top of the list was two hours ago. Under security alerts it read:

A new device has logged into this account from Jacksonville, FL.

A second notification was under the first, this time under account activity:

Seed phrase match confirmed. All assets recovered.

Richie stared at the screen, the phone's white light reflecting off his face in the dark bac seat making him a headless ghoul in Vic's rear view mirror.

Richie tapped back to the Coinbase home screen. Under the heading "my balance," where it had shown him to have three quarters of a billion dollars a moment before, it now read:

$0.

He tapped assets. None. He tapped account activity again. It read:

All assets recovered

Richie gulped for air. He broke out in a fierce sweat. He felt his pulse banging away in his temples. Air. He couldn't get enough in his lungs.

He choked in on his own saliva and started to cough.

Several things happened at once. Vic saw the grotesque disembodied head floating in the mirror and knew he was seeing a heart attack. He began to slow the car. Richie tried to scream at him to keep his eyes on the road.

A black shape appeared out of the fog on the driver's side, ahead of the car. It was nothing, a shadow cast by a streetlight on the other side of the highway, but Vic never knew that.

He jerked the wheel right, sure he was seconds from colliding with a car or a deer or something else stopped in his path.

The Face in the Grave

Richie gasped for a breath but none came. His heart was slamming to a halt, destroying itself like a careening freight train coming off the rails.

The right front tire of the Caddy left the road and the headlight shone crazily for a frozen second on a wall of white.

Then the car launched over the side of the mountain, a flightless metallic bird, engine whining.

The State police responding to the scene the next morning marveled at the perfect angle and spot the vehicle took leaving the blacktop, lacing neatly through the hardwoods stretching up between gray-brown rock outcroppings.

It was fifty feet before the Caddy touched a thing, landing nose down, sending its two occupants through the windshield as cleanly as if they'd been shot from a sideshow circus cannon.

But there'd been no net to catch these two, only a final face full of Afton Mountain and a wild tumult downhill, ending against scrubby pine trees.

The recovery team leader told his wife later that night that picking up the two bodies had been like lifting trash bags full of broken humanity. He said it reminded him of his first day in biology class when the prof lectured the class on the net value of a human body reduced to its chemical components.

Maybe five hundred bucks, the crusty old professor said.

He told his wife, "I doubt those two would bring that much. Funny thing, though. The driver? Dude's face was gone. Like the glass on the windshield just took it. Other guy. Old man. No. He was destroyed. Still a trash bag of broken bones. But his face, weird. Hard to forget that. He looked like he was surprised. Not afraid. Surprised."

Chapter 54 - A Final Accounting

Carla

So my old man stole the mob's money. Then he died.

You'd think those things would go together, right? Steal money from bad people and bad people will make your heart stop beating. And why steal bad people's money? Because you want their money. Greed.

But that's not the story.

I know this may not sound true, but I was there and I saw it myself so I don't care. When Sandy and I opened that casket, and I saw Tony's face, it was a peaceful face. Resting. Restful.

And I know that's the undertaker's job, but that's not what I saw. I saw it with more than my eyes. This is what makes the story so hard to tell and harder to live in.

The face in the grave. My father. Not a man who stole money out of greed, but out of love.

The Face in the Grave

And not a man who died violently because he stole the mob's money, but a man whose heart just stopped beating over breakfast one morning.

That was a peaceful face. My father.

Sometimes when I look at Sandy and he makes a particular face—mostly it's that tight lipped, no-teeth smile of his—I see Tony. I see our father. His biological father and my adoptive father.

A man who married two women and had two families that never knew the other existed. A bad man. But we never knew he was a bad man. He wasn't bad to us. We didn't know he was bad until he was peacefully lying in that casket with a face worth a billion.

Father. There's a name. We don't have anyone else who answers to it. My biological father couldn't be found by the IRS, not to mention CSE.

So what do you do about that? Honor your mother and your father? I'm going to need some help with that. We all need help trying to fit these pieces into our hearts.

My counselor used Tetris to explain trauma to me. She said the things come up on the screen and we turn them over and let them fall into place. If the pieces fit and the line is complete—poof—that set of experiences go off into the memory hole and there's room for new stuff.

But sometimes the pieces just won't line up or they fall into the screen too fast for us to get them sorted out. We get a pile up and start to feel some way about life.

But if we acquire some skills at Tetris, we know how to move things and to be patient and work our way through the pile up.

Eventually we get the lines to disappear and we have more room again.

But she said there are things that come along that shouldn't be in any game. They are like round balls or bubbles that won't ever fall into place no matter what you do. Move left, move right, rotate. It doesn't matter. They won't go into place because there is no place.

When these things come down they won't go away and stuff piles up around them and on top of them. You can still live with them but they take up room inside you.

She told me the dirty little secret is everyone has these bubbles in their heart. Everyone. Some are just better than others at keeping the game going.

I believe it.

Shirley and Rita look like they've got a pile-up. Thankfully they have found refuge in each other instead of hating and blaming each other. Makes sense. Who else can they talk to about this mess? Same with me and Sandy, I guess.

Another thing the counselor said: there's nothing like shared suffering to cement us together with another person. We'll see. It's weird wanting Sandy to comfort me and knowing he wants more and then getting those flashes of Tony.

It rattles my Tetris rows and makes me anxious. We'll see.

Is there a way to pop those bubbles and get some kind of normal back? Was there ever anything normal for any of us?

I have a hope. Something about that face in the grave, the peaceful face that didn't belong there.

Tony wrote a note in the margin of his billion-dollar Bible. It was next to the place where Jesus was getting ready to leave his disciples and he says to them "I will not leave you as orphans."

Written in his precise accountant handwriting was this:

"I am not an orphan. I am not alone."

There was a date next to it. The week Tony died.

I think that was what was on his face. I think that thought must have popped those trauma bubbles even in an old crook and bigamist like Tony Diderrick—in a life full of numbers that didn't add up.

And if he could have that, maybe I can too.

Maybe we can too.

Acknowledgements

We don't write out of our own lives as much as we write out of the accumulation of all the lives into which we've been invited. I've been invited into so many fascinating lives in my time it is hard to break out a few of them because the voice of the many speaks loudly.

Nevertheless, my wife and children made the space for me to be me, and no stories worth telling come out of inauthenticity, so I want to specially acknowledge them.

I had one of those teachers, the kind that stand out in the ebb and flow of subjects that make you love their subject more than others because they love it, or teaching itself so much it infects you.

Mine was a creative writing teacher named Mike Leonard.

He may not remember me, but I'll never forget him, and I'll never forget how he took all comers in a deep blue collar county in Virginia and made all of us believe we had something to say with the written word.

Thank you Leonard.

R. Kenward Jones is a disruptive teacher, writer, podcaster (who isn't these days?), counselor, husband, father and grandfather. He holds a bachelor's degree in mechanical engineering and master's degrees in biblical studies and counseling.

His debut novel, Buried at Sea, was published by Penmore Press in 2022. Daily, he writes proverbs, parables and prayers and shares them on his Facebook page and website to inspire and encourage.

R. Kenward Jones is a US Navy veteran and served as both an enlisted man and officer for 12 years before he left the military to become a pastor. After a 13-year long bout with treatment resistant depression he left the ministry to reset his life. He knows the Valley of the Shadow of Death and the power of personal Creativity as the way through it and out of it.

Currently he works as a counselor and teaches the 515A "zero excuses" bootcamp at the local YMCA. He and Tina, his high school sweetheart, have been married for 40 years, have two children and one grandchild, and live in Southeastern Virginia although they still consider the Shenandoah Valley to be their "home."

R. Kenward Jones enjoys life and joy tempered by suffering and more than anything wants to help other sufferers experience the same.

This work of fiction was formatted using 12-point Times New Roman font for the body, "Mustard" Font for the Cover and Chapter headers - with 1.15 line spacing, on 55lb cream stock paper.

The page size is 6.14" x 9.21." The custom margins are industry standard, 0.5" all around, and 0.00" inside, with no bleed, and 0.635" gutter. The margins are "mirrored."

Headers and footers are standard.

The cover is full color hardback in a glossy finish.

The binding is 'perfect.'

Milton Keynes UK
Ingram Content Group UK Ltd.
UKHW011822140624
444031UK00010B/154/J